DRAAKENWOOD

OTHER BOOKS FROM JORDAN L. HAWK:

Hainted

Whyborne & Griffin:
Widdershins
Threshold
Stormhaven
Necropolis
Bloodline
Hoarfrost
Maelstrom
Fallow
Draakenwood

Hexworld
"The 13th Hex" (prequel short story)
Hexbreaker
Hexmaker

Spirits:
Restless Spirits
Dangerous Spirits

SPECTR
Hunter of Demons
Master of Ghouls
Reaper of Souls
Eater of Lives
Destroyer of Worlds
Summoner of Storms
Mocker of Ravens
Dancer of Death
Drinker of Blood

Short stories:
Heart of the Dragon
After the Fall (in the *Allegories of the Tarot* anthology)
Eidolon (A Whyborne & Griffin short story)
Remnant, written with KJ Charles (A Whyborne & Griffin / Secret Casebook of Simon Feximal story)
Carousel (A Whyborne & Griffin short story)

DRAKENWOOD

(Whyborne & Griffin No. 9)

JORDAN L. HAWK

ISBN: 978-1546701507

Edited by Annetta Ribken

AUTHOR'S NOTE

Miss Lester's creepy grandfather is first introduced in the short story "Eidolon" (Whyborne & Griffin 1.5).

CHAPTER 1

Whyborne

"ARE YOU SURE this is going to work?" Persephone asked. She perched atop a bale of hay, her expression skeptical. Though we were twins, she had been given to the sea at birth, the inhuman side of our heritage brought to the surface so that she might survive. The stinging tendrils of her hair curled around her shoulders, and the pale portions of her dolphin-slick skin reflected the light of the lanterns set about the sheltered back yard.

In the past, Griffin had tended a small plot of vegetables and herbs here, but over the last few months we'd found another use for the space. The thick hedge surrounding the property—coupled with the propensity of Widdershins's inhabitants to turn a blind eye—had allowed us to transform it into a training ground of sorts. Now it was dotted with bales of hay and dress forms turned into practice dummies. We'd even dug out a shallow pond to have water on hand for spells.

The masters would return eventually. Last July, a cult known as the Fideles—Faithful—had sent a signal through the veil dividing our world from the Outside. They meant to summon back the inhuman creatures known only as the masters, who had once ruled our world. Entities of unfathomable power, they commanded sorcery of every kind. They'd shaped new orders of beings from the raw clay of earthly life: the umbrae, the ketoi, the rust, and doubtless more. And they'd twisted the arcane lines flowing across the world, to create a titanic magical vortex beneath what was now Widdershins.

But the umbrae and ketoi rebelled, and the maelstrom sought to thwart their return. I was determined we'd fight them again, drive them back to the Outside and seal them there permanently.

How…well, that was another matter.

I'd feared they'd seek to return last Hallowe'en, but nothing had happened. Not even the Fideles had troubled us lately. The holidays had come and gone, and the calendar turned from 1901 to 1902. A part of me wanted to believe that life would continue as it had; that the threat had somehow resolved itself.

But the rest of me knew better. We had to be ready when they returned. Which led to tonight's exercise.

"No," I admitted. "I'm not at all sure."

"I'm certain it will be fine," Griffin said. He held up his sword cane, which I had spent the last week modifying. The silver head and dark wood were now etched with sigils, and bore a crudely bound set of crystals and wire that detracted from its normal guise as a fashion accessory. "You might want to move, however, Persephone. I'd hate to set you on fire by accident."

She hopped off the hay bale. Her jewelry and gold net skirt glittered in the lantern light as she moved a prudent distance away.

Griffin took up position in front of the bale, poised to stab it with the blade of his sword cane. "Are you ready, Whyborne?"

I hesitated. This had seemed a good idea a month ago. Griffin's shadowsight meant he could often perceive things I couldn't, including the warp and weft of spells being used against us by enemy sorcerers. Unfortunately, he had no means beyond the mundane to deal with them.

I had magic, but no shadowsight. Last July, I'd touched Griffin briefly, while drawing on the arcane energy of the maelstrom. In that instant, we'd worked together—but the burn of magical fire through his purely human body had injured him.

Human sorcerers tapped into arcane lines as well, using wands to take the brunt of the power, rather than their own bodies. And eventually it occurred to me that there might be a way for Griffin and I to combine our skills after all.

Only now I wasn't so certain. What if something went wrong? What if I'd made some mistake, and Griffin was harmed due to my incompetence? "It might not be safe. I don't want you to get hurt. Perhaps—"

"I trust you, Ival," he said. "Now come. Cast the spell when I tell you."

I took a deep breath. "All right." I centered myself. Though our house wasn't on an arcane line, I could still feel the power of the enormous magical vortex rotating widdershins beneath the town. I took another breath; magic crackled along my skin, ached in the scars on my right arm. "I'm ready."

"Now," Griffin said, and thrust the sword cane into the hay bale.

At his signal, I spoke the true name of fire, all my will focused on the sword cane. The crystals sparked, and fire erupted from the blade.

"Well done!" Griffin exclaimed, grinning as he withdrew the blade. The hay burned merrily, flames growing larger and larger. "Er, though perhaps you overdid it a bit?"

"Oh dear!" I cast about, but the shallow pool had frozen over in the late January night. The flames were beginning to spread to the other bales nearby, and tendrils of smoke rose from one of the practice dummies.

"Unfreeze the water!" Persephone exclaimed.

I went to my knees by the pool and thrust my palm directly against the ice. I drew power through my scars, arm aching as I focused. But it worked; the ice dissolved under my skin.

Persephone touched a hand to the scars on her face, left behind by a mask made from the bones of a god. The water emptied from the pool, rose into the air—then cascaded down atop the burning hay. The flames went out, leaving behind only smoke.

I stood up. Griffin seemed fine, but I went to him anyway. "Are you all right?"

"I'm quite unharmed," he assured me. "I saw the magic, of course, but it remained contained in the sword cane as intended." He looked up at me, and a smile lit his features. "Well done, my dear."

I restrained the urge to kiss him, though only because of my sister's presence. "Thank you."

"We'll need to practice more," he added. "But it was a fine start."

Persephone glanced at the stars. "Practice all you like, but Maggie is waiting for me."

"At this hour?" I'd never intended for Miss Parkhurst to be exposed to the horrors populating my life, not even the ones I was related to. But my sister and my secretary had developed a friendship last year, and of course Persephone couldn't visit her in the daylight. I only hoped Miss Parkhurst wasn't allowing Persephone to impose too greatly on her time.

"Give her my regards," Griffin said, apparently not at all concerned over my secretary losing sleep. "We should get to bed as well, Whyborne. The workers from the telephone company will be here to install ours in the morning."

"Yes," I said, my mind still half on poor Miss Parkhurst. Then the import of his words caught up to me. "Wait. Did you say *telephone?*"

~ * ~~ * ~~ * ~

"I can't believe you brought this…*thing*…into our home," I said the next day. I gestured vaguely at the contraption now mounted on the wall of Griffin's study. "What on earth were you thinking?"

"We discussed all the reasons for us to have a telephone," Griffin reminded me, "and decided it was the most prudent course."

"Well, yes, but I didn't think you meant *now.*" I'd imagined he meant to have it installed sometime in the future. The very distant future. But of course Griffin was the sort of man to act, not dither about like me.

"It will be a boon to my business," he said. "Not to mention, being able to quickly contact your father or the museum could make all the difference should there be an emergency."

"Should the masters come bursting back into our world, you mean."

"Among other things, yes," Griffin replied. "I'm sure the telephone will prove its usefulness in many ways."

I snorted rudely. "I have my doubts. I've accepted all of the modern technology you've brought into our lives—electricity, the motor car, the replacement motor car—and not once have I uttered a single word of complaint."

Griffin made a choking sound. I ignored him.

"But surely a line must be drawn somewhere," I continued doggedly. "Being forced to talk to people—and in my own home! Surely a telegraph would be more than sufficient."

"Come now, my dear." Griffin pitched his voice soothingly, the same way he did when coaxing Saul down from a tree. "I'm sure once you understand its operation, you'll feel much more at ease. Let me demonstrate it to you."

I eyed the telephone warily. A Kellogg model, it had a handsome wooden case, a pair of black enamel bells, and a black receiver and transmitter. "Must I?"

"I'll relieve you of the burden when we're both here," Griffin said. "But there will be times I'll be out on a case or the like. And do recall, Bradley would have surely murdered you in this very room last July, had I not been able to place a call from Boston to Whyborne House."

Drat. Unable to argue, I muttered, "I recall quite clearly, thank you."

"Then you see its uses." Griffin smiled at me, and my heart softened at the sight. I didn't understand how I'd captured the interest of such a man, let alone his undying affection. The white pearl of his wedding ring gleamed warm in the light, and I absently ran my thumb over the black pearl in my matching ring.

I returned his smile. "Oh, very well."

"Good. Now, let's place a call to your father."

My smile transformed to a scowl. If Griffin meant to endear me to the wretched contraption, he'd chosen the wrong avenue to do so.

"I have the numbers for Whyborne House, the police station, and the museum recorded here," he said, indicating a piece of paper he'd posted on the wall next to the telephone. "Now, one simply picks up the receiver and tells the operator which number is wanted."

I stood with arms crossed while he did so. "Calling for Mr. Whyborne on behalf of Dr. Percival Endicott Whyborne," he said after a pause. Presumably one of the servants had answered the telephone at Whyborne House. "Thank you."

He took the receiver from his ear and held it out to me. "Your father will be along in a moment."

I took it gingerly. A few moments later, Father's voice barked directly into my ear. "Percival!"

I winced. "Yes." Griffin pointed at the transmitter, and I redirected my reply into it. "Yes."

"Griffin mentioned you intended to join those of us living in the twentieth century," Father said, sounding pleased about my newest hardship. "I'm glad you called—you've saved me the trouble of sending a message."

As though it were some inconvenience for him to order a servant to have a message sent. “About what?” I asked, though I doubted I wanted the answer.

“There’s a meeting tonight I wish you to attend.”

Curse the man. “How many times must I tell you, I’ve no interest in running Whyborne Railroad and Industries?”

“As if I could forget,” he snapped. “My own heir…well, never mind. It isn’t that sort of meeting.”

I was less than reassured. “Then what?”

“Come to Whyborne House no later than eleven o’clock tonight. I’m calling a gathering of the old families.”

CHAPTER 2

Whyborne

"SHALL I JOIN you inside, my dear?" Griffin asked as he parked the motor car along the street in front of Whyborne House.

His first motor car had exploded, thanks to the sorcery of my late and very unlamented co-worker Bradley Osborne. I'd thought that the end of my trials, but Father—determined as usual to make my life unpleasant—had replaced the accursed thing as a Christmas gift to us.

I rubbed at my nose, which had transformed into a block of ice thanks to the January night. The rug over our laps contributed to some comfort, but any parts exposed to the wind had frozen on the drive over.

"Please," I said. I was always grateful for Griffin's presence, but never so much as when forced to venture into what had been my childhood home. "They won't allow you to attend the meeting, I fear, but if you don't mind waiting for me…"

"Of course I don't." He climbed down from the seat, and I followed suit. "I'll find my way to the kitchen and have something warm to drink while I await you."

I wasn't certain how the servants would feel about that, let alone Father. The vows Griffin and I had spoken on a lonely beach bound us as surely as any uttered in a church. But the rest of society would never recognize him as my husband.

Father had treated him as such, though—that was one good thing I could say about the man, and in truth it made up for a great deal else. The servants weren't fools; Griffin had been invited to family gatherings for some time now, despite having no obvious reason to be there. Fortunately, they were loyal to the Whyborne family, so I didn't fear untoward gossip being spread past the walls of the house. But whether they saw Griffin as a member of the family they served, or more akin to themselves, or neither, I didn't know.

The butler, Fenton, greeted us at the door. "Master Percival," he said, "your father requested I show you to his private study prior to the meeting."

"I'll see you shortly," I told Griffin, as a footman appeared to take charge of him. Fenton led the way through the foyer and down the familiar hall to Father's study.

Father sat behind his desk when we entered. He wore an elegant suit that probably cost what would amount to several months' salary for me. The years had turned his beard and hair iron gray, but he still reminded me of an aging lion, not yet ready to give up control of the pride.

Our relationship had never been warm, but as of late I'd come to the reluctant conclusion that he cared about me in his own way. It didn't take away the ugly memories of my childhood, relentlessly bullied by my brother Stanford, with Father's only response to pat Stanford on the head and tell me to develop a spine. But I could believe Father had truly thought his actions the best for me. That someday I would thank him for making a man of me, instead of growing into what he saw as a womanish weakling.

Needless to say, that hadn't happened. I'd left Whyborne House at the earliest opportunity and charted my own path, funded by Mother's sale of the jewelry she'd inherited from our ketoi ancestress. Not that we'd known ourselves to be hybrid creatures at the time.

"Percival," Father said by way of greeting. He looked over my attire. I'd worn my best suit, even digging out the diamond cufflinks he'd given me for my eighteenth birthday, when he'd still hoped my rebellion would prove short lived. "Sit."

I sat. "What is this all about?"

He regarded me steadily across the desk. I'd sat here many times during my youth, letting my mind go blank while he lectured me on my every failing. A family portrait had hung on the wall: Mother, seated on a chair, my infant self in her lap, and my older brother and sister standing beside her, while Father loomed behind us all.

But Guinevere had died at our brother's hand, and Stanford would spend the rest of his life locked in an asylum in upstate New York. Mother took to the sea. Of those in the portrait, Father had been left with only me: the unfavored child, a disappointment from the moment of my troubled birth on.

Father had replaced the portrait a few years ago with a landscape depicting the Battle of Shiloh, which presumably had fewer bitter memories attached.

"I've been considering our war against the masters," he said. "The very fact we've heard nothing from the Fideles cult since October worries me a great deal."

"I have the same concerns," I said cautiously.

"They struck at both the land and sea, and were turned back," he went on. "By you and your sister."

"And?" I certainly didn't need to be lectured on events in which I'd participated.

"Don't be so impatient," Father snapped, his brows lowering. "My point is, we are at a disadvantage. They have surely not been idle these last few months, but we have no information on their movements. No spies, no means of gathering intelligence. You seem to have no plan beyond waiting for the next attack and hoping to survive it."

My eyes widened. Of course; this was my fault now. "I've been practicing with my magic. What else would you have me do? This isn't the War Between the States. I'm no general. I have no troops, no spies, no—"

"You have resources!" He brought his palm down on his desk in emphasis. "Griffin still has contacts among the Pinkertons—have them on the lookout for anything otherworldly. For that matter, have him expand his detective agency—hire men who can be trained as the Pinkertons are, to defend the town against physical threats. There are scholars at that museum of yours who could be put to work cracking the code of the Wisborg Codex. We live in a modern age of newspapers and telegrams—hire a service to sift as many as possible, seeking any hint as to what the Fideles might be doing."

I gaped at him. "What…I'm meant to just start ordering people about? You greatly overestimate my influence if you imagine anyone would listen to me."

His face darkened. "You're wrong, Percival. Do you think no one has noticed your actions? Those mad librarians have already fought for both you and your sister, though I'm not entirely clear why."

"Because Mr. Quinn knows," I said, a bit dejectedly. "About Persephone and me. How, I'm not sure, but he realized we're a part of the maelstrom even before I did."

I'd been dismayed when I'd first discovered my heritage to be not entirely human. But that was as nothing compared to the revelation of last July. That Widdershins—the maelstrom—in its semi-sentient fashion had gathered and shaped our family for generations, until it had two receptacles for…well, itself. Tiny fragments, but still linked to it, to be its eyes and ears and hands in the world. To keep it free when the masters returned.

Father brought his hand down on the desk, startling me. "And that gives you *power*. You view it as some sort of disadvantage, but it's quite the opposite!"

Of course he didn't understand. Command came naturally to him. It had allowed him to lead soldiers in the war, and later to build the family wealth from respectable to staggering. But I wasn't like him. If the maelstrom needed such a leader, it had chosen its vessel poorly indeed. "And why isn't Persephone receiving this lecture?"

"Because she doesn't need it. I've spoken to her, and she's already sent word to the other ketoi cities, to have the hybrids loyal to them act as our spies. Since the Fideles killed one of their gods and wiped out a city in the Bering Sea, most of the ketoi chieftesses are more than eager to assist." He stabbed a finger at me. "But the Fideles are human, which means the majority of their actions will take place on the land. Which means *you* must act." He dropped his hand and glanced at the clock. "Which is why I've called this meeting of the heads of the old families and their heirs. They have resources we can take advantage of."

"In exchange for what?" I asked sourly.

"The old families have worked together since the founding of Widdershins. We used to meet as part of the Brotherhood of the Immortal Fire, but…well." He waved a hand. "After you became my heir, I should have called a meeting. At the time, it didn't seem likely you'd come."

Because it was Stanford who'd been a member of the Brotherhood alongside our father. Stanford who had been meant to stand at his side, to take the reins of family and business when Father grew too old.

God knew, I would have preferred Stanford had kept the position. I wished he hadn't let himself be consumed by greed and jealousy and the desire for power, until he murdered Guinevere and shattered our already broken family for good.

Perhaps Father had similar thoughts, because he rose rather abruptly to his feet. "Come—it's midnight. They'll be waiting for us."

CHAPTER 3

Whyborne

THE MEETING TOOK place in what had been Mother's room, before she went to the sea. I hadn't set foot here since she left, and was startled to see it entirely redecorated. The long room ran along the front of the house, overlooking High Street. Heavy cloth-of-gold drapes shrouded the windows, as if to reinforce an air of secrecy. Scarlet wallpaper covered the walls, and the portrait of Mother as the Lady of Shalott no longer hung above the hearth. All of her books and bookcases were gone as well, no doubt returned to the library two stories below.

I paused at the doorway, feeling an unexpected pang. This place had been a sickroom for Mother, a cage to which her broken health had condemned her. But for me, it had been a refuge. The one place I'd felt accepted and loved. The lone room where I could let down my guard and simply be…me. And now it was gone.

Mother's bed had been replaced by a heavy oak table. I pitied the footmen who'd had to carry it up the stairs. Matching chairs surrounded it, upholstered in crimson. The only illumination came from the flickering flames of the enormous gold candelabrum in the center of the table. Its candles at least were white; I'd half expected them to be red or black.

Five of the seven chairs drawn up around the table were occupied already. Miss Lester sat nearest the door, dressed all in white as usual. Beside her were Joseph Marsh, his aged spine bent into a curve, and his grandson Orion. Sterling Waite and his son Fred sat opposite.

The Marshes, Waites, and Lesters had helped the necromancer Theron Blackbyrne found Widdershins, alongside the Abbott family and the Whybornes. After his death, they'd availed themselves of whatever black magic proved necessary to keep their stranglehold on the town. Though other families had risen to prominence since, the old families had always formed a core of uncontested power, answerable to no one.

At least until the elder Abbott died during the fall of the Brotherhood. His son had proved inadequate to the task of either maintaining the family fortune or learning sorcery, and left town over two years ago.

Well, to be fair, my Endicott cousins and I had chased him out. I still winced to recall the memory of my rather poor behavior that night.

"Thank you for joining us," Father said. He took his place at the head of the table, leaving the empty chair at the foot for me. A servant slipped from the shadows and offered me brandy. I nodded, feeling rather as though I might need something to brace me for this. "You all know my son Percival."

Four pairs of male eyes fixed on me, none of them friendly. I knew Orion and Fred from my youth, though they'd been part of Stanford's set. I'd never had a set, let alone any interest in the rumored wild parties at their exclusive club, even after I'd been old enough to attend.

Once everyone had refreshment, Father said, "That will be all. We'll ring should we need anything further." The servant bowed his head and left, shutting the door firmly behind him.

"You may be able to guess why I asked you here," Father began.

"Hopefully not to waste our time," the elder Marsh said in a rasping voice.

Miss Lester's dark eyes glanced in my direction. "I know why," she said, tipping her head to me. "Widdershins knows its own."

I—or the maelstrom—had touched her last July, just as we touched so many. The experience had faded to the quality of a dream, but I still recalled some of what I'd seen of her thoughts.

I also now suspected her family were ghūl hybrids. Which was rather disturbing, given they ran the town's mortuary service.

"Yes," I said, because I couldn't exactly deny it.

"Perhaps you'd like to inform the rest of us, then," said Waite, his voice chilly. Fred nodded his agreement.

Father launched into what sounded like a prepared speech. "Outside forces have aligned against Widdershins. And by 'outside,' I mean both from beyond our town…and beyond our world. We of the old families must band together to face them if we are to preserve our city and our lives."

Marsh and Waite exchanged glances. "I see," Waite said. "And I suppose you are the one who will lead us to victory against these nebulous enemies?"

"Nebulous?" I exclaimed. "The Fideles are anything but 'nebulous.' I know the newspapers claimed it was an earthquake that broke windows all across Widdershins last July, but surely you of all people know better."

Waite's eyes narrowed. "If you refer to your inexcusable display on the Front Street bridge, it did not escape our notice. Or anyone else's."

Miss Lester drew herself up. "Inexcusable?"

Marsh glared balefully, first at her, then at me. "Those of us who matter in this town keep our secrets, not flaunt them in public. Your indiscretion has put us all in danger."

"I-I didn't have a choice," I protested.

"And did you have a choice when your actions destroyed the Brotherhood and led to the death of my eldest son—Orion's father?" Marsh's voice remained low, but his words cut through the air between us like a knife. "Rather than appeal to the Brotherhood, you took matters into your own hands and disrupted the ceremony on the island in the lake. My boy *died* there, torn apart by Guardians—"

"Joseph," Father said, his tone stern, "you know very well that Blackbyrne's plot went farther than any of us knew. I explained it to you at the time."

"And that's part of the problem, isn't it?" Waite asked. "*You* explained, Niles. Three of the other old families were represented that night. James Abbott, Marsh's son, and *my* father. They all died, while you and both your sons survived. We had no choice but to rely on your version of events."

"Are you calling me a liar?" Father demanded. His face flushed red at the insult, and a part of me cringed at his anger, even though it was directed at others for once. "My word was good enough then. Yet suddenly it isn't?"

"Not suddenly. We aren't fools," Marsh growled. "We've been watching the events of the last four years with growing alarm. First the Brotherhood was wiped out after centuries of success. Then this one —" he pointed at me "—destroyed the lunatic asylum at Stormhaven."

I didn't at all care for the direction the conversation seemed to be taking. "That wasn't my fault. Or, it was, but again, I had no choice. Or would you rather the dweller in the deeps walk the land, in thrall to a madman with a grudge against the Brotherhood?"

"Again, we have only your word as to what happened," Marsh said. "How convenient for you the doctor died, and all evidence was lost amidst the rubble of the asylum."

"Then there came the debacle at the museum on Hallowe'en." Waite picked up the thread of accusation. Clearly he and Marsh had discussed this beforehand. "I imagine you were dismayed when Stanford revealed your most closely held secret, Niles. You brought the blood of those of the sea into your family, then hid the fact from the rest of us."

Father's mouth pressed into a thin line. "I didn't know," he said stiffly. "Heliabel herself didn't know of her heritage."

"And we're to believe that?" Waite shook his head scornfully. "Perhaps we would, if it didn't advantage you so clearly. Let's begin with the matter of Percival's sister, supposedly dead all these years, and now 'the queen beneath the flood.'"

"She's a chieftess." I sat forward in my chair, gripping the arms. "It isn't the same."

"She commands an army of fish creatures." Marsh's voice dripped with contempt. "Things which have no loyalty to us."

To the old families, he meant. "Persephone is on our side."

"And what side do you consider to be *your* side?" Waite asked. I felt as though he and Marsh were a pair of hunting dogs, hounding me from either flank. "After the Hallowe'en gala, we looked into the prophecy." His gaze slid to Miss Lester. "Despite one of our number having somehow learned of it far earlier, it doesn't belong to the old families. It was a promise made to the ones who came after, who crept into the town *we* made."

"Now see here." This was the very attitude that had always most maddened me about the old families. They built a pedestal, put themselves on it, and declared that anyone like Griffin, whose ancestors hadn't arrived in Widdershins at Blackbyrne's side, weren't up to their standards.

But it wasn't their place to say who belonged here. The maelstrom decided who to collect, not them.

Miss Lester's flat, black eyes narrowed in anger. "Widdershins knows its own," she repeated. "You *cannot* deny it, Sterling."

"We were here first," he insisted. "We ruled this town for two centuries. And now, we are confronted by this bit of awful doggerel some insist on calling prophecy. One line of which, again most conveniently for Percival, states that *the town will rise to his hand.*"

My fingers tightened on the carved armrest. Despite the fact the windows were tightly shuttered and the drapes drawn, a breeze stirred through the room, guttering the candle flames and ruffling the white fur trimming Miss Lester's dress.

"What the hell are you implying?" Father asked.

"A coup," Marsh said. "Meant to break the old families and leave the Whybornes the sole power in Widdershins." His gaze stabbed at me from the forest of wrinkles surrounding his eyes. "Led by this one."

The scars on my right arm ached. I took a deep breath, willing my face to remain an expressionless mask, betraying nothing of my anger. "That's absurd."

"Niles chose a wife with the blood of the sea in her veins," Waite said. "But you, Percival…well, I have to wonder just how long you've planned this."

Orion spoke up for the first time. He was a pale, sleek man who reminded me vaguely of a ferret. "You never seemed interested in the same things as the rest of us. Even when we were boys, Stanford said you spent all day studying. At the time we laughed at you, but in retrospect your knowledge of languages both living and dead proved rather useful for learning the dark arts. While we studied business and politics, you went first to Miskatonic, then took up employment at the Ladysmith Museum. Both places infamous for owning many rare books on sorcery."

The wind grew stronger, and some of the candles winked out. The hearth fire flared, sparks flying away up the chimney. "How dare you." I bit off each word to keep myself from shouting. The one thing in my life that was my own, that I had fought for with every scrap of my being, and Waite dared to imagine it was part of some lifelong scheme to come to power?

Marsh straightened as far as his bent back allowed. "You destroyed the Brotherhood. When a rival sorcerer tried to interfere with your plans, you tore down Stormhaven. Your older sister died under mysterious circumstances, and your brother is confined to a sanitarium, leaving you the sole heir to a vast fortune."

All the air seemed to have vanished from the room. "This is madness," Father snapped. "You were at the Hallowe'en gala—you saw what Stanford did. What he confessed to."

"Every event has worked to Dr. Whyborne's advantage," Marsh went on implacably. "Hasn't it, Percival? Rumor claims you and your sister command a cult of librarians headquartered in that museum of yours."

"We have watched you." Waite leaned forward, his eyes glittering in the light of the candles. "Every step of the way, you have obliterated anyone who stood before you, while adding to your own power. And now you and Niles come to us with yet another tale no one else can verify. Wanting us to fall in line, to obey your orders. But we are not spineless women, eager to hand over our power to another." Miss Lester hissed in outrage, but he ignored her. "We have seen through your charade. It will be a cold day in hell before we bow our heads to you."

The thin strands restraining my temper snapped. I rose to my feet, even as a thin layer of frost raced across the table. "You are fools. The masters are coming back, and they won't give a damn about your so-called power. They won't *care* who any of our ancestors were—who founded this town, or who commands it. If we don't prevent them from returning from the Outside, we'll all die screaming together in the dark."

Waite rose to his feet and seized my wrist. "Do you think to frighten us with your little tricks, sorcerer? Tell me, if you can—what exactly are these 'masters?'"

My lips parted…but I had no answer for him. We knew they were beings of great power, but that was all. I was utterly ignorant as to their nature, or what abilities they might have, or even when they would return.

I tore my wrist free from his grasp. His hand curled into a fist. "I don't know the details, but I assure you, they are very real."

"I don't believe you." He turned to his son. "Come, Fred. I think we've heard enough, don't you?"

The two representatives of the Marsh family rose as well. I hadn't wished for this meeting in the first place, but to have them walk away, after impugning my character, was too much. I took a step toward them as they reached the door. All four froze, eyeing me as they might a dangerous animal.

"The masters *are* real," I repeated. "And I will fight them. With or without you."

"I choose without," Waite said coolly.

The door shut behind them. At the table, Miss Lester stirred. "Well," she said. "This has certainly been an entertaining evening. Thank you for the invitation, Niles."

CHAPTER 4

Griffin

"I SIMPLY CAN'T believe it," Whyborne concluded as I shut the door to our house behind us. "They think I'm some kind of...of diabolical mastermind." He started to remove his coat, then cursed. "And I've lost one of the blasted cufflinks."

I'd found my way to the kitchens, having given Fenton the slip after he left me in a formal parlor, and been speaking to the cook when a footman had rushed in to find me. "Dr. Whyborne is ready to leave," he'd gasped, and the look of pallor on his face had me running for the foyer almost before he'd finished speaking.

Ival had been pacing back and forth, in as high dudgeon as I'd ever seen him. Of course, he hadn't looked furious in any obvious way. But I—and apparently someone among the servants—knew the signs well enough for alarm. The way his face closed into an expressionless mask, skin white and dark eyes narrowed, his hands clasped tight behind his back, all told me in an instant that something had upset him deeply.

Of course, the fact the chandelier had begun to swing in a wind with no obvious source might have been the root cause of the servants' alarm.

He'd told me what happened on the way home, shouting to make himself heard over the engine. It seemed to have calmed him somewhat, at least. His hands no longer clenched, and the normal color had returned to his cheeks.

"Hopefully you lost your cufflink at Whyborne House," I said, taking off my hat and coat and hanging them up. "Let's go up to the study. I'll pour you a drink."

He led the way to the stairs, and I followed him to the study on the second floor. We spent most of our time there, and the room reflected it. Our two chairs were drawn up to the fire; a stack of scholarly books beside his and the latest volume of *The Casebook of Simon Feximal* by mine. Our cat Saul curled on the couch; he opened one sleepy eye at our entrance, then closed it again.

The fire had burned down in our absence. Whyborne poked it back to life, while I poured two whiskeys. We sat together on the couch, squeezed in beside Saul, who declined to move to make more room for us.

"I'm sorry," I said. "It sounds as if the meeting wasn't very productive."

"I just don't see how anyone could think such a thing." He glowered at his drink, and I hoped he didn't accidentally set it alight.

"I can," I admitted.

His eyes went wide, and I realized belatedly I'd said the wrong thing. "You…fine. This is some grand plot I've been conducting all along, cleverly hidden even from you. You're nothing but a-a pawn. Perhaps—"

"Ival, please." I put down my whiskey and grabbed his hand. He kept it curled on his knee, making no move to clasp mine in return. "*Listen* to what I'm actually saying. Marsh and Waite don't know you, save as Niles's son. Their sons were friends of Stanford's which would hardly endear you to them. None of them have been at your side, fighting, for all these years. Moreover, they have no particular reason to trust you. Yes, you saved their lives and countless others from Stanford's schemes that Hallowe'en. But as they said, doing so benefited you." I grimaced. "And again, if the sons were friends of Stanford, or even merely enjoyed getting drunk together at their club, they might ask themselves what happened to the man they thought they knew. If you had anything to do with his change."

Ival didn't say anything, but his hand relaxed beneath mine. He turned his palm up, and I laced my fingers through his. "They know their relatives died along with the Brotherhood," I went on. "But none of them saw you ready to fling yourself through a hole in reality to save the world. They weren't with you when you fought Nitocris, or kept the tidal wave from destroying Widdershins, or prepared to die alone beneath the mountains in Alaska because you feared unleashing the umbrae might lead to disaster."

"At least I was wrong about that," he said in a low voice.

I leaned against him, slipping my other arm around his shoulders. "They don't realize the extent of the threat. To them, the Fideles are just another cult. They look at you and see a powerful, dangerous man. And..." I hesitated, trying to think of some diplomatic way of putting it. "You do have a tendency to come across less than warmly, especially in situations where you're uncomfortable. They've reached the wrong conclusions about you, but there is a certain logic behind them."

His shoulders slumped beneath my arm. "If you say so. It's just...to have them throw such an accusation in my face, after everything that's happened. The blood and the tears, the struggle. As though none of it mattered. As though I had done it for my own advantage." A sigh escaped him. "I suppose it's a good thing they don't know about my connection to the maelstrom. I imagine they'd see it as more proof this was some sort of coup begun by Father long ago, to be ultimately carried out by me."

"Probably," I agreed ruefully.

"As for Father, he doesn't think I'm taking an active enough role preparing for the Fideles. He seems to believe I can just go ordering people around." Whyborne shook his head. "That might work for him at Whyborne Railroad and Industries, but I have no control over what goes on at the museum. He behaves as if I'm the director, or the president, rather than a lowly scholar of languages."

"You have more influence than you realize," I said. "The other museum staff are neither blind nor stupid. Neither are the board of directors. Even if no one speaks of it, they know they owe you their lives for saving them from Stanford and Dives Deep."

"That only goes so far," he objected. "A new office and a private secretary are one thing, but..."

I wanted to shake him. Where once he'd hidden unnoticed in corners at museum galas, now he could barely escape the presence of the director and president. They wanted to be seen with him, even if Whyborne didn't wish to believe it.

But an argument wouldn't make him see it. Niles often called Whyborne stubborn, and although he'd misjudged his youngest son at almost every other turn, he was entirely correct on that point.

Whyborne leaned his head against mine. "I wish none of this had happened. I wish I was…normal. That I could go to my job at the museum, and come home to you, and not have to worry about sorcery, or things from the Outside, or any of it." He sighed gustily. "I wish the maelstrom had found a different vessel."

I wanted to point out that we would never have met, had that been the case. Remind him how grateful I was it had chosen to collect me. But I sensed he sought a different type of reassurance. "I wish our lives were quieter, no doubt. But as for the rest of it…I love you because of who you are."

"Flaws and all?"

"You have flaws?" I asked in mock surprise.

He snorted and butted his shoulder against mine. "Devil."

"I'm an angel," I protested.

"A fallen one." But it drew a grin from him.

I pressed a kiss to his forehead. "Let me help you forget your troubles for a while, Ival."

The grin turned into a chuckle. "And how do you propose to do that, I wonder?"

"With something I'd meant to save for Valentine's Day," I said. "But I think you have more need of it tonight."

Whyborne arched a brow. "What do you want of me?"

"Everything." I tugged his hand to my lips, kissing his knuckles. "But for the moment, strip and wait for me in front of the fire."

"Don't be long."

I hastened into what was ostensibly my bedroom, though we both slept here on alternate nights. One of my recent cases had taken me to a bathhouse near the docks. I had stopped in just long enough to slip a few coins to one of the contacts I cultivated among the staff, and to procure a bottle of what claimed to be oil for use in therapeutic massage. Which, to be fair, was a possible use for it, if not the one most frequently put to at the establishment.

I returned to find Whyborne sitting on the rug in front of the fire, his clothes neatly placed on one of the chairs and a throw drawn up around him to keep off the chill. "You're tense and upset," I said, holding up the bottle for him to see. "Perhaps a massage to loosen the muscles?"

He looked at me skeptically. "And since when are you a masseuse?"

"I'm a quick learner. Lie down on your belly."

He did as requested. I divested myself of my clothing, then paused to admire the view. My husband lay stretched out before me, bare skin brushed in ochre by the light of the fire. A knot of scar tissue decorated his left shoulder, and a complicated pattern of scars stretched from his right shoulder to his fingertips. His dark hair stuck out in spikes, defying the attempt of any hair tonic to tame it. The last few months of worry had etched more lines around his eyes, and I glimpsed the first gleam of a gray hair at his temple.

I saw beneath the surface as well. My shadowsight was attuned to magic, and it burned in him. The coals might be banked for the moment, but the glow was still there. The fire in his blood.

Last autumn, we'd traveled to Fallow, the town I'd been raised in. And there, in a field, I'd learned the truth about that glow within him.

I'd learned, too, something even more important in its way. The maelstrom had collected me, brought me here. It had chosen me at my lowest point. When even I didn't believe I had any value, the maelstrom did.

It brought me here and gave me a home—a *real* home, with someone who would never turn his back on me. With someone I loved beyond my words to tell. And now, every time I looked at him and saw that glow, I remembered, and I smiled.

"Are you going to do anything, or just stare at me all night?" Ival asked, sounding amused.

I swallowed against the emotion threatening to choke me and unstoppered the bottle. The faint scent of roses wafted out. I straddled his hips, my cock going half-hard at the touch of his skin. The boyish smile I so adored curved his lips in response.

I poured some oil into my palm, warming it between my hands before applying it to his shoulders. The muscles were tense beneath my fingers, so I gently kneaded them as I spread the oil.

"Mmm," he mumbled, eyes drifting closed.

"Relaxing?" I asked.

"In some ways." He bucked his hips slightly under mine. "Less so in others."

I grinned. "Patience, my dear."

I ran my hands over his back slowly, reverently, pausing occasionally for more oil. Gradually the tension faded from his shoulders, and I worked my way down. After more than four years together, I knew every inch of his skin. But I took the opportunity to get reacquainted, studying everything from the shape of his vertebrae, to the mole over his left hip.

The slide of skin on skin had its natural effect on us both. His breath grew heavier, and arousal brought a flush to his cheeks. I shifted off of him, and he parted his legs slightly, the head of his erect cock poking out between them.

My fingers skimmed over his spine, down his crease, to his balls. "Do you want me to fuck you?"

"God, yes."

Sometimes I would make him ask for it, in as much filthy detail as I could get him to speak. I loved seeing him blush, even as desire darkened his eyes. But tonight was about releasing all the tension I could from him.

I position myself between his legs and retrieved the oil. I poured a generous amount on his crease, just to see it run down over his skin.

"Griffin," he said, the words almost a whimper. He started to lift his hips, but I put a hand to the base of his spine.

"Shh. Relax. Let me do all the work."

I wrung a moan of pleasure from him when I slid a finger inside. When I judged him ready, I slicked myself and gripped his hips, lifting him to a workable angle.

"Ah. Yes." His fingers gripped the rug as I pushed in, his eyes squeezed tight. "More."

I gave him more, supporting his hips even as I began to thrust. The oil was wonderfully slick, and our heated skin released the scent of roses into the air. The only sound was the slap of skin on skin, punctuated by his short, sharp moans.

He let go of the rug, no doubt meaning to reach for his cock. "Don't move," I growled. "Just enjoy."

I bent over him, sliding one arm around his hips to hold him in place, while I wrapped my other hand around his prick. Oil still coated my hand, and he gasped at the sensation.

My cheek pressed against his back, and I inhaled his scent: salt and ambergris. I wished I could see his face, but I contented myself with listening to his breath quickening. “Griffin,” he said. “Yes, please.”

I increased the pace of my strokes. “Don’t hold back, Ival. Come for me.”

He shuddered and clenched beneath me. I closed my eyes and gave myself over to my own pleasure, sensation cresting like an oncoming wave, until I could hold it back no more and spent inside him.

“God,” he murmured, half into the rug. I sat back, saw him blink a few times, eyes slowly returning to focus.

I stretched out by him, pulling a throw over us both. “Feeling more relaxed?” I asked.

He snuggled in close. “If I were any less tense, I’d melt straight into the floor.” His lips pressed a kiss to my shoulder. “Thank you. You take such good care of me.”

“And you of me,” I said, because it was the truth. He’d always been there for me, from the very beginning. He’d held me through my fits, lent me his strength when my parents turned their backs on me, supported me in every way.

Given me a home. A place to be my imperfect self without fear.

Though he’d deny it, I sometimes thought the exchange an unequal one. And never more than now, when the concerns that preyed upon his mind were so enormous. The very fate of our world might hang in the balance.

I wished I could take this burden from him, even though I doubted my ability to hold up beneath it even half as well as he had. But no one could take the place of him or Persephone.

Still, I would stand by him in any way I possibly could. I would give him anything he needed from me, do whatever I might to lift the weight from his slim shoulders.

I could only pray it would be enough.

CHAPTER 5

Whyborne

AN ODD RINGING sound awoke me. I blinked awake, reached for the alarm, and discovered it silent. What the…

Oh. The blasted telephone.

I jabbed Griffin in the ribs. "Griffin."

He mumbled something incoherent and rolled over the other way.

I repeated the action, harder, this time. "Griffin!"

He blinked, sluggishly. "Wha…?"

"It's the telephone." A glance at the window showed the sun not yet up. "You didn't say they put calls through at such an hour!"

Muttering something I couldn't quite catch, he snatched up a thick winter robe and slid out of bed. I considered burrowing back under the covers, but I was now wide awake thanks to the incessant ringing.

I pulled on a nightshirt and robe, and followed him down. I arrived in the study just in time to hear him say, "Griffin Flaherty speaking."

He blinked—and then the sleepy look in his eyes vanished. "I see. Yes. Of course. We'll go straightaway."

Curse this infernal contraption. I wanted to hear the other side of the conversation. I hovered behind him, until he replaced the receiver in its cradle.

"What's wrong?" I asked.

"That was your father," Griffin said.

Of course it was. "What on earth did he want at this time of the morning?"

"He was calling about Thomas Abbott."

"Abbott?" I hadn't thought of the man in years, and now he'd been brought to mind twice in a handful of hours.

"It seems he returned to Widdershins." Griffin started for the stairs, and I followed in his wake. "Though apparently he failed to improve his fortune during his absence. His body was found a few hours ago, in the room of a rather questionable boarding house near the docks."

"Oh." Abbott had fled Widdershins thanks to me. I'd mistakenly believed he'd murdered Guinevere. That hadn't proved the case, but he had been plotting blackmail and sorcery alike.

Still, my reaction had been a bit…extreme. Though admittedly not as extreme as my Endicott cousins, who wanted to kill him even after learning he wasn't behind Guinevere's death.

"That's unfortunate," I said. "Still, it's nothing to do with us."

"I hope it's nothing to do with us," Griffin said. "Because Abbott was murdered. And it looks as though sorcery was involved."

An enclosed wagon with *Lester Mortuary Services* stenciled on the side already sat in front of the boarding house when we arrived in Griffin's Oldsmobile. A carriage waited behind it, also with matched black horses and black harness.

The street was narrow, lined by decrepit buildings, all of which leaned to the side, and none in the same direction. Grime covered every window, and there were no lamp posts of any kind, gas or electric. Most of the businesses appeared to be either saloons, gambling halls, brothels, or some combination thereof. At this relatively early hour, all were shuttered. A lone fishmonger stood behind a display of fish packed in blood-tinted ice. He watched us as we passed, bringing down a cleaver and severing the head from a codfish without so much as a glance downward. I wondered how many fingers he still possessed.

"Mr. Abbott certainly came down in the world," Griffin remarked after he'd shut off the noisy engine.

"Yes." The Abbotts had owned a mansion on High Street for generations, not far from Whyborne House. But their fortunes had dwindled, and much like my own family, only a few children had been born into any generation. Thomas had been the last of their line.

If his father had lived, perhaps things would have been different. But the elder Mr. Abbott died along with most of the Brotherhood of the Immortal Fire. Thomas found himself in possession of a fortune he didn't know how to manage properly, without the resources of the Brotherhood to buoy him up while he found his footing. He'd frittered the money away until he owed more to his creditors than he could hope to pay.

Griffin picked up his carpetbag, and we left the motor car. As we approached the door to the boarding house, the curtains hanging over the carriage window pulled back to reveal Miss Lester's pale face. Griffin let out a surprised hiss. I shot him a glance, but his expression had settled back to neutral, giving away nothing of his thoughts.

"Miss Lester," I greeted her, touching the brim of my hat. "I wasn't expecting to see you here."

"Whatever he may have become, Thomas Abbott was still the last of one of the old families," she said. "Once you've completed your investigations, I will see he is properly interred. Niles will inform you as to the particulars of the funeral."

I hadn't the slightest desire to attend Abbott's funeral. But it seemed as though I wasn't going to be given the choice. "I see."

"Had you had any contact with Mr. Abbott recently, Miss Lester?" Griffin asked. "Or heard any rumor of him? Any reason he might have returned?"

Her lips turned up in a cold smile. "They always return, Mr. Flaherty. I told you, when we first met, that this town collects people. And Abbott was of the old families, his ancestor among the first it claimed. He couldn't leave for long."

This was a conversation I truly didn't want to have. "We should view the body, so you can do your work," I said with a nod to Miss Lester. "Excuse us."

"She has ghūl blood, I believe," Griffin said, once we were away from the carriage.

Ah—that explained his startlement upon seeing her. I'd forgotten he didn't know. Otherwise, I would have warned him of what his shadowsight might betray. "Yes," I agreed.

"You knew?"

"Last July. When I perceived the world as the maelstrom does." I didn't like speaking of the experience, but seemed unable to avoid it. "I don't remember every detail, but her family came here to be free of the Outside. Nitocris, in their case, but they won't bow to the masters, either."

"Ah."

"I didn't think to mention it to you." I winced. "There's been rather a lot going on."

He chuckled ruefully. "Indeed there has. Think no more on it, my dear."

The interior of the boarding house was every bit as disreputable as the street outside. Newspaper patched broken or missing window panes. Green wallpaper peeled off in great strips where water had leaked down from the roof. The floor looked to have been only indifferently swept.

A woman with a hard face stood in the door to the parlor, her arms crossed over her chest and her countenance fixed in a glare. "You come to gawk at the body?" she asked. "Fine gentlemen like you got nothing better to do?"

"I'm sure this has been terribly distressing," Griffin said, offering her a winning smile. His hand dipped into his pocket, producing a few dollar bills. "For your trouble."

She plucked them away adroitly, and her expression became far more welcoming. "Well, at least you've got manners. Not like those blasted policemen. Offer you a drink to warm the blood?"

"I shouldn't wish to put you out," he replied. "I'm certain you have quite a lot of work to do, maintaining a house like this."

I glanced around again, but found no evidence to support Griffin's claim that the house had been maintained in any fashion whatsoever. The landlady gave him a smile though, revealing several missing teeth. "That I do. It's been hard since the mister died, but with the Good Lord's help I get through the day. You know the dead fellow, then? Called himself Mr. Arnold, but that damned policeman says he was somebody important."

"My friend knew him," Griffin said with a nod to me. It wasn't strictly a lie, though Abbott had been of the set Guinevere and Stanford socialized with. Parties in Newport, yacht races, nights at the club, and heavens only knew what else. They'd been bright and happy, drinking champagne and spending their parents' money as quickly as they could.

In some other world, I might have been one of them. Had I not been born sickly; had my interests not been so strange. Or had I been more inclined to please father, to pretend to be someone I wasn't. I might have laughed and drank with Fred and Orion, with Thomas and Stanford. Play-acted an interest in the fairer sex, though I doubted my ability to have done so with any success. Griffin might enjoy intimacies of that sort with women, though he preferred men, but they left me utterly unmoved.

"How long was he here?" Griffin asked.

The landlady considered. "Oh, 'bout two weeks, I'd say. Most of my boarders are sailors, you know, so he stood out a bit. He talked like a book and drank like a fish, but for the most part he kept to himself. Muttered about sorcery once or twice, and how he was going to get even with somebody. But who doesn't, from time to time?"

"Who indeed?" Griffin agreed with a grave nod. "Did he happen to mention a name?"

Her brow creased in thought. "Once, I think. Peter? No. Pat? No." She snapped her fingers. "Percy—that was it."

Oh, heavens. I did my best to keep my dismay from showing on my face. As for Griffin, his pleasant smile didn't waver at all. "Thank you for your help, ma'am," he said. "If you recall anything of interest about the deceased, please, don't hesitate to contact me." He passed her one of his business cards. "Your time is valuable, so of course you will be compensated."

She took the card and nodded in the direction of the stairs at the end of the hall. "Fourth floor. There's a policeman outside the door."

As we mounted the steps, I said, "So Abbott wanted to get even with me."

"It seems likely," Griffin agreed. "Perhaps we should be grateful some ill befell him before he had the chance."

A lone policeman stood outside one of the doors on the fourth floor. Upon seeing us, he tipped his hat respectfully. "Detective Tilton has gone back to the station, Dr. Whyborne, Mr. Flaherty, but I've got orders to help you in any way I can. He also said if you need him, just send word."

I'd spent my life avoiding the police, afraid to draw their attention even when I'd lived as celibate as a monk. After Griffin had set up shop here in Widdershins, he and Tilton had clashed on more than one occasion. It seemed unspeakably strange therefore to receive such deference now.

What *did* Tilton know about me? He'd survived for years as a police detective in Widdershins, so presumably he had a finely honed instinct concerning when to look more closely into a situation, and when to avert his eyes. At some point, I had been shifted into the latter category.

Then again, as a member of the old families, maybe I'd always been in that category. The detective had sparred with Griffin from time to time, but merely suggested I keep better company.

"Thank you," Griffin said to the policeman. "Has the scene been disturbed?"

"No, sir. The patrolman who answered the landlady's cry for help took one look inside and sent for Detective Tilton. He recognized Mr. Abbott, checked to make sure he was dead and not just unconscious, and sent a runner to Whyborne House. He figured this was a matter for the old families to take care of."

"Quite right," Griffin agreed. "And no one else has been inside?"

"No, sir." The man shook his head. "You'll pardon me for saying so, but what I glimpsed before the detective shut the door was all I want to see of the matter. Unless you have some need of me, I'll stay out here."

"Of course." Griffin put his hand on the latch, then glanced up at me. "Shall we?"

I nodded. The door creaked open on unoiled hinges, revealing a shabby room scarcely larger than a closet.

Abbott lay inside, sprawled on his back on the floor. A tangle of chalked sigils surrounded his body.

"Oh dear," I said. "This isn't good at all."

CHAPTER 6

Griffin

I PUT MY hand out. "Wait here," I told Whyborne.

He didn't object. I stepped cautiously into the room, careful not to tread on the chalk lines scrawled on the floor. Magic yet clung to them, glowing a pale, nacreous green in my shadowsight. But it was faint and fading, whatever spell had been cast over and done with.

The room was tiny, with only a bed and a single chair for furniture. The blankets were threadbare and stained, and the chair hadn't seen polish in years. An odd scent hung in the air, a sort of acrid fetor I couldn't quite place.

Abbott lay sprawled on his back in the center of the floor, his eyes wide. I'd only been in the same room with him twice previously. Once at the party welcoming Guinevere back to the states, and the second time when I'd kept Whyborne and the Endicotts from killing him out of hand. He'd been well dressed, clean, his figure firm.

The last two years had not been kind. The refined man I'd met was long gone. Hunger hollowed his cheeks, and it had been some time since he'd bathed, judging by the layer of grime on his skin. His clothing might have belonged to any poor laborer. His shirt hung open almost to the waist, exposing skin the color of marble. Large, sucker-like marks showed on the bare flesh of his chest and throat.

"His coat and vest are hanging over the chair," I observed aloud. "Which suggests he removed them voluntarily."

"What do you think happened?" Whyborne asked. "What are those marks on him?"

"I'm getting to that." I crouched down by the body, observing it closely. All the buttons still remained on Abbott's threadbare shirt; it hadn't been torn open, at any rate. I peered closely at the marks, searching for any trace of magic. But if there had been any, it had faded beyond my ability to perceive.

"My shadowsight doesn't tell us anything we didn't already know," I said. "You might as well come in."

He shut the door behind him, then crossed to me. "Is that why you had me remain outside?"

In the last year, I'd grown used to seeing him with my shadowsight. I no longer expected to find gills when I kissed his throat, or feel tentacles wiggling against my fingers when I threaded them through his hair. Most of the time, anyway. But he still burned, the fire I'd sensed from the first now revealed.

"You're a flame, my dear." I opened my carpetbag and took out a magnifying glass. "Or, rather, you're an arc light, and what magic remained in the room a candle guttering in a pool of wax. I feared you'd overwhelm any clue they might have left behind."

"Oh." He studied the sigils. "These seem familiar—I'm certain I've come across something like them before. I wonder if Iskander would be willing to photograph them, once the body has been removed?"

"I'm sure he would." I examined the strange marks on the corpse through the magnifying glass. Seen up close, they were even more baffling. In the center of each was a deep puncture wound, surrounded by mottled bruises, as though suction had been applied to the injuries. "Look here, Whyborne. Abbott's been stabbed, multiple times, but there's no sign of blood."

An uneasy look passed over his face. "Was he already dead when it happened?"

"No. The bruises wouldn't have formed in that case." I lifted his arm, or tried to. Rigor mortis had set in, and the body was as pliable as the marble it resembled. "Help me lift him, would you?"

"I'd rather not," Whyborne muttered. But he came to my side, careful not to disturb the chalked lines. His lips fixed in an expression of distaste, he helped me lever Abbott up so I could shove the dead man's shirt aside to look at the skin. "What are we doing?"

"Checking for the settling of blood. Once the heart stops beating, gravity takes over, and blood pools in whatever body parts are lowest. In this case, his back should be much darkened." I signaled to Whyborne to lower the body back to the floor. "It isn't."

Whyborne frowned. "Why not? Was he moved?"

"I don't think so." I shook my head slowly. "Between that and the lack of blood around the wounds…I think Mr. Abbott died from exsanguination. Something sucked all the blood out of his body."

CHAPTER 7

Whyborne

"DRAINED OF BLOOD?" Christine exclaimed the next day at the museum. "Surely Griffin doesn't mean to suggest Abbott was killed by vampires."

I didn't bother to look up from my desk. Iskander had kindly not only photographed the sigils, but developed the prints as well in his darkroom at the house he and Christine shared not far from our own. Christine had brought them into the museum to give to me, then promptly planted herself in the guest chair in my office.

"Don't be absurd," I said, shuffling through the photographs. "There's no such thing. Er, I hope."

Miss Parkhurst appeared at my door. "I've brought your mail, Dr. Whyborne."

"Just put it on the corner of the desk, if you would," I said.

"I say, those are lovely pearl earrings, Miss Parkhurst," Christine remarked.

A few of the letters tumbled from Miss Parkhurst's hands. She hastened to pick them up. "Oh, er, th-thank you, Dr. Putnam-Barnett. They were a gift from a friend."

"I'm sure," Christine said dryly.

"Do stop bothering my secretary, Christine," I said, glancing up. "That will be all, Miss Parkhurst."

Once she was gone, Christine said, "Odd, isn't it, how much new jewelry Miss Parkhurst has of late?"

What on earth was she going on about now? "Don't be absurd. I haven't noticed a thing."

Christine snorted. "Of course you haven't."

"You know as well as I do that she assisted the ketoi while we were in Fallow." I took the *Liber Arcanorum* from my desk drawer and began to flip through it. "Gold and pearls are mere trinkets to them. It's hardly odd they would give her some to show their appreciation."

"She rents a house by the river now, doesn't she?"

"How in the world should I know?" I cast Christine a vexed look. "Don't you have work to do?"

"I still have hopes of being granted the firman to excavate the fane in Egypt," she said, rising to her feet. "In the meantime, though, I should finish my latest article. Do let me know when you need me to come stake your vampire for you."

"It isn't a vampire. It's a..." I cast about for a less lurid term. "Hematophage. A blood eater."

"Vampire," Christine whispered from the doorway. I leveled another glare at her, but she was already gone.

I stared at the photographs spread on my desk, trying to recall where I'd seen similar sigils before. The Pnakotic manuscripts? The *Al Azif?* The Wisborg Codex?

Hopefully not the latter. So far as I had been able to tell, the codex contained information about the masters, their creations—earthly and otherwise—and the Restoration which would usher them back into the world they'd once ruled. But the codex was encrypted in some fashion I'd been unable to fathom. The Fideles held the key to deciphering it, but I didn't. Meaning it remained an enigma, taunting me with the fact that knowledge of its contents might make all the difference in the upcoming struggle.

Miss Parkhurst knocked tentatively. "Dr. Whyborne?"

I bit back a sigh—apparently I was doomed to endless interruptions this morning. "Yes?"

"Detective Tilton is here to see you."

"Tilton?" He must have some new information about Abbott's murder. "Of course. Show him in."

Tilton entered with an air of reluctance, his hat clutched in his hands. "Dr. Whyborne," he said. "Accept my apologies for disturbing you."

I'd never seen him look so worried. Something must have gone very wrong with his investigation. "Have a seat," I said, indicating the chair. "How can I help you?"

"I have a few questions to ask you. I…well, I wouldn't if it were up to me, of course." He eased himself into the seat, looking increasingly nervous. "You read about our new chief of police in the papers, I'm sure."

I tried and failed to remember. "Er, not really. Can you refresh my memory?"

"He's not from Widdershins," Tilton said. "But after the last chief died in…unusual circumstances…it was difficult to find a local replacement."

"Oh dear," I said. *Unusual circumstances* could cover any number of terrible fates.

"Chief Early doesn't understand how things are done here." Tilton shifted uncomfortably in his seat. "I have to follow orders, but…" He trailed off.

"And what did he order you to do?" I asked cautiously.

Tilton took a deep breath. "Dr. Whyborne, where were you the night of January 26?"

I stared at him blankly. "In a meeting at Father's house. Several members of the old families were there."

"And after?"

At home, making love with Griffin on the study rug. My face burned, and I prayed Tilton didn't notice. "In b-bed."

"And are there any…um…witnesses?"

My hands went ice cold. I'd always feared the police would find some reason to look more closely into my living arrangements. But as time passed and nothing ever came of my fears, I'd begun to relax.

"Of course not," I snapped. Griffin said I looked cold when upset, so I did my best to project an icy demeanor. It must have worked, because Tilton visibly flinched. "I cannot fathom why you would ask such a question, sir."

"Because…" Tilton cleared his throat. "One of Abbott's fellow boarders said you'd threatened to kill him if he ever returned to Widdershins."

~ * ~

For a moment, I felt only relief. This wasn't about my relationship with Griffin after all.

Then the import of Tilton's words fully registered. "What?" I exclaimed.

"Please, Dr. Whyborne. I'm only doing my job," he said, holding up his hands. "If Chief Early hadn't ordered me to, of course I wouldn't disturb you."

Dear God, no wonder he was so nervous. He thought I might put a curse on him, or set him aflame. Or that he, too, might disappear in *unusual circumstances.*

I forced myself to sit back in my chair. "Of course. I...I understand."

"Thank you." He paused. "So, is there any truth behind the accusations? Did you threaten to kill Thomas Abbott if he returned?"

Not one of my finer moments. "He'd tried to blackmail my sister Guinevere," I said. "I was understandably upset."

Tilton didn't look at all reassured by my response. "I see. Did you have any contact with Mr. Abbott after he came back to Widdershins?"

"No. I didn't even know he had returned, until Father informed me he'd been killed."

"Of course," Tilton agreed. He rose to his feet. "I've taken up enough of your time. Unless you have anything else you would like to add?"

I couldn't imagine what else I could say. "No. But we are trying to discover what killed him." I indicated the photographs on my desk. "I may not have been fond of the man, but I'm certainly not going to let his death go without doing everything possible to find out what happened. And if there's any continuing threat."

Tilton gave a curt nod. "Thank you. Good day, Dr. Whyborne."

CHAPTER 8

Griffin

THAT EVENING, I listened with growing horror as Whyborne detailed his encounter with Detective Tilton.

"You admitted you threatened Abbott?" I asked when he finished.

Ironically, we were in the midst of preparing ourselves to go to Abbott's funeral. Whyborne sat in front of the mirror, trying and failing to tame his hair with Brilliantine. "Well, yes," he said, frowning at his reflection. "I didn't explain all the extenuating circumstances, but the blackmail threat would surely be reason enough."

I resisted the temptation to clutch at my own hair in frustration, though only because I'd just finished combing it. "Ival, did it never occur to you it would be a bad idea to offer the police a motive for murdering Abbott?"

He turned to face me, blinking in surprise. "I told him the reason I said such a rash thing. Surely no one believes I actually killed a man, do they?"

I tipped my head back, willing patience. "You *have* killed men, Whyborne. More than one, in fact."

"Not that the police know of! Besides, they were all trying to kill us first." His chair creaked as he shifted his weight. "I would never murder anyone in cold blood."

"I know that. You know that. The police do not know that."

"Oh. I suppose you're right." The chair creaked again. "Will you not even look at me?"

I turned my gaze on him. A strand of his hair broke free of the Brilliantine and slowly rose back to its normal position. "All right," I said, forcing myself to think past my fear. "Motive alone isn't enough. Perhaps if you were anyone else, but the son of Niles Whyborne isn't getting hauled into jail without actual evidence of wrongdoing."

Predictably, the reminder failed to cheer him. "I wish you had been there. I was so relieved he hadn't come to ask questions about us, I discounted any other threat."

"Understandable." I put my hand on his shoulder and gave a gentle squeeze. "But if Tilton—or any other police officer—returns, refuse to speak to him without a lawyer present. I'm certain Niles will be more than happy to give you the name of his most ruthless solicitor."

"No doubt." He touched the back of my hand with his fingers. The black pearl on his wedding ring shone softly in the light, revealing a host of hidden colors. "I'm sorry, darling."

"You have nothing to apologize for." I bent and kissed him swiftly. "Tilton has no desire to pursue this line of questioning. With no evidence to link you to Abbott's death, the investigation will be quietly shelved."

Ival didn't seem convinced, and in truth neither was I. I'd noted the hiring of the new police chief, but not paid especial attention. Perhaps that had been a mistake. If the man thought he had something to prove, it could mean trouble for us.

I couldn't help but wonder if the maelstrom had collected Chief Early for its own inscrutable reasons, or if he had come on his own. The latter, I suspected.

A knock sounded on our door. "That will be Father," Whyborne said. "Or a footman, more likely, doing the actual knocking. We shouldn't keep him waiting."

Rather than bringing his new touring car, Niles had arrived in a carriage with the Whyborne family crest painted on the side. No doubt he felt it more appropriate for a solemn occasion. At my suggestion, Whyborne told his father about the visit from the police. Niles's face darkened, and I had the feeling Police Chief Early was about to have a very bad day. But when he spoke, he directed his vitriol elsewhere.

"Blast Thomas Abbott for a fool." Niles's mouth tightened with disapproval. "His father had enough sense to leave sorcery to the sorcerers."

"Like the rest of you left it to Blackbyrne?" Whyborne asked. "Oh, yes, that worked out so well."

Niles glowered. "Thomas at least shouldn't have summoned something he couldn't control—"

"Like the Brotherhood resurrecting Blackbyrne?"

Niles shut his mouth with an audible snap. I directed my attention out the window and pretended to have been struck temporarily deaf.

The carriage joined the short processional just outside the mortuary. The Lesters had provided a catafalque, drawn by four black horses. "That was kind of Miss Lester," I remarked. "To give Abbott such a sendoff, when I'm sure she's not being compensated for it."

"Anywhere else, he would have ended up in an unmarked grave in potter's field," Niles agreed. "But he was the last surviving heir of one of the old families. His bloodline helped to build Widdershins from an uninhabited wilderness into what it is today."

"A horrible murder town," Whyborne agreed.

Niles glared, and I sighed. "Whyborne, you're being difficult," I said.

For a moment, his lower lip stuck out rebelliously. Then he sagged. "Forgive me. The interview with the police has left me in a poor mood." He glanced out the window. "Who are they?"

Despite Abbott's fall from fortune, a number of mourners waited at the gates to the cemetery. They lined either side of the road, their clothing ranging from that of respectable businessmen to something more appropriate to sailors. As the catafalque passed, they solemnly removed their hats. I recognized some members of the Marsh and Waite clans, both from branches that had clung to respectability and those which had slid into poverty.

"Inhabitants of the town," Niles replied with barely a glance. "Natives all, for many generations. As I said earlier, Abbott's ancestors helped shape Widdershins. The obliteration of one of the old families is not something to be taken lightly."

"What is the connection between the old families and the town?" I asked. "Is it only that they helped Blackbyrne found Widdershins, or is there something more?"

"Some arcane tie, you mean?" Whyborne asked.

"Perhaps." Niles stared out the window at the mourners. "Blackbyrne was steeped in necromancy, and even those of his followers who weren't sorcerers aided in his rituals. Once he was gone, the heads of the five families banded together and made certain their descendants would prosper here. Continuing the work of the Brotherhood of the Immortal Fire was one method they used to do so."

The iron gates to the cemetery stood wide, and the procession wound its way up the hill, toward where the oldest graves lay. At last it came to a halt, and we stepped out into the icy air. Pallbearers carried Abbott's casket toward the row of mausoleums, and the rest of us fell in behind.

The cemetery ended at the very edge of the Draakenwood. I'd set foot in the forest once, but only for a short time. Though it seemed a prime spot for bird watchers and other nature enthusiasts, I'd soon learned no one who'd lived in Widdershins long would willingly set foot there. Every year, the newspapers featured an article on the disappearance of some visitor, who chose to go on a walk in the forest despite the warnings. Whyborne usually read these with a sad shake of his head, and in time I'd learned to do the same.

One of the arcane lines feeding into the maelstrom cut through the cemetery, its blue fire visible to my shadowsight. It ran directly beneath the extravagant monument with BLACKBYRNE carved into it. The grave rested nearly beneath the eaves of the wood—though of course, no body lay there any longer. He'd been swallowed up by the Outside, fallen into the opening he'd torn in the veil to summon horrors. Undone by his own magic, much like Abbott.

Less ostentatious graves surrounded the monument, radiating out like the spokes of a wheel. Most were worn to nubs from time and weather, but the names Whyborne, Marsh, Abbott, Lester, and Waite could be made out on a few.

At some point, fortune had allowed them to build family vaults, which stood a bit farther out, alongside those of other families like Rice and Mathison, who had arrived later in the town's history. The procession stopped outside the Abbott mausoleum, and Miss Lester stepped forward to unlock the chain holding it shut. Her normal white furs were replaced with mourning black, and a veil shrouded her face from view. A priest from First Esoteric spoke a few words as Abbott was borne within. The wind sent the priest's robes flapping about his legs, the weak sunlight glinting from the golden tiara he wore.

The mourners began to disperse as soon as the mausoleum door was shut and locked once again. I glanced at Whyborne, only to find him staring at Blackbyrne's monument, his lips in a pensive moue.

"We'll find our own way back," I told Niles.

He glanced at Whyborne, then nodded. "As you wish."

I waited until we were alone, before approaching my husband. "Ival? Is something wrong?"

He blinked, as if coming out of a reverie. "I…no. Nothing."

I took his gloved hand in mine. "Something is obviously bothering you. Beyond what might be expected, I mean." I glanced at the monument. "Is it something to do with Blackbyrne?"

His shoulders slumped beneath the weight of his woolen coat. "I suppose. It's just…the thing that bothers me most about the maelstrom is it isn't…moral?" He shook his head. "I'm not sure the word is adequate, but it's the best I can come up with. It drew you here, and Christine most likely…but it also drew Blackbyrne, and the Abbotts, and my own ancestor, who barely escaped the hangman back in England. It collects people not because they're good, but because they're *useful* to it in some way, or because they…fit? I'm not sure how to explain it better than that."

"Widdershins knows its own," I said. "For which I, at least, am profoundly grateful."

His dark eyes met mine, troubled. "It isn't human. It doesn't have a sense of right and wrong. Or if it does, it isn't like ours."

I considered his words carefully. "I suppose that makes sense. It would be asking a great deal to expect a massive, semi-sentient magical vortex to view the world the same way as we do. Even as humans, we cannot always agree on right and wrong, after all."

"But I'm a part of it," he said unhappily. "So what does that make me?"

"Human," I said. "Well, a ketoi-human hybrid. A man, anyway." I squeezed his hand. "The best man I've ever known."

His cheeks pinked from more than the cold, and he ducked his head shyly. "You speak such nonsense."

"My husband," I pressed on. "My love. Of course you aren't perfect, but neither am I. You might have come from the maelstrom, but it doesn't define you. No more than where I came from—Ireland or Fallow, whichever you prefer to count—defines me."

"It isn't the same," he protested.

And perhaps it wasn't. I wouldn't claim my understanding of his circumstances was entirely accurate, but from what I'd gleaned, his soul, for lack of a better word, was a fragment of the maelstrom.

Whyborne, a thorough-going atheist, would hate the comparison. But it was the best I could make. And perhaps some would consider his condition damning, but if I believed in divine providence, then it was hardly a stretch to accept God had ordered this as well.

"Look at how your brother turned out," I said. "He carries no spark of the maelstrom. And yet you're a better person than he could ever hope to be." I hesitated, wondering if I could ever make Whyborne truly understand. "I know your connection to the maelstrom has troubled you ever since you realized the truth. But in bringing me here, it saved me, in a way I didn't even know I needed to be saved. The fact you're a part of it makes you more wonderful to me, not less."

He blushed even more fiercely, but squeezed my fingers. "I love you."

"I know. I love you, too." I tugged on his hand. "Come. It's getting dark."

"All right." He glanced at the shadows gathering beneath the nearby trees. "It probably isn't wise to linger too close to the Draakenwood after nightfall anyway."

"No doubt." And perhaps it was merely my imagination, but as we walked hand-in-hand away from the woods, I couldn't help but feel as though unseen eyes watched our backs, until the bulk of the hill hid us from view.

CHAPTER 9

Griffin

THE NEXT MORNING, the telephone rang in the midst of setting out breakfast. Whyborne was pouring our coffee; at the sound of the bell, he jerked, spilling hot liquid onto his hand. "Blast that thing!" he exclaimed.

"Run cold water over the burn, my dear," I advised, even as I hastened down the hall to my study. Picking up the receiver, I said, "Griffin Flaherty speaking."

"Hold for Mr. Niles Whyborne," advised the voice on the other end of the line.

My heart sank. There could be no good reason for Niles to call in the middle of breakfast.

"Griffin," Niles barked. "Is Percival there with you?"

"Yes. Do you wish to speak with him?"

"No. Just…making certain." He sighed. "It happened too late to make the papers, but Sterling Waite is dead."

Whyborne came into the room, nursing his sore hand. "The head of the Waite family is dead?" I said aloud. "How?"

"Murdered in his own home, possibly by whatever killed Abbott."

"That isn't good," I said.

"No, it isn't," Niles replied grimly. "The body has already been removed, but I imagine you'll want a look at it. Meet me at the mortuary in an hour."

The Lester mortuary stood on Cemetery Road, not far from the family's colonial mansion. I'd been inside the mansion once, when Miss Lester hired me to retrieve a strange talisman belonging to her grandfather. The experience had been unsettling, to say the least.

Niles's motor car was already outside. I left my Oldsmobile beside it, and knocked on the mortuary door.

A thin, hollow-faced man dressed in a somber suit answered. After a moment, I recognized him as the driver of the catafalque that took Abbott's body to the burying ground. He didn't ask my name, or even speak, merely stepped back and gestured for me to enter.

Niles and Miss Lester waited in the front parlor, which was decorated in muted tones. Niles sipped a cup of coffee, but Miss Lester sat very still, her ivory hands clasped in the lap of her white dress. With her black hair and eyes, the only spot of color about her was the red of her lips.

"Ah, Mr. Flaherty," she said. "Good morning."

My shadowsight betrayed what I hadn't perceived when we first met. Even though I knew she passed for human, I now felt certain I would see jackal teeth behind her parted lips, or that her eyes would become crimson between one blink and the next.

God. What would her grandfather look like, could I see him now? He'd been horrible enough to ordinary vision. I suppressed a shudder at the thought and inclined my head. "Good morning, Miss Lester. Niles."

"Percival didn't accompany you?" Niles asked.

I shook my head. "He had a staff meeting at the museum. I told him I'd send for him, if there was need." I paused. "Were there sorcerous marking around the body, as with Abbott?"

"Not that I know of," Niles said. "But the Waites are being devilishly tight-lipped about all of this. With me, at least."

"Because they think Whyborne is plotting a coup of some kind?"

Niles didn't seem surprised he'd told me. Neither did Miss Lester. "At least I'm not banished from their presence," she said, contempt lacing her voice. "Though only because they want Sterling embalmed. Such a waste."

A little chill crept up my back, but I kept my expression composed. I couldn't guess how Miss Lester would react, if she realized I knew inhuman blood ran in her family. Had it been there from the beginning of Widdershins? Or had some ghūl hybrid made its way across the Atlantic later, to marry into the Lester line?

Not that it mattered. "If I could view the body…?"

"I'll remain here," Niles said.

Miss Lester led me from the parlor to the back of the house, away from the area where any clients would tread. A set of stairs led to a large basement. The scent of damp earth wafted from the aged brick of the walls, and an odd chill touched me.

This was no ordinary basement. Though the room at the foot of the stairs held modern steel tables and a gleaming embalming machine, its walls were of ancient brickwork. Low, arched tunnels branched off from it. The largest ran in the direction of the cemetery, and my hands went cold.

The underground warrens, the smell of damp…it all reminded me a bit too forcefully of the tunnels beneath Chicago, where my partner had died and my mind been cracked open by a captive umbrae. My pulse quickened, and sweat slicked my palms.

Miss Lester's nostrils flared ever so slightly. "There is no cause for concern, Mr. Flaherty," she said. Her voice echoed in the vaulted room, the darkness of the tunnels. "The dead cannot harm you." I didn't know whether to be grateful she thought my reaction a mere common phobia or not.

She led the way to one of the tables. A body lay on it, covered in white cloth. She whisked the cloth away without ceremony, revealing Sterling Waite's nude corpse.

As with Abbott, there seemed no blood remaining in his body. The same pattern of sucker marks and puncture wounds covered his chest and abdomen. Closer inspection of his hands revealed some thick, blackish substance beneath the nails.

"He fought back," I murmured. There had been no signs of violence on Abbott, no indication he'd struggled with whatever had killed him. "Do you have Mr. Waite's clothes?"

"The police kept them for evidence," Miss Lester replied.

Damn. "Did you get a look at the room where he died?"

"No." She folded her hands before her. "The family had already removed his body to his bedchamber. I'm not certain where he was killed, but it wasn't there."

I bit back a curse. I would have thought the death of their patriarch reason enough for the Waites to abandon their hostility toward Niles and Whyborne, but apparently not. I was going to have to find my answers another way.

"Thank you, Miss Lester," I said.

She drew the shroud back over the body. "First Thomas, and now Sterling. What do you think is happening, Mr. Flaherty?"

I hesitated. I was no sorcerer, and anything I said at the moment would be pure conjecture. Still… "I'll have to ask Whyborne about the likelihood, but it seems to me Thomas Abbot summoned something he couldn't control. And rather than return to the Outside after killing him, it's now on the loose in Widdershins."

CHAPTER 10

Whyborne

AS THE CLOCK struck five, I shuffled the papers on my desk into slightly neater stacks. After an interminable staff meeting to start the day, I'd escaped to my office to find a note from Griffin. The same monstrous creature that killed Abbott had murdered Sterling Waite. Griffin meant to try and learn more; though he didn't go into detail, I assumed he would attempt to get information from the servants at the Waite mansion. He advised me that he might be late for dinner, and not to worry overmuch if he was.

I'd spent the rest of the day divided between legitimate work for the museum, and studying various tomes in an attempt to guess what sort of horror Abbott had called up. Although there seemed an unending catalog of potential awfulness, I'd yet to find any reference to a creature that killed by draining the blood of its victims. Short of Christine's vampires, that is, but I wasn't yet ready to entertain quite such an outlandish suggestion.

Now my head ached, and a crick had developed in my neck. I leaned back in my chair for a stretch, and contemplated whether I was likely to accomplish anything if I remained here for another hour or two.

There came a rap on my door. Miss Parkhurst stuck her head in; she'd already donned hat and coat in preparation for leaving for the day. Before I could tell her I wouldn't be needing anything further, she said, "Dr. Whyborne, the p-police—"

A short man with a large mustache shoved her out of the way. I shot to my feet, outraged at her rough handling. "What the devil? Apologize to Miss Parkhurst this instant!"

"Dr. Percival Endicott Whyborne," said the man, as if relishing every syllable. An ugly smirk twisted his face as he looked me up and down. He strolled in, followed by Detective Tilton and no less than six uniformed policemen. Tilton appeared utterly wretched; he met my gaze, then looked at the floor.

Dread pooled in my stomach, but I forced my spine straight. "What is the meaning of this?"

"Let me introduce myself," said the newcomer. He wore a sack suit and several heavy rings on his fingers. "Moses Early, Chief of Police. And you, Dr. Whyborne, are under arrest for the murders of Thomas Abbott and Sterling Waite."

"Wh-what?" I stammered. "I did no such thing!"

"Then you've nothing to worry about, do you?" Early's smirk remained fixed on his face. "But I think you do." He took a step closer to me. "It's a new era here in Widdershins. You aren't above the law anymore." He glanced at the uniformed police. "Cuff him."

"Surely that isn't necessary," Tilton said.

Early's smirk transformed into an annoyed scowl. "I say it is." When no one moved, he snapped, "Do you all have wax in your ears? Do it!"

One of the policemen took out his cuffs, while another approached me cautiously. Both of them looked pale and sweaty. My head spun. I took a step back, trying to think. I could cast them aside with a blast of wind, or set fire to the powder in their bullets, or—

The policeman with the handcuffs reached out toward me, then stopped. His eyes locked with mine. "I-I've got a wife and children."

I took a deep breath, calming my racing pulse. There had been some sort of mistake. Everything would be cleared up in no time. The police chief might be insufferable, but he had no evidence against me. On the other hand, if I fought back, assaulting a group of police officers with sorcery would leave me squarely on the wrong side of the law. Better to go quietly and let one of Father's lawyers deal with the problem.

"Yes," I said, holding out my wrists. "Of course."

They marched me out of my office, past a horrified Miss Parkhurst. Though the museum was closed to visitors, a great many of my colleagues were in the process of leaving for the night. A murmur rose in the foyer at the sight of the police, growing even louder when they saw the cuffs on my wrists. "Is that Dr. Whyborne?" a taxidermist exclaimed.

Heat suffused my face, and I did my best to keep my humiliation hidden. Curse Early for arresting me at my own desk, making a spectacle of me in front of the rest of the staff. By morning, I'd be the subject of gossip in every department, from Antiquities to Natural History.

"Widdershins!" shouted Mr. Quinn from behind us. "Unhand him at once, you cretins."

Blast. I twisted about, the grip of the policemen on each arm tightening, as though they feared I sought to escape. Mr. Quinn's pale face had gone white, his eyes wide with outrage on my behalf.

I didn't dare imagine what he might try to do. "It's all right," I called. "Just a little misunderstanding. Nothing to worry about."

Then we were out the main doors. A patrol wagon waited at the bottom of the steps. Tilton and one of the uniformed men climbed inside, then helped me in after. Early joined us.

"I'm sorry for the rough accommodations, Dr. Whyborne," Tilton said. I'd been in the back of this wagon once before, when I'd been trapped in Bradley's body. At least this time I could sit on the narrow bench, instead of being flung on the floor.

"Stop apologizing to the prisoner," Early snapped.

"This has all been a mistake," I said, in as reasonable a tone as I could.

The wagon lurched into motion. Already, the museum would be abuzz with word of my arrest. With a sinking heart, I realized my name would surely be emblazoned on the front page of every morning paper in Widdershins. Possibly the entire northeast, given the reach of Whyborne Railroad and Industries.

Father was going to kill me.

"So you keep saying." Early leaned forward, resting his elbows on his knees. "Tilton, take notes."

Tilton took out a notebook and pencil. He kept his eyes fixed on the paper, as if to distance himself from events.

"Where were you last night, between the hours of midnight and three a.m.?" Early asked.

At least I could answer that easily enough. "At home in bed."

"Were you?" Early sounded skeptical. "Any…companions…who might swear to that?"

"Of course not." Heat suffused my face. Once again, I couldn't give him an honest account, without convicting myself of a wholly different crime—and dragging Griffin down with me. "But you can ask my landlord. Mr. Flaherty would have heard the door open and shut, if I'd left the house."

"Oh, we'll ask him." Early's smile turned nasty, and fear raced through my veins. Had he heard some gossip or whispered suspicion about us?

The cuffs around my wrists went cold, frost forming on the metal. I had to calm down, but it seemed impossible.

"Mr. Joseph Marsh says you quarreled with Mr. Waite only a few days ago," Early went on. "At your father's house."

Curse Marsh. "We had a minor disagreement, nothing more."

"Mr. Marsh seemed to think it more than minor." Early removed something from his pocket. "Do you recognize this?"

In the palm of his hand lay a familiar diamond cufflink.

"Yes," I said stiffly. "I lost it the same night, probably at the meeting at Father's. Mr. Waite seized my wrist. It must have come off in his hand."

The wagon drew to a halt. "That's one possibility," Early said. "The other is that he tore it free last night in the struggle for his life."

I swallowed hard. "You don't have anything," I said. "A cufflink isn't proof. You have no murder weapon, no witnesses. Nothing."

"It's enough to hold you." The doors opened, and Early started to climb out, then paused. Leaning closer to me, he fixed me with a smile that chilled my blood. "I know your type of man, Dr. Whyborne. You think you're above the rest of us. You believe your money and your heritage makes you better than us common folk. But you're wrong. I'm going to be famous as the police chief who brought low the son of one of the richest men in America."

He left the wagon. Two officers helped me down, and Tilton clambered out and shut the doors behind us. As the policemen hustled me into the station, Early said, "Tilton, I've another job for you. Take the warrant and some men, and go search the house where Dr. Whyborne rents a room. Bring anything suspicious to me."

CHAPTER 11

Whyborne

THE JAIL WAS relatively small—serious crime in Widdershins seldom made it to the court room—with only a few cells. Two of the three cells were already occupied; I found myself in the middle one. A thin layer of grime coated the masonry block walls, interrupted here and there with brighter patches where inmates had scratched obscenities into the walls. A bare electric bulb near the guard station provided the only light, revealing a water tank, sink, and bucket, whose lack of cleanliness made me feel faint. The furniture consisted of a single bed, and I loathed the very thought of touching the worn and stained blankets. Were they disinfected between prisoners, or did I run the risk of vermin? At least I was alone in the cell. Though I feared that would only be temporary.

A search of our house wouldn't reveal anything connected to Waite's murder. But it would reveal far too much otherwise. Valentine's Day cards, anniversary gifts, photographs of Griffin and me with our arms about one another.

Early had come to Widdershins to make his name. If he couldn't convict me of murder, perhaps he'd settle for a different crime.

I'd used the station telephone to place a call to Father, hoping a lawyer might arrive quickly enough to put a stop to things. But Father had gone to Boston for a meeting with his man of business there, and wouldn't be back until late this evening. Early refused to let me make any more calls, and ordered me locked in this wretched cell.

What would Griffin think, when the police arrived on our door with a warrant to search the premises? How would he feel, standing there, while Tilton and his men ransacked all our more private belongings? The thought was agonizing enough to make me consider breaking out of the cell and…

What? Become a wanted fugitive? Attack Tilton before he could return with any evidence?

Early wanted to make his name…but he couldn't force the city prosecutor to bring me to trial. Murder was one thing, but Father's wealth, plus a clever lawyer, would hopefully be enough to prevent a charge of sodomy from being brought against Griffin and me. I just had to avoid doing anything to make the situation worse.

Using sorcery against Early, for example, no matter how much I might long to do so.

The door leading to the jail opened, revealing Griffin's familiar figure in the light of the electric bulb. My heart started in my chest, but he was alone. Not being dragged in by police, under arrest. Thank God.

Griffin paused and spoke to the jailer, who sat at his station reading the newspaper. The jailor shook his head, and Griffin nodded, before coming to my cell alone.

"Griffin?" I asked as he approached. I couldn't help but note the grim expression on his face.

My voice must have betrayed my worry, because he managed a smile. He didn't speak until he reached the bars, wrapping his hand around one. Though I longed to touch him, it would be the height of foolishness given the circumstances. I merely put my own hand around the bars below his, just close enough for our skin to brush.

"Ival." He pitched his voice low, so no one else could hear. "How are you holding up?"

My heart felt as though it would beat out of my chest. "I'm fine, but Tilton—Early told him to search our house. He had a warrant!"

"Keep your voice down, my dear." Griffin glanced back at the guard, but the man had no interest in anything beyond his newspaper. "It's all right. This new police chief might not understand our town, but Tilton does. He sent a note ahead, while delaying at a saloon with his men. With Christine and Iskander's help, I was able to remove anything remotely incriminating to their house for safe keeping. Including the Occultum Lapidem. It didn't seem wise to risk the police making off with a powerful magical artifact."

I sagged in relief. "I suppose that means Tilton doesn't think I'm a murderer, since surely he wouldn't have alerted you if he did."

"Perhaps." Griffin gave me a rueful smile. "Or perhaps he's wise enough not to involve himself in the business of the old families."

"Probably," I agreed.

"But why are you still here?" he asked, all traces of the smile slipping away. "I would have thought a lawyer would have you out by now?"

I winced. "I couldn't reach Father, but I left word." Now that one anxiety was eased, another took its place. "Oh dear heavens, do you think I'll have to spend the night here?"

"Calm down." He pressed his hand more tightly against mine. "Unfortunately, given the hour, even the best lawyers may not be able to locate a judge to free you. Chances are, yes, you'll have to pass the night in jail."

My mind flinched from the thought of the rusty bars, the squalid sink, and the possibly verminous bed. "I can't!"

"Whyborne," he said in the tone he used when he thought I was overreacting, "You've spent time in far worse surroundings. Recall Alaska."

"That was different," I insisted. "Do you know what the papers will say tomorrow? It will be a scandal. Father will kill me with his own hands."

"I doubt that." Griffin glanced over his shoulder and reaffirmed the guard was still reading the newspaper. He reached between the bars quickly and clasped my hand. "The case they have against you is flimsy at best. They can't accuse you of using sorcery in open court, and any competent lawyer will demand to know what sort of weapon you're meant to have used to extract Waite's blood and make off with it. Or how you could have escaped from the third-story room in which Waite was found, complete with locked door and a window with no ledge as the only possible access. The cufflink means nothing."

"But I don't want to stay here," I said plaintively. "I want to go home with you." After my earlier fright, all I desired was to hold and be held by him.

"I know, my dear. But it's all right. We're safe." He leaned his forehead against the bars, and I longed to kiss him. "In a few days, or a week, we'll get our things back from Christine and Iskander. Restore our home to its proper state."

"I don't think Early is just going to give up," I said. "He didn't strike me as that sort of man."

"Then he should be glad he chose you to harass. If he crosses the Waites or the Marshes, or even the Lesters…" Griffin shook his head. "Widdershins will take care of him, one way or another."

"That's not comforting, Griffin."

The newspaper rustled. "I'm sorry, Mr. Flaherty," the guard called. "Your time is up."

I wanted to beg Griffin to stay with me. But of course that was impossible, not to mention rather selfish. I forced my spine straight and managed to approximate a smile. "Don't worry about me. I'll be fine."

"Indeed you will," he agreed. "And I'll be back first thing tomorrow morning, with the lawyers. And hopefully with a judge's order to release you. Ordinarily you'd have a court appearance for bail to be set, but I'm sure Niles's lawyers will find some way around that." Meaning a hefty bribe, no doubt.

"I'll see you in the morning, then."

Despite his confident words, I thought he released his grip on the iron bar only reluctantly. But he spoke cheerfully to the guard on his way out, and didn't so much as glance back at me.

I knew why, of course. Still, I wished we might have had more time together. Or more privacy. Or simply that I was leaving with him.

Stifling a sigh, I turned to the bed. It seemed I'd have no choice but to lay my head down on the thin mattress, and hope I wasn't sharing it with too many companions of the insect variety.

CHAPTER 12

Whyborne

I COULDN'T SLEEP.

The mattress was so thin I could feel the ropes beneath. The blanket was no better, doing little to keep out the January cold. I'd removed my suit coat and laid it over top of me in an attempt at both warmth and comfort. It succeeded at neither. As if that wasn't enough, the light remained on, presumably so the guard could make certain none of us attempted an escape under the cover of night.

Although the walls separated me from the other prisoners, I could still hear them. A low moan echoed from the cell to the left, and thunderous snores from the one to my right. I had no book to keep me company, and my pocket watch had run down without my notice, so I lacked even a way to mark the time.

How many hours until morning? Surely my release would come soon after sunrise. Although I hated to rely on Father, his lawyers were absolutely cut-throat. I'd be a free man soon enough.

The guard left his station, footsteps echoing as he made his way past each cell in turn, peering inside. I pretended to sleep, as though that would somehow lessen the humiliation of my predicament. Apparently satisfied we weren't going to cause trouble, he went to the door leading from the jail to the rest of the police station, and let himself out.

I opened my eyes and sat up. Was it normal for the only guard to just leave? I had the impression someone would keep an eye on us throughout the night, but perhaps that wasn't the case. After all, the cells seemed secure enough. Even with my sorcery, I'd have difficulty freeing myself. Wind, water, frost, and fire would all be useless. Possibly I might use the earth spell to soften the mortar around the bars on the window—if I had some means of reaching the high, narrow slot in the wall.

The electric lightbulb dimmed, flickered—and went out.

"Whazzat?" mumbled one of my fellow prisoners. "Bulb burned out."

Something more than the freezing air coming through the window made the hair on my arms stand up. I stared into the darkness, willing my eyes to adjust to the faint moonlight. There came a soft click, and the door to the jail swung open. I hoped it was merely the guard returning—and found myself utterly unsurprised when it wasn't.

The man who stepped inside was a short, rather fussy looking fellow in a neat suit. He carried a small lantern, which he raised so its beam fell across the cells, as though he searched for someone.

I had the horrible feeling it was me.

"Who the fuck are you?" yelled the man on my right, woken from his sleep.

The newcomer ignored him. "Dr. Whyborne?" he asked. He stopped perhaps ten feet back from my cell, a bemused look on his face. "You take after your mother."

Did he mean my looks, or my ketoi blood? I rose to my feet, mind racing. "I don't believe we've been introduced," I said coldly. "Are you with the Fideles?"

"Hardly an astonishing guess," he replied. "You, Dr. Whyborne, are coming with me."

I'd never imagined I'd want to remain in my cell, given the chance to leave. "I think not. The bed here is so luxurious, you see."

"Shut it!" shouted the prisoner to my left. "Some of us are trying to sleep."

The cultist cast him a wearied look. "Just as well I already meant to eliminate the witnesses."

He pulled a slender bronze wand from his coat pocket and began to chant in Aklo. I backed up, away from the bars, until my legs fetched against the bed. I didn't recognize the spell he used, but I had to keep him from finishing it. I centered myself and reached for the wind—

Too late.

Two clouds of black smoke appeared, followed closely by a third. Except they weren't smoke, not really. Rather, a twisting darkness hung on the air, seeming to billow outward from a distant point, all laws of perspective suspended.

Something moved in the depths of the smoke.

One moment, the shapes were too far away to make out. The next instant, they were *here*, stepping out as if through a portal, emerging into our world. They were dog-like—or, at second glance, perhaps dragon-like. Though possessing the size and general form of mastiffs, their skin was scaly and black as pitch, their tails those of a lizard. Great claws scored the stone floor, and their gaping mouth revealed teeth like knives. A nacreous glow clung to them, burning in their baleful white eyes.

"Christ preserve us!" screamed one of the prisoners.

Two of the Hounds started toward the other cells, but their movement was like nothing I'd ever seen. They seemed to flicker and stutter, here one second, then vanished, then back again several feet closer. Like a malfunctioning kinetoscope, or one with missing images.

The iron bars of the other two cells proved no barrier to them. The screams of my fellow prisoners cut off abruptly.

The sorcerer smiled. "Good dogs," he said. "Now fetch Dr. Whyborne."

The third and largest Hound made for my cell.

I stumbled back, until my shoulders collided with the outside wall forming the rear of my cell. The Hound blinked in and out of existence, each time drawing closer. Greenish drool dripped from its teeth, and a foul reek filled the air.

I dropped to my knees and pressed my hands against the floor. Frost spread out, racing to coat the rough flagstones, walls, and bars. An ordinary dog would have leapt back from the sudden bite of frost on its feet, but this hideous thing failed to react at all.

Damn it.

The other two Hounds joined the third, their jaws coated in blood.

An abnormally long, round tongue slid from the mouth of one and licked splashed gore from the back of its head.

Earth was the hardest element for me to shape, but I could do it. I took a deep breath, centering myself. The maelstrom turned beneath me, its arcane fire waiting for my touch. The scars on my right arm ached as I drew from it, then sent the power out, binding the universe to my will. The very stones of the floor curved upward to trap the misshapen, taloned paws—

Only they weren't there any more, the Hounds blinking instantaneously from where they had been, to another point inches away. The stone closed on nothing.

I was in a great deal of trouble.

"Now, Dr. Whyborne," said the sorcerer. The largest Hound pressed its nose to the bars—then was suddenly on my side of them, with no transition in between. "I trust I have your attention. Allow me to make you an offer."

A pair of knives glinted in the lantern light behind the sorcerer. Blood sprayed from his throat, and he had only an instant to look surprised, before collapsing in a heap. I leapt to my feet, expecting to see Iskander and the rest of my friends come to my rescue.

Instead, I beheld a tall, blond woman dressed in men's clothing, her hair tucked beneath a low cap. "Bloody sorcerers never know when to shut it," she said, sounding as though she'd just crawled out of some London gutter. "Lucky for us, though, ain't it?"

"Pay attention, Hattie." A black man, whose speech and dress hinted at a far more refined upbringing than hers, stepped to her side. "We still have the Hounds of Tindalos to deal with."

At the death of their master, the Hounds turned on the newcomers. The one closest to them made a flickering, jerky rush in their direction.

Looking utterly unperturbed, the man flung a handful of powder at it. There came a flash, and abruptly the creature ran like a normal four-legged beast, rather than blinking in and out of existence. The woman whooped and met its charge with her knives.

The Hound in my cell let out a growl and rushed toward the bars. The man turned on his heel and flung another handful of the strange powder. An instant later, the thing screamed. Its body thrashed madly, and I realized the iron bars were now embedded in its flesh. There were no wounds, however—it was as though the Hound had simply materialized around them.

"Don't just stand there—kill it," the man exclaimed, even as he moved to deal with the third Hound.

"How?" I demanded. "I have no weapon!"

"You *are* a weapon, you fool." The powder had missed the last Hound, and the man hurled himself away from the swipe of its claws. Fortunately his companion had dealt with her Hound. Her knives described glittering arcs through the air. The Hound blinked, there one moment, then a foot to the left the next.

I turned my attention to the Hound speared on the bars of my cell. Well—it seemed here was the opportunity to put the last few months of practice to use.

The scars on my arm ached as I focused my will. Not giving myself too much time to dwell, I laid my hand on the thing's scaly flank.

A cry of startled pain escaped me. Its flesh was cold, bitterly so, my fingers going numb almost instantly. It thrashed, snapping at me but unable to reach, pinned as it was. Its dragonish tail struck my legs, nearly knocking me to the ground, but I clung to it doggedly.

Then I made my will into a weapon, reached for the arcane fire burning beneath the city—and pulled.

It hurt, like flames hollowing my bones. The scars on my arm flared with pain, and the scent of burning fabric filled the air as my shirt sleeve began to char. I gritted my teeth, making my body into a conduit, letting the magic flow through me and into the Hound.

The creature let out a screech like metal on metal. Its black body began to flake apart beneath my hand. Blue light welled up through the cracks in its skin, until suddenly it collapsed altogether. I fell back, the stone floor bruising my tailbone painfully. The last flakes of ash crumbled into nothing, and the Hound was gone.

"Take that!" the woman exclaimed gleefully. Greenish ichor dripped from her blades, and the final Hound fell to the floor. A moment later, its body seemed to fold in on itself, as though someone crumpled a wad of paper. It grew smaller and smaller—then, with a soft pop, vanished from our dimension altogether.

Silence descended momentarily on the cells. The woman scooped up the sorcerer's fallen wand and tucked it into a pocket. The man carefully brushed powder from his coat, then removed his gold-rimmed spectacles and cleaned them with a handkerchief. Apparently satisfied, he turned to me at last. "Ah. And here we have the abomination."

The woman came to the bars, peering in at me, as though I were an animal on display at the zoo. "Lord, it looks human don't it? You'd never guess." She eyed me critically. "Not very smart though, is it?"

"I beg your pardon!" I exclaimed. I rose to my feet, dusting off my trousers as best I could. "Not to suggest I don't appreciate your timely arrival, but who are you?"

"How rude of us. Allow me to present Miss Hattie Endicott. I am Mr. Rupert Endicott." The man smiled, a flash of white teeth in his dark brown face. "We're your cousins."

CHAPTER 13

Griffin

I DROVE THROUGH Widdershins as fast as the motor car would allow, throwing aside all thought of safety for myself or others. Pedestrians dove out of the way, and a teamster yelled obscenities at me, but I didn't care. The moment the police station came into view, I threw on the brake, coming to such an abrupt halt I nearly lost control and struck a lamp post out front.

"Where is he?" I shouted, as soon as my foot crossed the threshold. The officer at the front desk stared at me as though I'd lost my mind. I didn't give a damn what he thought. "Whyborne—where is he?"

The officer shrank back. "Er, sir, if you'll just give me a moment to fetch Detective Tilton."

I rushed past him, through the front part of the station. The man shouted something at me, but the words held no meaning.

Dawn had barely broken when Tilton called this morning. His words remained jumbled in my memory, only a few standing out with any importance. A disaster at the jail. Blood. Bodies. Murder.

I'd left Ival here, certain the worst he would have to face would be an uncomfortable night in a cell. I'd never thought that whoever—*whatever*—had killed Abbott and Waite would come for him as well.

Certainly not in such a public fashion.

God, how could I have been so stupid?

I hadn't thought, and I'd left him here, trapped and helpless, with no friend to defend him. I'd been lying alone in our bed, missing him, while he'd been…

The door to the cells stood open, the stench of blood wafting out. I broke into a run.

"Hey!" exclaimed one of the policemen. I shoved him aside, snarled an imprecation, and tore free from grasping hands. My eyes went to the middle cell, where I'd last seen my Ival…

Who perched morosely on the edge of his bed, his chin in his hands.

"Let him through," Tilton ordered from somewhere behind me.

The next thing I knew, I gripped the bars in an attempt to hold myself upright. Ival's eyes widened at the sight of me, and he sprang up from the bed. "Griffin?"

"You're alive," I managed to say. I wanted to say so many other things. I wanted to beg his forgiveness for not seeing the danger, for abandoning him here.

"Yes." His expression softened, and I knew we were giving away too much, but I couldn't bring myself to care. "Quite alive. And ready to be out of here. I don't suppose you brought a lawyer with you?"

I shook my head. "No. I came the instant Tilton called me. He said someone died, several someones, and…"

I trailed off. "Well, yes," Whyborne said, with a nod to the room behind me.

I looked back over my shoulder. A body covered in a sheet lay only feet away; it was a wonder I hadn't tripped over it. The other two cells stood open, and their contents were covered by several sheets apiece. The air reeked of death, and bile clawed at the back of my throat.

"The policeman who was on duty is dead, too," Whyborne said, pitching his voice quietly. "His relief found him this morning."

I stared at the blood soaked sheets. Now that I could think straight again, I realized something must have ripped the men apart. Not at all like what had killed Abbott and Waite. "It wasn't the hematophage?"

"No." He glanced at the police. "I'll tell you later. Hopefully the lawyer will arrive soon, and I can come home."

At least Early could hardly accuse Whyborne of murdering anyone from inside his locked cell. I wanted to demand the police let him out now. I wanted to sweep him up in my arms and whisk him away home. But I couldn't do any of those things. I was as useless now as I had been last night.

"I'll wait for the lawyer," I said. "We'll…he'll have you out of here immediately."

Still, it took every ounce of willpower I had to unlock my fingers from around the cell bars. To leave him again, even if only for a little while, even though a small army of police officers milled about.

Thankfully, the lawyer arrived soon thereafter. He swept past me and into the heart of the station, like a paladin heading into battle. I found a seat near the door, where I was at least somewhat out of the way, and waited.

The station door burst open, and Christine strode in, her face like a thundercloud. "Whyborne!" she bellowed in a voice she'd used to command hundreds of workers in the Egyptian desert. "Where the devil are—oh, hello, Griffin."

Iskander caught her by the arm and drew her away from the rather scandalized looking officer at the desk. "We stopped by your house, but when no one answered, we feared…"

He trailed off, but I took his meaning. He worried I'd been arrested after all, and the two of us were in danger of standing trial on sodomy charges.

"I'm fine," I said. "And I've already seen Whyborne this morning—he's doing well, if impatient to leave." I swallowed. "Something happened here last night. Two other prisoners are dead, along with a policeman." I tried to remember how many sheet-draped shapes there had been, and failed. All my attention had been on Whyborne. "Possibly another man. I'm not sure."

"Oh dear." Christine sat down beside me. "Well, then. You'd best tell us what's going on."

As predicted, the lawyer had Whyborne released within the hour. I was certain Tilton was as desperate to get him out of the jail as we were. Whatever Whyborne had told him about the deaths last night, the detective had to realize they'd only occurred because of Ival's presence. I doubted Early would agree, but we made our escape before he appeared.

Whyborne declared himself in desperate need of a bath and breakfast, so the four of us retreated home. The bath would have to wait until after Christine and Iskander left, as we relied on a tin tub and the kitchen tap, but I set about making breakfast the moment we arrived. It seemed the least I could do.

I'd already told Christine and Iskander everything I knew. Whyborne filled in the gaps while I cooked. When he reached the part about the Endicotts, Christine let out an explosive oath.

"Not them again," she exclaimed with such force she startled Saul away from his food dish. "And you trapped! How on earth did you fend them off?"

Whyborne accepted a cup of coffee from me with a grateful smile. A sleepless night had left dark rings around his eyes, and his hair was more disheveled than ever. "Believe it or not, they didn't come to kill me," he told Christine. "They wanted an alliance."

"Well, I hope you told them to take their alliance and—"

"I didn't."

Her eyes widened. "Have you lost your senses, man? They've tried to murder you on multiple occasions, and now you're seriously considering joining forces with them?"

Iskander stood up and helped me distribute pancakes onto the plates. We'd both learned it was easier at times to let Whyborne and Christine argue themselves out, before offering our own opinions.

"The fact they'd just saved my life did come as something of a recommendation," Whyborne replied. "You weren't there, Christine. The way those Hounds moved…" He shook his head. "Mr. Endicott called them Hounds of Tindalos. I've read of them before. From what I recall, they can shift back and forth between our world and other dimensions—the Outside—with ease. Going by my observations last night, the ability allows them to evade injury and pass through obstacles."

"But this mysterious powder fixed them in place?" I asked, setting plates full of pancakes on the table. Iskander fetched the syrup and butter, and we tucked in.

Whyborne took up his knife and set about primly cutting his pancakes into neat squares. Christine rolled her eyes at the habit; as usual, he ignored her. "So to speak. I don't wish you'd been exposed to danger, of course, but I do wonder how they would have appeared to your shadowsight, Griffin."

I'd far rather have been exposed to the danger than have him face it alone. But I only said, "I'm equally curious. Hopefully I won't have the opportunity, as the sorcerer is dead."

"And you didn't recognize him?" Christine asked.

Whyborne took a sip of his coffee. "No. Not that it means anything. He was one of the Fideles. At a guess, Abbott was working with the cult."

Christine frowned. "Then why not just use the vampire—"

"Hematophage."

She rolled her eyes again. "Fine. The *hematophage.* Why not just use it to kill you?"

"Because the Fideles sorcerer wasn't there to kill me outright." Whyborne shrugged. "Threaten me, yes. But he spoke of making an offer." He scowled. "Of course, one of the Endicotts—Hattie, I believe her name was—killed him before he could say what it was."

"And what about the Endicotts?" Iskander asked. "Why on earth would they seek an alliance? I thought they wanted nothing more than to see you dead?"

"It seems we aren't the only ones the Fideles are causing problems for." Whyborne stabbed a bit of pancake with his fork more viciously than needed. "Whatever else one might say of my cousins, they truly believe themselves the saviors of humanity. They aren't the sort to simply stand by while the Fideles undertake this Restoration of theirs and welcome the masters back into the world. As much as they hate me, the Endicotts realize there is a much bigger threat."

"So they want to work together to stop the masters?" I asked.

"Yes. After that, presumably they'll immediately attempt to stab me in the back." Whyborne stared unhappily at his plate. "But quite honestly, that's the least of our worries right now."

"We can't trust them," Christine said. Her fork scraped the plate as she finished her breakfast. "I say we send them packing back to England."

"I think if we're cautious," Whyborne began.

"And I don't!" Christine shoved her plate away with a scowl. "Damn it, Whyborne, this isn't only about you. Theo and Fiona tried to wipe Widdershins off the map. The Endicotts might want you dead, but they won't rest until the entire town is destroyed along with you. What if they decide that killing you and annihilating the rest of us is the best way of stopping the masters?"

"I'm not an idiot, Christine," he snapped, shoving his plate away as well. "But destroying the town won't do anything to the maelstrom. It will still be here, waiting for the masters to use—only without opposition. The Endicotts would be doing the Fideles' work for them"

"Do the Endicotts know that?" Iskander asked.

"I'll make it very clear," Whyborne said. "They wished to set up a meeting, to which I agreed. I suggested the museum, after hours. That way Persephone can join us. And Mr. Quinn and the librarians will be on hand, should the Endicotts change their minds and decide to cause trouble."

Christine didn't seem appeased. "Sensible," I said. "And if we conclude they have nothing to offer us—at least, nothing outweighing any potential treachery—we'll send them back to England empty handed. Agreed?"

"Agreed," Iskander said. Whyborne nodded, and, after a long moment, so did Christine.

"Very well," she said, and pushed her chair back from the table. "We'd best get to the museum, before anyone notices our absence. Whyborne?"

"A bath first." His shoulders slumped. "After being humiliated in front of half the staff yesterday, I rather think I need to look my best."

CHAPTER 14

Whyborne

GRIFFIN KINDLY OFFERED to draw my bath, while I went upstairs and removed my clothing. Even at a cursory glance, I noticed the items missing from our home: a picture from the study here, a book from the shelf there. My anger toward Early deepened, and I hoped Tilton wouldn't suffer for allowing me to leave before his superior arrived.

I pulled on a robe against the chill, then hurried back downstairs. Griffin had filled the bath using a rubber hose from the taps, and steam rose from the water's surface. When I entered the kitchen, he crossed the room swiftly and caught me in his arms for a desperate kiss.

I returned the kiss, burying my fingers in the soft curls of his hair. "I'm so glad you're all right," he whispered against my lips. "I'm sorry I wasn't there. I should have kept watch, or-or not left you there to begin with."

"You didn't know," I said. But the guilt didn't fade from his green eyes. "I'm fine, Griffin. Though if you'd care to make a personal inspection, just to reassure yourself…?"

He kissed me again, then shoved my robe from my shoulders onto the floor. His hands were cool against my skin, but his mouth was hot. "The floor is too cold—sit in a chair."

I obeyed. He paused for a moment, just looking at me, his eyes dark with hunger. Then he went to his knees and shoved my thighs apart.

My cock was nearly hard already, and the heat of his mouth brought it to full attention. I let my head fall back, gripping his hair with on hand. The sensation of his clever tongue on the head was bliss, and when he took me to the root, I didn't bother to suppress a groan.

He worked me for a few minutes, then pulled away. I whimpered and raised my head to look at him. He'd drawn himself out, cock red and leaking with need. A bit to my surprise, he climbed into my lap. "I want to see you," he whispered, bracing himself against my shoulders.

I wrapped my hands around our members, holding us together. He moved, long rolling thrusts that sent waves of excitement all the way to my toes. "Yes," I said. "Griffin, please."

His breath was ragged with desire. "When Tilton called…I was so afraid for you. I can't lose you. I won't lose you."

"You won't." Perhaps it was an empty promise, but I made it anyway. "I love you."

He kissed me aggressively, tongue demanding entrance. I sucked on it, hard, felt him stiffen against me. A moment later, hot spend spilled over my fingers. I released him, stroked myself a few times, and moaned my climax into his mouth.

We were silent and unmoving for a long moment. Then he pulled back and kissed the tip of my nose. "I love you, too. My dearest Ival."

"Only yours," I said. My left leg was starting to fall asleep, so I shifted a bit. Taking the hint, Griffin climbed off me and inspected his trousers.

"I think I'll have to change after all," he said.

"Was that a complaint?" I challenged.

"Not in the slightest." He kissed me again, then left to go upstairs.

Drowsy and content, I slipped into the bath. The water was still warm, and I sank gratefully down into its embrace.

The telephone began to ring.

"Griffin?" I called hopefully.

He didn't answer, and the blasted telephone kept ringing. Muttering a curse I'd picked up from Christine, I dragged myself dripping out of the bath. After wrapping a towel around as much of my body as possible, I hurried to the study.

"Percival Endicott Whyborne speaking," I snapped into the transmitter.

"Dr. Whyborne?" asked a timid voice. "It's Maggie Parkhurst. The director asked me to call, since you haven't come in yet. He wants to see you in his office as soon as possible."

"I'm very sorry, Dr. Whyborne," Dr. Hart said, "but we—the president and I—feel it may be best—for you, not just for the museum—if you take a short leave of absence."

I sat in the chair across the director's wide desk, a creeping numbness making its way through my limbs. I'd finished my bath, dressed in my best suit, done everything to present myself as a respectable member of society.

But it seemed my fate had already been decided.

"A leave of absence," I repeated.

Dr. Hart nodded encouragingly. "Exactly. Just until your current legal troubles are resolved. This way, you can concentrate on…whatever it is you need to clear things up."

"Oh." All the air seemed to have left my lungs, and I could manage nothing more.

"Your work for us has always been exemplary," he said, as though he thought it would somehow make me feel better. "Your dedication to the museum is above reproach."

But I'd been dragged out by the police, in front of my colleagues. My name was splashed in headlines from Widdershins to New York. A crowd of reporters had been waiting on the front steps of the museum; I'd been forced to sneak around the back and enter through a service door to avoid them.

The Ladysmith would, and had, tolerated a great deal from its employees. That was one of the reasons working here had so appealed to me, even before I'd met Griffin. But it drew the line at public scandal.

I understood why, of course. The museum had to look after its own reputation, to make certain donations continued to flow in. And there might be other factors as well, at least in this case. "There are members of the Marsh and Waite families among the trustees, if I recall correctly."

Dr. Hart looked pained. "Yes. I hope you understand. Mr. Mathison and I—all of us—know what you've done for this institution. It's just that…"

The Marshes and Waites had influence, and weren't afraid to use it. Anger flashed through me—perhaps the maelstrom should have ordered things so that one of *them* carried the right bloodline for it to inhabit. Like Father, they were used to telling other people what to do.

"I…of course." I rose to my feet. "Let me just get a few things from my office."

"I'm certain we'll have you back with us soon," Dr. Hart called after me. I let the door shut between us without a reply.

How I was to research a way to stop the hematophage stalking Widdershins without access to the library, I didn't know. Perhaps Mr. Quinn would allow me to sneak in afterhours—but then I'd have to avoid the night watchmen. If I tried and was caught, would Dr. Hart fire me outright?

I had no choice but to attempt it, at least for tonight. But after…

I looked around at the familiar corridors as I made my way back to my office. Would I ever see them again? My work here had been the fulfillment of a lifelong dream. How happy I'd been, when I was first shown to my little office in the basement. Even when I'd been at my loneliest, when Christine had been in the field and I'd gone for days without speaking to another person, there had been the simple joys of piecing together fragments of clay tablets, of reading an ancient phrase no one else had read in millennia.

I never wanted the sorcery and the monsters. I'd only ever wanted this.

And now I was in danger of losing it, perhaps forever.

Miss Parkhurst leapt up from her desk when I came into view. "Dr. Whyborne! Are you all right?" Her hands fluttered, as though she was uncertain what to do with them. "I knew the police would let you go. I told Persephone—that is, Miss Whyborne—they'd probably already released you. She wanted to mount a rescue, but I thought it might do more harm than good, honestly."

Dear heavens, how much of poor Miss Parkhurst's time was my sister monopolizing? I'd have to give Persephone a stern talking-to this evening. "I had to spend the night. There were…complications."

"Oh." She looked at me worriedly. "But you're all right, aren't you?"

"I fear I have some bad news." No sense holding back. "The director has given me a leave of absence. At least until I can clear my good name."

"Oh no!" She paled. "But—they can't believe you'd do such a

thing!"

"It doesn't matter whether anyone believes it," I said glumly. "I suppose I should be glad Dr. Hart didn't suggest I resign outright."

"I should hope not!" She straightened her spine, her eyes flashing fire. "If he does, I-I'll resign in protest!"

"There's no need." Dear heavens, she was starting to sound like Christine. "I appreciate your loyalty, but I should hate to deprive you of a job."

"I don't care," she said. "But, in the meantime, what is it I can do? Do you need me to smuggle books out of the library to your house?"

"Not yet." I hated to involve her with our doings, as they so often turned dangerous. But with any luck the meeting tonight would offer little in the way of risk. "I do have a favor to ask of you, though, if I may be so bold."

"Of course, Dr. Whyborne." She nodded firmly. "You can rely on me."

CHAPTER 15

Whyborne

Bereft of any further excuses to avoid visiting Father, I made my way to Whyborne House. Most likely I should have called on him earlier, as he had paid for the lawyer who had freed me, but I'd hoped to put the moment off for as long as possible.

As usual, I found him hard at work in his study. The glare he fixed on me made me feel as though I were thirteen again, and caught in some wrongdoing. I straightened my shoulders with effort and took the empty chair across from him without waiting for an invitation. "Father. Thank you for sending the lawyer so promptly."

"This is not acceptable, Percival." He snatched up a newspaper from among the pile on the desk and brandished the headline at me. As though I hadn't seen it on every street corner in Widdershins already. HEIR TO WHYBORNE EMPIRE ACCUSED OF MURDER blazed in enormous type across the top, followed by *Victim Businessman Sterling Waite.* "Businessman" was certainly one way to put it, though not the one I would have chosen.

A side column, its headline only comparatively smaller, added *Older brother Stanford Whyborne a criminal lunatic. Does madness run in the family?* I couldn't bring myself to read the article, but I could imagine it well enough.

"It's not acceptable to me either," I replied stiffly. "Thanks to the Marsh and Waite families, I've been asked to take temporary leave from the museum."

Father tossed down the paper and leaned back in his chair. "One question, and I expect an honest answer. Did you kill Sterling?"

"Good lord, no!" Father and I had never been close, but I never imagined he'd think I'd actually commit such a crime. "He had the cufflink from the other night, when he grabbed my wrist. He probably put it in his coat and forgot about it. I assure you, I don't go about murdering people on a whim."

Father glowered. "Then I won't bother to reprimand you for your carelessness."

"How kind."

"The lawyer informed me there was some sort of incident at the jail overnight," Father went on. "One policeman and two prisoners dead, along with an unknown man."

No outward show of concern for me, of course. "Yes." I briefly told him of the incident, and the Endicotts.

"More sorcerers," he said with distaste, once I finished. "This is why we hired others to do our sorcery for us in the Brotherhood, Percival. To keep their interference at a minimum."

I bit back a comment that would have only resulted in an argument, and instead said, "Speaking of the Brotherhood, you once mentioned the Hounds of Tindalos. I've read of them in the *Arcanorum,* of course, but perhaps you have some practical suggestions for dealing with them in the future?"

"We sent them against others, not defended against them ourselves," he said, without any indication his words were in the least horrible. I'd resigned myself to the fact he'd never admit the Brotherhood had done anything wrong, using black magic to crush their enemies. "Though not often. They move easily between dimensions, and so are summoned with less effort than some creatures. But they don't remain in our world long, so their quarry must be close at hand."

That was at least somewhat comforting. It didn't sound as if the Hounds could be used to track their prey over distances. "With any luck, we won't encounter them again." The memory of the dying prisoners, their echoing screams, sent a shudder through me.

"This nonsense with the papers and police can't be allowed to continue." Father lit a cigar, his expression thoughtful. "Detective Tilton must know he has no case that can hold up in court."

"I'm certain he does. The problem is with the new police chief. Moses Early." I waved away the cigar smoke that drifted into my face. "He admitted he's hoping to use my arrest and prosecution as a stepping stone to bigger and better things. I'm sure he's quite pleased with the headlines this morning."

Father tapped the ash from his cigar into the gilded standing ashtray by the desk. "It should be easy enough to rid ourselves of him. Allow me to handle the matter—I don't want there to be the possibility of tracing his death back to you."

"What? No!" I stared at Father in horror. How could he just sit here, calmly discussing killing a man? Even someone as odious as Early? "I won't allow it."

"You're too soft, Percival. This is why I placed my hopes in…" Father trailed off, and his expression lapsed into some emotion I couldn't quite discern.

"In Stanford?" I asked.

He didn't answer for so long I began to wonder if he would at all. "I did what I thought best," he said at last. His gaze went to the painting on the wall, where the family portrait had once hung. "For all of us. But my judgment proved faulty, disastrously so. In particular, I misjudged you at every turn. I swore I wouldn't make that mistake again. Yet here I am, falling back into bad habits."

Was I hearing aright? "Father…"

"Let me finish." He picked up his cigar, discovered it had gone out, and set it back down. "I will follow your lead. Police Chief Early will come to no harm from me."

I didn't know what to say. At length, I nodded. "Thank you, Father." I gestured vaguely. "I should return home. Tell Griffin what happened at the museum."

I made my way to the door. But before I could open it, he said, "Percival."

I stopped. "Yes?"

"Don't imagine I never ask myself what I might have done differently with you boys." The sadness in his eyes shocked me. "Whatever else you may think of me, I've never been one to shirk responsibility. There must have been something I could have said or done to put Stanford on the right path. I missed it, and Guinevere paid the price."

I'd never thought to hear him say such a thing. "Perhaps. But in the end, Stanford's choices were his own. Just as mine have been."

He shook his head slightly in disagreement, but said nothing. Sensing the conversation was at an end, I slipped out the door and shut it carefully behind me.

"I can't say I'm pleased with the idea of working with these cousins of yours, Whyborne," Christine said that night, as she let Iskander and me into the museum through the staff door. As part of my "leave of absence," I'd been forced to surrender my keys. "Where's Griffin?"

"Fetching Persephone," I replied. "The motor car only seats two, and I had no desire to ride all the way from the coast with her in my lap."

Griffin had been oddly reluctant to let me make the trip to the museum alone. Indeed, he'd been upset to learn I'd gone from the museum to Whyborne House, then back to our home without asking him to drive me. I'd tried to explain I didn't think it likely I'd be attacked in the streets in broad daylight, but he'd remained unmollified. As for making my way to the museum under the cover of darkness, I'd ultimately persuaded him only by agreeing to walk over with Iskander.

Clearly, last night's attack at the jail had upset my husband deeply. We'd faced danger many times, both together and apart. Perhaps he was more shaken because of having to empty our house of anything that could be considered incriminating. The incident had left me feeling vulnerable; no doubt it was even worse for him.

The museum had closed some hours ago, and night pressed against the windows as we made our way to the library. Before taking my leave this morning, I'd asked Mr. Quinn if he might be willing to lend assistance. His glee at my request had been a bit unsettling.

The doors stood open, and Mr. Quinn hovered near the entrance, looking rather like an undertaker at a wake. Griffin arrived a few moments later, accompanied by a junior librarian but without my sister. A look of relief flickered over his face when he saw me.

"Where is Persephone?" I asked.

"I let her out as near as I could to the window into your office. That way she'd be less likely to encounter any patrolling guards than if she'd come in through an outer door." He frowned. "She should have been here by now, though."

Curse it. Possibly she'd become distracted, or even lost. The museum was something of a maze, after all. "Wait here. I'll find her."

The door to my office was shut. Perhaps no one had explained door knobs to Persephone? I would feel foolish if she was inside, trapped by a simple latch. I reached for the knob, which turned easily beneath my hand.

My first thought was that Persephone was inside, as expected. Only Miss Parkhurst, who I thought was making coffee, was there as well. She was perched on my desk, and—

"Oh dear lord!" I shouted. Clapping a hand to my eyes, I flailed in the opposite direction. My shin collided hard with Miss Parkhurst's desk. I let out a yelp of pain, hopping on one foot and trying to massage the injury without lowering my other hand from my eyes.

"Dr. Whyborne!" Miss Parkhurst cried in alarm.

If I fled down the hall now, would it be possible to pretend none of this had happened? It didn't seem likely, so I uncovered my eyes and turned back to the open door of my office. Miss Parkhurst stood there, her face scarlet, wringing her hands frantically.

"I'm so sorry," she squeaked. "I-I can explain. I can…"

Persephone strolled out, looking insufferably smug. "It's only my brother, Maggie."

"I'm quite aware." Miss Parkhurst's shoulders slumped miserably. "I'm sorry," she said to me again.

Of course. I saw what was happening now. "Oh no, Miss Parkhurst," I said, drawing myself up. "You have nothing to apologize for. I quite understand." I jabbed a finger at Persephone. *"You* on the other hand…"

Persephone's eyes widened and the tendrils of her hair lashed. "Me?"

"Yes, you! How dare you?" I took a step forward, and so did she, until we were only inches apart. I did my best to use my height to loom over her. Unfortunately, she was also rather tall, which rendered the tactic ineffective. "You befriend my secretary, monopolize her time, and then come into my museum, and-and debauch her! On *my* desk!" Dear God, I'd never be able to do work there again.

"Dr. Whyborne," Miss Parkhurst said in a small voice.

We both ignored her. Persephone's eyes flashed, and a low wind sprang up, sending papers cascading from inside my office. "I made no secret of our relationship."

"Well, you certainly didn't mention it to me!"

There came the sound of running footsteps from the corridor. "Ival?" Griffin called. "We heard shouting."

"Of course I did," Persephone said to me, ignoring Griffin. She poked me hard in the chest, her claws pricking through my shirt. "Is this some land-dweller foolishness? Because you're acting stupid, brother, even for you."

"Even for me?" I exclaimed, outraged. "Miss Parkhurst is an innocent young woman, and you've taken advantage—"

"Good gad, Whyborne, shut up," Christine interrupted. She'd come with Griffin...and Iskander, of course.

Miss Parkhurst let out a small sob and hid her head in her hands. "Oh God."

"Christine, this is none of your concern." I could at least do whatever possible to preserve poor Miss Parkhurst's modesty in front of everyone.

"No, this is none of *your* concern," she shot back. Before I could argue, she said, "First of all, you're a man. Second of all, you're literally the only person in this room who hasn't slept with a woman. I assure you, no one here is interested in your opinion."

I gaped at her. Before I could inform her of her rudeness, she barreled on. "Now, apologize to poor Miss Parkhurst and your sister at once."

"It—it's all right, Dr. Putnam-Barnett," Miss Parkhurst managed. Her eyes were red, and she blinked rapidly, but she didn't move away from Persephone's side. "I'll just...just clear my desk..."

Had my sister ruined everything? "What?" I exclaimed. "You aren't leaving me, are you?" Where would I possibly find another secretary who suited me half so well?

Her eyes widened, and a soft laugh escaped her. "I...I'm sorry, but..." She caught Persephone's hand in hers and squeezed it. "I have to choose...and I can't choose you."

"Choose me for what?" I asked, baffled. Out of the corner of my eye, I saw Griffin put his face in his hands. He seemed to be hiding laughter, though God only knew what the man found amusing about this debacle. "I thought you were happy as my secretary. Do you require a raise?"

Miss Parkhurst and I stared at each other in mutual incomprehension. Griffin finally chose to take pity on us. "You're not being fired, Miss Parkhurst," he said.

She looked tremulously hopeful. "I'm not?"

"Fire you?" Persephone bared her teeth at me. "You're threatening Maggie?"

"Not set her on fire," I snapped. "No one is setting anyone on fire. Or doing any other sort of firing." I tried to find some way to salvage what was left of any of our dignity. "It's only that you, sister, have trouble understanding there are boundaries. For example, my *desk."*

Miss Parkhurst turned scarlet again. Persephone only laughed.

"Whyborne, if you're done being dramatic, can we return to the library?" Christine demanded. Without waiting for an answer, she left, followed by Iskander. Griffin glanced at me, and I motioned him to go ahead.

As I trailed after him, Persephone tugged on my coat. She held hands with Miss Parkhurst, who was still rather pink. "Griffin told me you're in trouble with the police." She said the last word as if tasting the unfamiliar concept.

"They think I murdered two people," I said unhappily.

"Then tell them you have not."

If only it were that simple. "I did. But the murders happened in the middle of the night, when I was in bed. No one can vouch for my whereabouts."

"Why not?" Persephone asked. "Are you and your husband fighting?"

Oh God. I froze, glancing reflexively at Miss Parkhurst. For a moment, she seemed only puzzled—then her eyes widened.

"H-husband?" she said.

Persephone frowned. "Of course. Didn't you know my brother and Griffin are married? I brought their wedding rings up from the depths myself."

Griffin sighed. "Come, Miss Parkhurst, let's make some coffee," he said. "I think the twins are about to have another exchange of words."

CHAPTER 16

Whyborne

THE REST OF us gathered in the library, awaiting Griffin and Miss Parkhurst's return with the coffee. I didn't know what he meant to say to her and likely didn't wish to.

Now that the shock of it was past, I felt wretched for frightening my secretary as I had. If there had been even the slightest sign of affection between her and Persephone, perhaps I would have been more prepared for the sight which had greeted me when I opened the door.

No. No, there was probably nothing which could have prepared me for that. I was going to have to get a new desk.

But I understood the need to conceal such an affection, far better than most. Certainly far better than my wretched sister, who blurted out private matters heedlessly. And what on earth did she mean when she said she'd made no secret of it? I'd never suspected a thing.

She perched on the edge of a desk across from me, swinging her legs back and forth like a child. Mr. Quinn had ensconced us in a small room normally used for book repair, generously furnished with desks and chairs. He hovered near the door, his pale eyes going from me to Persephone, then back again. At least someone was pleased with this gathering.

Iskander and Christine had taken two of the chairs. Christine was unruffled, but poor Iskander seemed to be wondering how his life had brought him to this point. I rather sympathized.

I heard Miss Parkhurst's laugh echo from elsewhere in the library. Griffin had once again worked his charm, it seemed. Persephone looked up at the sound, her eyes shining and a little smile touching her lips.

They entered, bearing the coffee. Miss Parkhurst returned Persephone's smile…then glanced at me. Her entire face flushed crimson, and I feared she'd drop the coffee altogether.

My ears turned hot as well. No doubt she was even now putting a new interpretation on all the times Griffin had come to visit me at the museum. Or the times he had exited my locked office, cheerily thanking me for consulting with him on a case.

My poor desk.

This would quickly become an untenable situation if something wasn't done about it. "Please, Miss Parkhurst, accept my apologies. It was never my intention to cause you a moment of distress. Nevertheless, I did so. I hope you can find it in your heart to forgive me in the spirit of our many years together."

Thank heavens, it produced a smile from her. "Of course, Dr. Whyborne. I…I'm glad to continue my work with you. Once the director allows you to return, I mean."

"Aren't you going to apologize to me?" Persephone asked.

"No." I glowered at her. "Not unless you apologize first for all the things you've done to me. Climbing in my window, knocking off my hat, setting my shoes on fire—"

"The shoes were an accident." She glanced at Miss Parkhurst. "I was still learning the fire spell."

I made a noise to indicate my disbelief and accepted coffee from Miss Parkhurst. But the mention of magic reminded me of why we were here to begin with. "Miss Parkhurst, you may wish to take your leave. I fear we've gathered to discuss somewhat unsavory matters."

"But that's why I'm here," she said. "I want to help. I know I'm not…not a sorceress, or a soldier, or anything like that. But there may be something I can do. I assisted Persephone—I mean, Miss Whyborne—in October."

"I think you can call her Persephone, all things considered," I muttered.

Footsteps sounded from the open door. A moment later, one of the librarians stopped just outside. He offered Persephone and I a bow, nodded at Mr. Quinn, and stepped aside to reveal my cousins.

Hattie came in first, still outlandishly dressed, her knives sheathed prominently on her hips. Her eyes went straight to Persephone, and she cocked her head. "Oi, take a look, Rupert. This one don't pretend to be human at all."

"Quite," Rupert agreed. He watched the room as well, one hand hovering near his pocket. I doubted he had anything so mundane as a gun concealed within. Had he suspected an ambush?

I rose to greet them, clinging to manners to guide me. "Mr. Rupert Endicott, Miss Hattie Endicott." I began to introduce my friends, but Hattie interrupted me.

"I know you," she said, her eyes fixed on Iskander.

Iskander looked faintly alarmed. "I assure you, we've not met."

She waved a dismissive hand. "No, I mean, you're Barnett, ain't you? I knew your mum."

"What?" Christine exclaimed.

The blood seemed to have drained from Iskander's face, lending his bronze skin a grayish tinge. "I…that's not possible."

"Sure it is." Hattie patted the knife on her right hip. "Who do you think taught me to fight?"

CHAPTER 17

Griffin

"Enough, Hattie," Rupert said. "We have more important matters to speak of at the moment. You can catch up with Mr. Barnett later."

"It's Putnam-Barnett now," Iskander said faintly. I wished I weren't on the other side of the room from him, so that I might put a supportive hand on his shoulder. But if I made too obvious a gesture, the Endicotts would surely see it as a sign of weakness.

They'd done this to shake us; of that much I was certain. The Pinkertons had trained me to take the measure of people quickly, and though I was sometimes wrong, in this case everything about the Endicotts put my hackles up. And not just because of what their family had done to us in the past.

Though Rupert didn't much resemble Theo and Fiona physically, he spoke with the same refined accent and had the same easy bearing. His clothing was far more stylish, though whether from personal taste or because it would earn him a level of respect his black skin would not, I couldn't yet say. Behind his gold-rimmed glasses, his eyes gleamed in my shadowsight, the sure mark of a sorcerer.

I'd been surprised when Whyborne mentioned one of his cousins was black, but perhaps I shouldn't have been. I knew from past experience the Endicotts valued sorcery above all else. They also didn't give a damn for society; as they saw it, doing exactly as they pleased was their reward for keeping humanity safe.

Whatever Hattie's roots—clearly she hadn't been raised at the family estate, given her manner of speech—she was a capable woman. The way she held herself, like a fighter, made me wonder if she'd been sent as Rupert's bodyguard. Or if the task of killing Whyborne and Persephone, should the alliance founder, would fall to her.

Widdershins would be afire with whispered gossip about them. A woman wearing trousers and carrying knives, in the company of a well-dressed black man, would catch eyes even here. And if they were anything at all like Theo and Fiona, they'd blaze a careless path through the town, using magic against anyone who dared stand in their way.

"I assume the abomination has told you of our purpose here," Rupert said. Miss Parkhurst, who'd poured him a cup of coffee, looked as though she considered throwing it in his face at the insult. Instead, she put it aside, well out of his reach.

"Good gad, enough," Christine snapped. She'd transferred the scowl she'd been giving Hattie to Rupert. "Whyborne says you want an alliance, but I trust you about as far as I can throw the museum. If you have nothing more to offer than insults and half-baked lies, then leave."

Hattie frowned, but the only emotion Rupert showed was a slight tightening of the lips. "Perhaps you are right," he said. "Very well, then, *Dr. Whyborne.* Have there been any new developments since last night?"

Whyborne sat with his arms folded over his chest. His face had settled into aloof stillness. "No."

"Then it seems to me we have two questions. Beyond what the Fideles have planned, that is." Rupert paused, as if expecting one of us to jump in. When we all merely stared at him, he sighed, like a schoolteacher with disappointing students. "It seems that they, perhaps with Mr. Abbott's help, summoned something ghastly. This hematophage, as you call it. Whether Abbott was meant to die is a question we likely won't have answered easily."

"Meant to die?" Whyborne asked.

Rupert sighed again. "I'd heard you were a sorcerer. Surely you're aware that things summoned from the Outside often must feed in order to remain here."

Unpleasant memory clawed up from the back of my mind. "When Blackbyrne was resurrected, he needed fresh blood to sustain himself." And the Brotherhood had meant my blood to nourish the arisen Leander.

"Precisely." Rupert nodded in my direction. "It's good to discover you're more than decorative, Mr. Flaherty."

I showed no expression at the attempted insult. Christine muttered something in Arabic, and the line between Whyborne's eyes deepened.

Curse it. We were giving away too much. But there was nothing to be done about it now.

"The question is," Rupert went on, "why they sent the creature after Mr. Waite, rather than Dr. Whyborne, or even Miss Whyborne. Did he pose some sort of threat to them?"

"I wouldn't think so," Whyborne replied. "Other than being the head of one of the old families."

"I shudder to imagine what 'old families' implies in this case," Rupert said. "I take it they have some influence in this helltown. That could be reason enough, I suppose."

His casual slander of Widdershins irked me, but I kept it from my face. "But his heir has already stepped into place," I said. I'd spoken to the servants at the Waite mansion, and been assured Fred Waite had assumed his father's mantle with little disruption. "Waite may have had dealings with the Fideles we don't know about, of course."

"Whatever their grudge against Waite, another, larger, question remains." Rupert cocked his head slightly to one side. "What precisely did they want with Dr. Whyborne? Hattie and I overheard the sorcerer speaking at the jail. He had not come to kill Dr. Whyborne, but to make him an offer."

"I suspect his 'offer' would have consisted of something along the lines of 'come with me or die,'" Whyborne said. "Especially as I can't imagine the Fideles think for a moment I'd cooperate with them after all that's happened."

We had struck a—very—temporary alliance with one of them in Kansas. But that had lasted only long enough for Creigh to save her own skin.

"Nonetheless, they want something from you." Rupert gazed at Whyborne, as if he could discern what, if he only looked hard enough.

"Something beyond merely your death."

I felt as though I'd swallowed a chunk of ice, only to have it lodge behind my heart. Whatever the Fideles wanted, it would be terrible, of that I had no doubt.

I couldn't let them come near my Ival again. I had to protect him, as I'd failed to do last night.

"If we kill the hematophage," Christine said, "and then kill the Fideles, we won't have to worry about what they want."

Hattie laughed gleefully. "I like her. She ain't bad, for an abomination's minion."

Christine's eyes bulged. Before she could do more than draw breath, I said, "And what do you propose we do to remove either monster or sorcerers, Mr. Endicott?"

In other words: what, if anything, do you have to offer us?

The look he gave me suggested he'd heard the implication clearly. "I am an alchemist of no small skill. I may be able to locate the hematophage, wherever it lairs during the day. In order to do so, however, I'll need something of its essence. Which won't be easy to obtain, as creatures from the Outside tend to dissolve into nothingness quite quickly."

"Waite had some blackish ichor beneath his nails," I said. "I imagine his body was well cleaned at the mortuary, however."

Rupert looked surprised. "Indeed? That's rather odd. Perhaps it has some earthly aspect, and isn't entirely of the Outside, then."

"Like those possessed by Nitocris?" Iskander suggested.

"In a way. Perhaps we shall be lucky, and something will remain in one of the wounds," Rupert said. "Very well, then. Fetch me his body."

Whyborne's eyes widened. "Pardon me?"

"I'm certainly not mucking about in some filthy crypt." Rupert brushed at his sleeve, as if just the thought might have summoned a bit of dirt. "Go get his body and bring it to the house. I've set my laboratory up already, so I'll be able to get to work as soon as you have it."

So, they'd been here for more than a few days. No doubt they'd been observing us the entire time. The thought sent a shudder down my spine.

"I'll go with them," Hattie volunteered unexpectedly. "Be a chance to get the lay of the land and all that."

Christine looked as though she meant to object. Before she could, however, Iskander said, "Yes. I think you should."

"The funeral is tomorrow morning," I said, before an argument could start. "We'll go to the cemetery tomorrow night."

"In the meantime, we should attempt to discover what, precisely, these sorcerers are about," Rupert said.

"We have photographs of the magical sigils drawn around Abbott's body," Whyborne said. "I didn't recognize them, but you might. I can bring them by tomorrow, if you'd like."

"A good suggestion." Rupert glanced at Whyborne and Persephone. "The Fideles may simply be here to kill you, of course. But Candlemas is less than three days away, and if your enemies are planning to conduct some unholy rite against you or this town…that is when they will do it."

CHAPTER 18

Whyborne

"I DON'T LIKE this," Griffin said, shutting the door to our house behind us.

"What part?" I asked. Heaven knew, he had plenty to choose from. "Working with the Endicotts? Grave robbing? The fact I'll never be able to use my desk again?"

A chuckle escaped him. "I won't comment on the latter. All of these things worry me, of course. But the fact the sorcerer wanted to take you alive…that shouldn't be more alarming than him wanting to kill you, and yet…"

"Considered the Fideles have already tried stealing first my body, then my free will, I quite agree," I replied, hanging up my hat. "Unless they couldn't easily bring the hematophage into the jail. Perhaps the sorcerer meant to coerce me to go with him, then set it on me the moment we were elsewhere."

Griffin frowned. "I'm not reassured." He stepped closer and grasped my lapels with his hands. "I won't let them hurt you. I swear it."

Before I could ask him about his strange mood, he hauled me down by my lapels and silenced me with a fierce kiss. I could feel the press of his teeth through his lip, and the aggressive manner in which he thrust his tongue into my mouth sent a curl of desire through me.

"Griffin," I whispered, when I could speak again.

"Shh." He shoved me against the wall, his thigh sliding between my legs. I moaned encouragement into his mouth as he rocked against me. His suit coat fell to the floor, and he reached for the buttons on my trousers. I threaded my fingers through his thick hair as he thrust his hand into my clothes, fingers curling around my length—

The telephone began to ring.

"Devil take it!" I exclaimed.

Griffin's eyes were wild, irises thin rings of emerald around pupils gone wide with lust. Still, he stepped back reluctantly. "It might be Niles, with important news."

"It had better be damned important," I muttered. Driven by annoyance, I stalked into the study and snatched up the accursed receiver. "Percival Endicott Whyborne speaking."

The voice that came through the receiver wasn't the expected tones of Fenton, telling me to wait for Father. "Dr. Whyborne," said a man. His words sounded labored, as though some affliction of the lungs stole his breath.

"Yes?" I frowned at the telephone's wooden case, though of course whoever was on the line couldn't see me. "Who is this?"

"I must speak with you. Meet me at the Devil and Cat…room eight…as soon as you may. There isn't much time left."

The line went dead.

Christine was less than pleased when we rapped on her door shortly thereafter. I took it as revenge for all the times she'd beaten on the door of my locked office. I felt sorrier for Iskander, but Griffin was adamant we not go alone.

"Where did the call come from?" Iskander asked as we drew close to our destination. "Certainly not from here."

The Devil and Cat was in the same questionable part of town as the boarding house where Abbott had died. A saloon occupied the first floor, with rooms to let at an hourly rate on the three stories above. Like many of the establishments in the area, it was a favorite of sailors. And definitely not the sort of place to have a telephone.

"A department store, according to the operator," Griffin replied. "Presumably, our mysterious caller broke in to use their telephone.

The exchange printed in the newspaper gave him our number."

"And what is the likelihood of this being some sort of trap?" Christine asked. She'd brought her pistol, and Iskander carried his knives beneath his coat.

Griffin hefted his sword cane. "Rather high, I'm sure. Which is why we disturbed you."

"I suppose I can't complain, then," she said. "There's the saloon. Let us see what awaits us."

At this late hour, only a few drinkers were inside. They were all rather shabby, with stained pea coats and tattoos showing from beneath their cuffs or collars. Even though none of us were dressed in our finer clothes, we stood out painfully in the run down saloon.

"I think you're in the wrong place, friends," said the man from behind the rough plank that served as a bar.

I rather agreed. Nevertheless. "We're meeting someone," I said, with a nod at the stairs leading up.

He didn't reply, just kept staring at us as he wiped a mug with a dirty rag. Griffin led the way to the stairs, his gaze sweeping purposefully over the scattered drinkers. Looking for sorcerers with his shadowsight, no doubt, in case this proved to be an ambush.

Room eight was on the uppermost floor. "What a depressing place," Iskander murmured, glancing around the squalid hallway. The walls were of bare wood, and previous occupants had carved a mixture of initials, symbols, and pornographic images into them. A layer of filth covered the floor, sticking unpleasantly to our shoes. The air reeked of spilled liquor from below, and the questionable hygiene of those paying the hourly rate for the rooms above.

Griffin paused outside the door, glancing at the rest of us. Iskander gave a nod and stepped back, drawing his knives as he did so. Christine quietly took up position on the other side of the door, her pistol at the ready.

"Whyborne?" Griffin prompted.

I knocked on the door, which rattled in its frame. "Hello? It's Dr. Whyborne. You wished to speak to me?"

A shuffling sound carried through the thin wood. The bolt drew back, and the door swung open. A single candle shed only the dimmest illumination over the room inside, but I could make out the outline of a table, chairs, and bed.

The figure who had opened the door was shrouded in a cloak that reached to the floor, its hood casting such deep shadow over the face I couldn't tell if the features belonged to a man or woman. Its back was bent, and when it stepped aside, it moved slowly, as though in pain.

"Come in," rasped the voice I'd spoken to on the phone.

I hesitated. There was not yet any sign of a trap, but that didn't mean there wasn't one to be sprung. Iskander clearly had the same thought, because he said, "I'll keep watch on the hall."

We crowded into the small room. Iskander stayed at the door, edging it nearly closed and peering out the gap. If anyone came up the stairs or emerged from one of the other rooms, at least we'd have some warning.

The cloaked man lowered himself into one of the chairs with a deep groan. There were two other chairs, even more rickety than the first. I sat in one, and Christine the other. Griffin took up position in the far corner, sword cane held loosely in his hand.

"Who are you?" I asked our host, squinting at the shadows beneath the hood. "You said you had some urgent matter for me, that there wasn't much time left."

"No," he said in his labored voice. "It is I who don't have much time remaining."

A tentacle unfurled from beneath the cloak and fell limply onto the table.

CHAPTER 19

Whyborne

"DEAR LORD!" I shoved my chair violently back from the table. Spells sizzled on my tongue, waiting to be unleashed. The blade of Griffin's sword cane rasped free, and Christine snatched out her pistol.

But the cloaked figure didn't lunge across the table and attack, as I'd expected. "Repulsive, isn't it?" he wheezed. "It is my punishment."

The hair on the back of my neck stood up. I'd seen such punishment before, when the Fideles failed to steal the Wisborg Codex and kill me last July. I held up a hand, and Griffin stilled, the blade of his cane poised to strike.

"The Man in the Woods did this to you?" I asked. "Nyarlathotep?"

"Yes." The tentacle withdrew, tucked away again beneath the cloak. "My name is Montgomery Downing. I was a friend of Reverend Scarrow."

Scarrow had been the only sorcerer I'd met who didn't want to kill me. Naturally, he'd ended up murdered himself. "You're a member of the Cabal?"

"Yes. I studied sorcery. When I was young, I went to the Man in the Woods to learn." As Blackbyrne and so many others had before him. "But there is always a price."

I'd wondered why a being from the Outside such as Nyarlathotep had any interest in communing with human sorcerers. "What price?"

"Obedience." Downing let out a wet laugh. "I was a fool. Young. Stupid. I made the bargain willingly. But now the time has come. Nyarlathotep demands we act. He visits us in our dreams."

I exchanged an uneasy look with Christine. "And what exactly is it that he wants?" she prompted.

"Can you not guess?" Something squirmed within the shadows of the hood. I desperately hoped it was only tentacle hair like the ketoi had, and nothing more nauseating. "He is the emissary of the masters. All who learned sorcery from him must obey…must aid their return. Or face his wrath."

"This happened because you refused?" I asked.

"Yes." He paused to cough, a racking bout that ended with his shoulders hunched even lower. "I will not…open the door to creatures…who mean to reshape the world to their liking." He took a deep, gasping breath. "There is no promise of power that will make me betray humankind."

"Mrs. Creigh believed that cooperation was the only way to save humanity," Iskander remarked from the doorway.

"Making it easier to conquer us will not persuade them to spare us." Anger laced the labored words. "Humanity was too insignificant for notice when last the masters walked in this world. Now we are not. They will not care how many die when they remake our reality to better suit them. Our only hope is to resist. And so I have." The cloak rippled, as if he shuddered. "And this…is my reward. Each night I am visited in dreams. And each morning I find more of my body altered. My organs are not as they were. I can feel things moving in my lungs. But I will not surrender."

Horror rooted me to the chair. But it was mingled with admiration. "That is incredibly brave of you," I managed to say.

"Not many have that sort of courage," Christine agreed grimly. "I suspect most of those the Man in the Woods tutored, whether they originally favored the return of the masters or not, will have fallen into line by now."

"Yes." Downing's hood turned in my direction, though mercifully I couldn't make out anything within. "That is why I have come to warn you. They know about you and your sister."

More than the January cold seemed to settle into the unheated room. "Know w-what?" I'd hoped to ask casually, but the words stuck in my throat coming out.

"Nyarlathotep knows the maelstrom as does none other. He has seen you through the dreams of Mrs. Creigh. He knows that you are a fragment of the arcane vortex. Of Widdershins."

"I knew we should have killed Creigh when we had the chance," Christine said through gritted teeth. "Devil take the woman. I hope she ends up with a squid head."

I resisted the urge to rub my eyes in despair. I'd never intended to reveal myself in front of Creigh. But she'd tried to infect me with the rust, as she'd already infected poor Iskander. I'd had no choice but to draw on the power of an arcane line and burn it away.

Unfortunately, such an infusion of magic had affected my mental state, and I'd ended up ranting like some sort of poorly written stage villain. *I am the fire that burns in the veins of the world*—what on earth had I been thinking?

So she'd known there was something abnormal about me, though not precisely what. Certainly I hadn't told her. But it had never occurred to me that the beings she served might realize exactly what the maelstrom had done. That, like the ketoi and the umbrae, it had rebelled against its creators in the only way it could.

Well, I already knew Persephone and I were targets of the Fideles. It was difficult to imagine this bit of information could make things any worse.

"I see," I said at last. "Thank you for the warning, Mr. Downing." I directed my gaze at the space beneath the hood where I imagined his eyes to be. "Is there anything we can do? Perhaps there is some spell to reverse the effects or…"

"No." He sounded certain. Probably he'd spent what time he could looking into just that possibility. "I made my devil's bargain. Now, with my last act, I'll spit in his face." He settled back into the chair. "I have one more warning for you. The reason I called you here, in fact. Do you know why Nyarlathotep is called the Man in the Woods?"

"Because that was where cultists met him in medieval times," I replied. "And later, if any of the accusations leveled during the witch trials were true."

"Yes…and no." Downing's tentacle arm coiled and uncoiled. "It takes a certain amount of arcane power to pierce the veil and move between our world and the Outside. Lesser creatures such as the Hounds can do it easily. There is less…resistance, for want of a better word. But for beings of great power such as Nyarlathotep, it is more difficult. There are only certain places they can pass through."

The fine hairs stood up on the back of my neck. "The yayhos in West Virginia told me they could only come here at specific sites. Threshold Mountain was one of them."

"Precisely." Downing let out a wet, racking cough. When it ended, he said, "And the masters, the most powerful beings of all those to visit our world, require the maelstrom to pass back and forth. Nyarlathotep is but their servant, but much like the yayhos, can only enter our world in specific places. One of these is in the Draakenwood."

"Of course it is," Christine muttered. "Why wouldn't it be?"

"This is my warning to you." Downing reached across the table, and I had to force myself not to jerk back from the slimy touch of his tentacle as it wrapped around my wrist. "Nyarlathotep's minions plot against you, but you *must* fight on your ground. Here, you have the advantage. But the Draakenwood belongs to him." He drew in a deep, whistling breath. "Do not let them lure you beneath its eaves, or you will surely be lost."

At least my lack of gainful employment at the museum allowed us to sleep in the next morning. As Griffin and I enjoyed a leisurely breakfast together, a smart rap came on the front door. Griffin answered it, and a moment later returned to the kitchen with Iskander in tow.

"I'm terribly sorry to interrupt your breakfast," he said. "I didn't want to miss you."

Ordinarily, I would have enjoyed the newspaper alongside my morning coffee. But as it was currently full of speculation concerning me, the murders, and whether or not my family was constitutionally insane, I'd busied myself with a cryptography book instead. I still hoped to translate the Wisborg Codex, though without a key, my prospects were slim indeed.

I set the book aside. "Not at all. Is there something we can do for you?"

"I don't have any work at the museum today," he said. "You'd mentioned taking the photographs of the murder scene to Mr. Endicott, and I wondered if I might accompany you."

"You want to ask Hattie about her claim she knew your mother,"

Griffin guessed.

Iskander's mouth tightened. "Christine says it's just a lie meant to divide us. And I know she must be right. My mother would never have associated with the likes of the Endicotts."

"Of course not," I said staunchly.

Griffin looked less certain. "Surely an outright lie would be easily dismissed. Not to say there is more than a small grain of truth to it, of course. But your mother did keep some rather large secrets from you."

"About being from a family of monster hunters, you mean." Iskander's shoulders slumped fractionally. "Which the Endicotts also style themselves as."

Griffin winced. "I do agree with Christine in part, though. They mean to divide us."

At that, Iskander straightened. "If so, they'll be doomed to disappointment."

"Indeed," Griffin agreed, and clapped him on the shoulder.

I remained silent. Theo and Fiona had known exactly what to say, what to do, to divide us. And their cousin Turner had set Griffin's brother Jack against me, again using just the right words as bait.

Rupert and Hattie wanted an alliance…but so had Theo and Fiona, before they'd learned of my inhuman bloodline. Still, perhaps forewarned was indeed forearmed in this case. So long as we were on guard, surely any ploys to sow dissent in our ranks would be easy to avoid.

As there were now three of us, we opted to take the trolley to the address Rupert had supplied. The neighborhood was a comfortable one, the houses large and well-kept. Children strolled with their nannies, and servants returned from market with full baskets. We passed the house belonging to Dr. Hart, and an ache started in my chest. What if I never got my job back? I didn't *think* the police could possibly have enough evidence to convict me, especially as there was no chance of them producing—or even identifying—the murder weapon in court. But what if I was wrong?

I couldn't flee Widdershins. Not with the masters coming. I had no intention of allowing the police to jail me, no matter what means I had to resort to. I'd have to go into hiding in some fashion.

Which meant no more job at the museum. No more articles in the *Journal of Philology*.

No more quiet nights at home with Griffin.

"It's going to be all right, my dear," Griffin said in a low voice.

I glanced down at him. "You don't know that."

He didn't reply verbally, but allowed the back of his hand to brush against mine. I took it to mean he knew I was correct.

A maid answered the Endicotts' door. She was neatly dressed, her apron perfectly white and her black hair pulled back into a tight bun. She took my card and left us in an unremarkable parlor to wait.

Hattie joined us almost immediately. "Rupert said you'd be along today." She glanced at Iskander. "Good to see you, Mr. Barnett. Putnam-Barnett, sorry."

"Miss Endicott." Iskander offered her a small bow. "If I might have a moment of your time."

"Guessed you'd have some questions for me."

Griffin cleared his throat. "Perhaps Whyborne and I should call upon Mr. Endicott while you speak privately?"

"No." Iskander stood as if bracing himself against something. "I'd prefer it all out in the open. You said you knew my mother, Miss Endicott. That she, in fact, taught you to fight with the knives."

"Taught you too, didn't she?" Hattie dropped into a chair, her pose casual. I wondered what the servants made of her—or had they brought their own servants from England? That seemed far more likely. "But I'm getting ahead of myself. You might've guessed I wasn't raised at the family estate. My old man ran away—one of those who didn't inherit any inclination toward sorcery and all that. Figured he could do better on his own. He took off to London, met my mum, and cashed in his stack a few months before I was born. Life wasn't too easy after that, so I learned to brawl early on. Good at it, too. Good enough to impress the family when they finally found me. But punching don't work so well against sorcerers, so they wanted me to learn something different." She leaned forward with a grin. "That's where your mum came in."

Iskander shook his head. "How would she have even known the Endicotts? No one by that name ever moved in our circles."

"What, you think the family don't keep track of others like us?" she asked.

Memory sparked. "Theo said you have records of the bloodlines of other families dedicated to fighting monsters," I said. "But I thought he only referred to English families."

"'Course not. What good would that do?" Hattie rolled her eyes at me. "Egypt, Abyssinia, even really foreign places like France. Not that your mum's folk made it easy, Iskander. Can I call you that?"

He blinked, taken aback. "I-I suppose so."

"Good, you can call me Hattie." She offered him a grin that brought forth a dimple in her cheek. "We actually thought your family had died out a couple of times over the years, but then there'd be evidence of a lot of dead ghūls, or somebody would come across a camp in the desert or the like. So of course when Mrs. Barnett came to England, we contacted her. Naturally we did it all quiet—lady like her, married to a landed gentleman and all, has her reputation to think about. Didn't want to expose her, in case her position became useful."

I couldn't imagine what thoughts passed through Iskander's mind at the moment. "I…see," he said, his expression rather fixed.

"She helped us out once or twice, when there was a problem local to her. But after the family found me, I spent a summer in your gamekeeper's cottage." She tucked a strand of pale hair behind her ear, seeming lost in memories. "Bribed him a hefty sum for the privilege, but it meant less sneaking around for both me and your mum."

Iskander said nothing. I hesitated, but the question had to be asked, "Forgive me, Hattie, but I have to wonder why Mrs. Barnett would keep such a secret from her own son."

She grinned impertinently at me. "You think I'm lying, don't you, abomination?"

"Don't call me that," I snapped.

"Monster, then. Easier to say."

"I know why she didn't," Iskander said heavily. "Her early life was hard. She never spoke of it in detail, but she always said she wanted something better for me. I think she hoped I'd follow in Father's footsteps and become a diplomat."

"Don't need diplomacy to fight monsters," Hattie said. "You have to *act.* Kill them before they can kill you. Nothing good comes of talking to them."

"And yet here you are, seeking an alliance with us," Griffin said.

"Strange times and all that." She shrugged. "Speaking of which, Rupert would like to see those photographs. Shall we take them to him, then?"

"Yes," I said tightly. I didn't want to hear any more of her words, and I was quite certain Iskander felt the same. "Let's."

CHAPTER 20

Whyborne

"THERE IS SOMETHING...odd about these sigils," Rupert said. He set aside the magnifying glass he'd used to study the photographs. "You said you didn't recognize them, but do they seem at all familiar to you, Dr. Whyborne?"

My cousin had converted the house's ballroom into an alchemical laboratory. Worktables took up much of the space, along with shelves filled with jars of chemicals and occult substances. A bookcase held a number of tomes, most of which I recognized. A Latin translation of the *Al Azif,* an incomplete volume of the Pnakotic Manuscripts, and other sorts of books normally kept under lock and key.

Griffin paced around the room, studying everything with a critical eye, though he kept his arms folded and touched nothing. Hattie and Iskander conversed about some mutual acquaintance from the village near Iskander's ancestral home. Though they kept their voices low, Hattie's bright laughter sometimes broke free.

"Yes and no," I said to Rupert. "They're quite reminiscent of some of the arcane signs in the *Liber Arcanorum* and the *Cultes des Goules,* but not precisely the same. At least not that I recall." Curse the Marshes and Waites for getting me banned from the museum, no matter how temporarily. If only I had unfettered access to the library, perhaps I might be of more use.

"You recall correctly. They've been altered in some way." Rupert frowned uneasily. Though still neatly dressed, his clothing was far plainer than before, no doubt in case of chemical spills or other stains. A thick rubber apron offered some protection. He worked in shirt-sleeves, the cuffs rolled up to expose strong brown forearms. A pair of heavy rubber gloves lay on a nearby table, beside an unlit Bunsen burner. "This symbol, though. It's associated with alchemy. Usually used in formulae dealing with transformation. Ascension. Of moving past the earthly body."

"Abbott certainly moved past his earthly body," Griffin said.

"Rather unpleasantly, judging by these photographs." Rupert set them aside. "I don't suppose you have photographs of Waite's corpse?"

I shook my head. "No. Ordinarily the police would have taken some, but with one of the old families involved…"

Rupert sighed. "Theo's letter said this town was ill begun and ill run. I didn't realize…well, no matter."

I shifted uncomfortably on the hard wooden stool. I hadn't killed the Endicott twins directly—that had been the ketoi—but I was responsible for their deaths. Of course, Theo and Fiona had been preparing to sacrifice themselves in order to wipe Widdershins off the map, so I felt no guilt over my actions. Still, it was awkward to hear Theo's name from a man who had doubtless known him well.

A change of topic seemed in order. "Something else happened last night. What do you know about the Man in the Woods?"

Rupert's dark eyes sharpened behind his gold-rimmed spectacles. "A great deal less than you, I imagine, given your adventures in Egypt. Mainly, I know those who wish sorcerous power but lack the natural aptitude have two choices. Spend years in study, or go to one of Nyarlathotep's places of power and summon him. As such summonings tend to involve very nasty practices, we Endicotts destroy those sorcerers any time we come across them. Why do you ask?"

Hattie wandered over to listen while I related our encounter with Downing last night. I left out any references to the relationship between the maelstrom and me, however. What the Endicotts would do with such information I didn't know, and had no wish to find out. Most likely they'd take it as another reason to kill me.

When I finished, Hattie and Rupert exchanged a glance whose

meaning I couldn't decipher. "I would take his warning to heart," Rupert said to me. "Widdershins does seem to be your stronghold, as the family estate in Cornwall is ours. And yet I have the feeling there is more to it than that. There is something very *wrong* with you, isn't there, Dr. Whyborne? Something worse than ketoi blood."

"Go to hell," Griffin said, his voice almost a growl. "You don't know a damned thing about any of us."

Though Griffin's defense warmed my heart, it wasn't necessary in this case. "Does it matter?" I asked Rupert. "You already want to kill me. What more do you need to know?"

Rupert's full lips curved in a smile, catching me off guard. "A bold answer. At any rate, if this Draakenwood is indeed a place used by Nyarlathotep to meet with those who desire the power he offers, we would be foolhardy to set foot in it. Does it have a foul reputation, even for this place?"

"Yes," I said. "Those who venture too far in don't return. Well, I suppose except for the sorcerers."

"I'm not surprised to hear it." Rupert shook his head. "Don't let them lure you inside. Force them to come to you, to the ground where you have the advantage."

"Do we have time for that?" Griffin challenged. "Last night, you said they might be planning to conduct some sort of ritual on Candlemas. That's only two days away."

"Could they mean to summon Nyarlathotep in the Draakenwood?" Iskander asked.

Rupert and I both shook our heads. "No," Rupert said. "At least, not judging by the sigils you found around Abbott's body. At a guess, whatever they have planned involves this hematophage in some fashion. The problem is, we don't know enough about what they want at the moment. Hopefully, an examination of Waite's body will provide clarity."

"Which is interred on the edge of the Draakenwood," Griffin pointed out.

"Well then," Hattie said, patting one of the knives at her hip as she did so, "it's a good thing I'm going with you, ain't it?"

CHAPTER 21

Griffin

A FREEZING FOG enveloped the town as we drove a rented cart to the cemetery that night. It coated everything in a thin shell of ice, dampened our clothes, and chilled any inch of exposed skin. The world was reduced to the circle of our lantern light; objects appeared suddenly from the mist, and vanished just as quickly behind.

"Of all the mad things we've done, stealing corpses has to be a new low," Christine opined. She sat beside me on the driver's seat, her rifle beside her. She'd wrapped it in oilskin to protect it from the damp.

"Really?" Hattie asked, from where she sat in the back of the cart with Whyborne and Iskander. "I would've thought you lot would be old hands at this. Or do you usually just buy corpses off resurrection men?"

"I'm not a necromancer," Whyborne snapped. The expedition had put him in a foul mood already, and Hattie's endless jabs were wearying, to say the least.

"It's quite true," Iskander hastened to reassure Hattie. "Whyborne would never do such a thing."

Christine's mouth thinned to a tight line. Iskander seemed to be under the impression he could bring Hattie around, if only he could show her that Whyborne wasn't the monster she believed.

He was wrong, but I doubted I could convince him of it. Perhaps Christine would have more luck.

The cemetery gates loomed out of the fog. The sheen of ice clung to the weathered black iron, reflecting the light of our lanterns back at us. I urged the unhappy mules down the road running alongside the low stone wall. Even with the fog, entering through the gates seemed to court too much risk of discovery. The last thing Whyborne needed was for the police to catch him robbing the grave of a man he'd been accused of murdering. Not even the cleverest lawyer could keep him out of jail then.

When we reached a place near the river, where some of the stones had tumbled free of the wall, I drew the wagon to a halt. "This seems as good a spot as any," I said. "Is everyone ready?"

Christine swung down from the seat and tied the mules to the branches of a yew tree, which overhung the cemetery wall. When she was done, I handed the rifle to her, then collected my carpetbag and police lantern. Whyborne took the lantern hanging from the wagon. Iskander and Hattie removed the plank we'd brought to help carry Waite's body back out of the cemetery.

I held up my police lantern. "Whyborne? Would you be so kind?"

He lit it with a word. Hattie didn't so much as flinch; no doubt the Endicotts used sorcery on an everyday basis when at home.

We clambered over the low wall. Whyborne managed to snag his trousers on a patch of rough mortar, and muttered imprecations under his breath as we climbed the hill. Headstones appeared through the swirling mist like ghosts, and I had to stop twice to make certain we were still going in the right direction. The fog obscured even the dark bulk of the Draakenwood.

Eventually, we came across the arcane line, burning its way across the landscape. As I followed it up the hill, I murmured to Ival in a low voice, "This line runs into the Draakenwood."

Though he couldn't see the line, I knew he could feel its presence. "Yes. Presumably the sorcerers, or the Man in the Woods, draw from, if not this exact one, another which crosses the boundary of the woods."

The thought unsettled me, for reasons I couldn't entirely articulate. "Could you prevent them from doing so, somehow?"

He shook his head. His exuberant hair had wilted slightly in the damp fog. "No. If the maelstrom could do that, it wouldn't need…"

Whyborne trailed off, glancing back over his shoulder to where Hattie trudged behind us.

Wouldn't need him and Persephone, he meant. The great vortex beneath Widdershins had a sort of inhuman awareness, but its ability to act was limited. It needed eyes and ears, hands and mouths, to work its will on the world.

It collected people by shaping probabilities, or so we thought. It loaded the dice of the universe, so that I looked down at the paper on a whim and picked Widdershins as my destination, rather than having turned the page to a different news story and chosen New York instead.

But that wasn't enough. So it shaped more probabilities, found the right bloodline to contain it, and split off two fragments to become flesh. One for the land, and one for the sea.

It was up to them to keep it free. But there were only two of them; not enough to keep sorcerers from using its magic like parasites sucking blood, one little prick at a time.

I had the sudden urge to take Whyborne's hand. But this was neither the time nor the place for such a show of affection.

We half-groped our way through the mausoleums, until we found the one belonging to the Waites. A thin skin of ice coated the marble, thanks to the freezing fog, and cracked off the chain on the door when I touched it.

A heavy padlock guarded the door—but there were other wards as well. A thin line of arcane energy ran around the edge of the door.

"Get on with it, man," Christine said impatiently. "It's far too cold to stand about."

"There's a spell on the mausoleum door," I replied.

Hattie and Iskander put aside the plank, and Hattie crouched down to inspect the door. "How can you tell?" she asked.

Damn. I'd grown so used to my shadowsight, I'd forgotten to keep it a secret in front of her. "I can see magic," I admitted.

"Really?" she frowned at me. "How?"

"It's a gift." Which was true in its own way. "Whatever spell the Waites put here to guard their dead, we'll need to break it before opening the door."

"I thought they weren't sorcerers," Christine said.

"This is probably old magic." Whyborne laid his hand on the door, perhaps trying to feel the shape of the spell even though he couldn't see it. "Some curse to prevent anyone from…well, doing what we're about to do."

"Shall we use the curse breaking spell?" I asked. It should be a simple enough process, now that we'd turned my sword cane into a wand. "If I can just find the right spot…"

"Too complicated," Hattie said, drawing one of her knives. "This is quicker."

She thrust the blade of the knife into the crack between door and jamb, slashing down. The greenish glow dimmed, then vanished altogether. "Did that take care of it?" she asked.

My heartbeat quickened. "You have a witch hunter's dagger."

"Two of them." She cocked her head at me. "What, you think I'd just wander around, with no way of protecting myself from sorcerers who want to put an end to me?"

"I wouldn't have thought the family would tolerate anything that could be used against its most valued members," Whyborne said, eyeing the daggers with a new wariness.

She flipped the dagger into the air, caught it expertly, and put it back in its sheath. "Then I guess you don't know as much as you think."

I took my lock picks from my carpetbag and knelt in front of the door. "Whyborne, could you remove the ice from the padlock, please?"

He murmured the true name of fire. There came a little sizzle, the metal heating enough to melt the ice from the mechanism.

"Thank you." I set about working on the lock. The cold made my fingers stiff, but I was soon rewarded with a click. The chain rattled as I pulled it free.

The double doors swung open on squealing hinges, and I winced at the sound. "Christine, it might be wise for you to stay outside as lookout," I said.

"As though I could see anything in this dratted fog," she muttered. "Very well."

"I'll stay with Christine," Iskander offered. "Otherwise I fear it will be rather crowded within."

A large sarcophagus in the center of the floor dominated the interior of the mausoleum. Arcane symbols covered the sides of the limestone box, and the lid bore dates from early in the previous century.

The rest of the family dead lay tucked into niches in the walls.

"There," Whyborne said, indicating a niche near the back. The lantern light gleamed from a mahogany casket, the wood still polished and the golden hardware bright.

I set the lantern on the sarcophagus in the center of the small room. "Help me take it down."

Hattie added her strength to our effort, and we wrestled the casket from its niche and lowered it to the floor without incident. The pry bar from my kit made short work of the lead seal. As we removed the lid, I found myself grateful for the winter cold, which minimized any foul smells from the corpse.

Waite lay within, his body preserved by the embalmer's arts, though nothing could restore it to a semblance of life. The lips had drawn back slightly to reveal the teeth, and his cheeks were sunken. He'd been laid out in a fine suit, complete with shriveled marigold tucked into his buttonhole.

"All right," I said. "Now we just need to shift him onto the plank and get him wrapped, and we can leave."

"Thank heavens," Whyborne muttered. "I'll take his shoulders, if you can get his feet."

I nodded. He reached to grasp Waite's upper arms.

Blue light flashed in my shadowsight, surging from the arcane line and into the corpse. Before I could shout a warning, the dead man lifted his hand and seized Whyborne's wrist.

CHAPTER 22

Whyborne

I CRIED OUT at the touch of Waite's hand. For an instant, the horrible thought flashed through my mind that he was somehow still alive, despite embalming and interment.

But the flesh that closed around my wrist felt like clay: cold and malleable. Waite's eyelids slid open, revealing sunken orbs, the corneas soft and wrinkled.

I tried to wrench free, but Waite's grip was like iron. Griffin shouted my name and strove to peel the grasping fingers loose. Then Waite lifted his other hand, forcing Griffin to jerk back or risk being seized as well.

"Out of the way!" Hattie exclaimed. A knife flashed in the lantern light, neatly severing the hand that clung to my wrist. Thank heavens, its grip loosened, and I shook it off.

All around, the wooden coffins in the niches began to rattle, nails tearing free of rotted wood. The scrape of stone on stone announced the shifting of the sarcophagus lid. I snatched up the lantern before it could be hurled off. The last thing we needed was to be left in darkness.

We stumbled back toward the doors. "I thought Hattie destroyed the curse!" I exclaimed, as the first of the historic dead clambered free from its coffin. Little was left save for tendon and dried muscle stretched over bone, clothed in the tatters of attire popular eighty years ago.

"She did!" Griffin's face was white. "There was no trace of magic —and now it's everywhere! In all of the corpses."

"Someone cast a spell," Hattie said grimly. She buried her knife in the skull of a corpse trying to emerge from a coffin, and it collapsed like a puppet whose strings had been cut.

There came the crack of a rifle from outside. "Whyborne!" Christine bellowed. "You best come out here."

Blast it. No wonder she and Iskander hadn't responded to our shouting.

Christine stood with her back to the doors, her rifle raised. Iskander was poised at her side, his knives at the ready. Though the dense fog limited our vision, shapes moved within it. The doors of some of the mausoleums around us had begun to shake, and I heard the snap of rusted chains.

"I can't tell how many are out there—the arcane line is too bright," Griffin said. He'd drawn his sword cane; he and Hattie stood beside each other in the doorway, cutting down the Waites as they came.

And the damned fog prevented the rest of us from seeing anything. Well. At least that I could do something about.

This was no time for subtlety. Though I couldn't see the arcane line, I felt it in my bones. I drew from it, the scars of my arm aching with the sudden flush of power, and called the wind.

The roar of the trees of the Draakenwood heralded its approach. I heard branches snapping, trees groaning—and then the wind was on us, snatching away hats and forcing us to brace ourselves against its force. It shredded the fog, reducing the heavy blanket to mere wisps in a matter of seconds, and revealing our surroundings.

The earth above the oldest graves, those forming the spokes of the wheel around Blackbyrne's monument, heaved. Even as I watched, the first skeletal hands broke through, the dead clawing their way free.

The doors to the Marsh mausoleum burst open. Corpses clad in shrouds or fragments of clothing stumbled out, reaching for us.

Christine fired again, and one collapsed. "It's like the fane in Egypt," she said. "Do you recall, Whyborne?"

She was right. When we'd reached the Fane of Nyarlathotep, the dead interred in mastabas all around the lightless pyramid had come forth to attack both us and the ghūls.

"And like then, there are too many to fight," Griffin said. Leaving Hattie to dispatch the last two Waites, he drew his revolver and calmly shot one of the restless dead who had clawed its way from an earthen grave. "We need to find a gap in their ranks and run. Whyborne, is there anything you can do?"

At the fane, I'd managed to set one of them on fire—but it had been a resin-soaked mummy. These corpses wouldn't burn so easily.

I still clutched one of the lanterns in my hand. I doused the light, ignoring Christine's outraged protest—and flung it with all my strength at the nearest shambling corpse. The glass shattered, and oil spilled onto its lower legs.

I bent the world to my will, setting the spark to the glistening oil. Fueled by the power of the arcane line, the corpse went up like a torch.

Horribly, it began to flail, stumbling in circles. Was it the natural consequence of fire eating through tendons, shrinking already-dried muscle…or did some semblance of life still cling to the thing?

"Whyborne—my sword cane!" Griffin called.

I tore my gaze away from the burning corpse. I set fire in the sword cane, and the blade was instantly wreathed with flames. Griffin shoved it deep into the heart of one of the Marsh dead, and it collapsed with a sizzle of burning flesh.

Hattie whooped. "Come on, Iskander!"

She sprang to meet the advancing dead, and Iskander followed on her heels. They fell in back to back, knives flashing. It was clear even to me that their training had been the same. They moved together in a deadly dance, sharp blades sending hands, arms, and even heads flying from any of the dead who ventured near.

Christine fired again and again. So far as I could tell, none of the graves farther into the cemetery were giving up their dead. We could flee down the hill, as soon as we broke through the line of animated corpses around us. It would only take a few more to form a gap.

A mausoleum door behind me burst open, the heavy stone door nearly striking my back. I spun with a shout…then froze.

WHYBORNE was inscribed above the door. And the corpse now stumbling toward me belonged to my sister Guinevere.

~ * ~

Every muscle froze. I felt as though I'd been gut-punched, all the air knocked from my lungs.

Time had not been kind to what little remained of Guinevere. Still, I recognized her in an instant, despite the darkened flesh, the gleam of bone and teeth through a rotted cheek. The winding sheet she'd been wrapped in hung in decayed tatters, trailing behind her like some parody of a bridal train. Her dark hair peeled away from her skull in clumps, and her eyes were nothing more than empty sockets.

And yet she looked at me. Saw me.

We were never close in life, but she'd been my sister. Was my sister, still. Bad enough to have her cruelly murdered, but this—this mockery, this enslavement, this magic animating her remains piled horror onto horror.

She stretched out her hands to me. I could still make out the slashes on her fingers, where she'd tried to hold off the knife Stanford had plunged into her chest.

Bile coated my throat, but the rest of me went numb. She was getting closer and closer, her ragged fingers twisting into claws. I had to do something…but I couldn't.

"Ival!" Griffin called from behind me. "Close your eyes."

I obeyed him as though our nerves were wired together. I heard the hiss of magical flames on the sword cane's blade, smelled the unspeakable stench of burning rot. There came a wet thump from just in front of me.

Griffin's hand closed on my shoulder, forcibly turning me away. "Come on, my dear. We have our chance to flee. Can you run?"

I opened my eyes. The corpse I'd set alight had collapsed, and Iskander and Hattie had widened the gap, even as more dead lurched from the oldest graves. "Yes," I managed to say. "I-I can."

"Then for God's sake do it!" Christine exclaimed. She shot one last corpse, then lowered her rifle and sprinted for the opening in their ranks. Hattie followed on her heels, and Griffin and I fell in behind them. Iskander brought up the rear.

We ran blindly down the hill, making for the cemetery wall. Thank heavens these other graves remained quiescent around us. As we ran, the sound of laughter echoed from behind us.

From the direction of the Draakenwood.

Griffin cursed, but kept running, as did the rest of us. But as we ran, I wondered who had watched us from the wood…and why their laugh sounded so damnably familiar.

CHAPTER 23

Griffin

A FEW HOURS later, Whyborne and I sat in the parlor of the Lester's colonial era mansion, trying not to shiver.

Once we'd reached the cart, we'd waited for a time, to see if the corpses would follow us or return to their rest. When no shambling dead appeared, we decided to split up. Christine and Iskander would go home and get some rest. Whyborne and I would visit Miss Lester and warn her anyone venturing into the cemetery in the morning would find part of it in a rather disturbed state. And Hattie would return to Rupert and tell him of our failure.

Unless the entire incident had been some plot of the Endicotts. Rupert had been the one to send us to the cemetery in the first place, after all. The laugh we'd heard hadn't belonged to him, but I couldn't be certain more of the family didn't lurk about.

Still, I didn't think it likely. Hattie had been in as much peril as the rest of us. Not to mention such a ruse would be foolishly elaborate on their part; if they wished to kill Whyborne, they'd had their best chance already, the night in the jail. Even so, I couldn't entirely discount the possibility.

It was enough to make a man paranoid.

Though it was the middle of the night, Miss Lester had been dressed when we arrived, and seemed quite awake. We'd visited her house once before, and found it little changed from then. The air was still icy cold, though neither she nor the silent servants appeared to feel it. She led us to the parlor, which featured furniture in a style that had been popular a century before. A large mirror hung on one wall, the glass hidden behind a shroud.

We sat awkwardly in uncomfortable chairs, while the serving man brought coffee. I clasped the warm cup gratefully as I explained what had happened. We'd already decided to be honest about our intentions in visiting the Waite mausoleum, rather than concoct some less criminal explanation. I doubted Miss Lester would be much disturbed.

And indeed she wasn't. "You should have come to me," she said. Her coffee sat before her, untouched. "I might have offered another… approach…to the cemetery."

I shivered at the memory of the tunnels beneath the mortuary. "And the risen corpses?"

"Ah. That I would have been little help with, I'm afraid." She seemed to consider for a moment. "All cannot be restored as it was, but we can minimize the damage. Blame it on a freak wind storm."

She gave her servant a significant look that seemed to convey some silent signal. He bowed slightly and departed.

"If you will indulge me," she went on, "did all the dead rise against you? Or only a few?"

"Not all." I paused, careful not to look at Whyborne. "In fact, it seemed to me the only corpses who rose were those of the old families."

From above our heads came the muffled sound of a high-pitched giggle. I stiffened and looked up in alarm. I'd heard that sound before, when I'd undertaken a case for Miss Lester. Some shapeless *presence* had chased Whyborne and I in the dark, and it had made that same sound. Not the mirth of a child or a woman, but something darker. Corrupt.

The last time we'd heard it had been from the attic where Miss Lester's grandfather dwelled. Or was caged.

"Excuse me for a moment," Miss Lester said. She rose to her feet and withdrew.

"What do you think her grandfather wants?" I asked Whyborne. "I hope he still has his talisman."

The talisman had been stolen shortly after I'd met Whyborne, and he'd helped me with its recovery. The thing was clearly magic, though I'd never been certain what, precisely, it did. Only that Miss Lester was adamant no one of their bloodline touch it after sundown.

In the brief time we possessed it, the talisman had drawn…something…to it. Something insubstantial, which attacked from the sky, only to be driven back by fire. I'd been extraordinarily relieved to return the talisman to Miss Lester's grandfather and have done with it.

Whyborne didn't reply. He sat with his elbows on his knees, staring blankly at the coffee he'd touched no more than Miss Lester had hers.

As we were alone, I put my hand to his shoulder. "I'm sorry, Ival. Whoever raised the dead at the cemetery was monstrous, to put you through such a thing."

He closed his eyes and took a deep breath. "I can't stop seeing her."

I'd seen the magic of the arcane line flow into the dead. Someone had perverted the power of the maelstrom, turned it against us and used it to hurt my husband.

How horrible it must have been for him, to confront the decaying remnants of his sister's body. It would haunt his dreams, no doubt, just as it clearly haunted his waking thoughts now. Anger tightened my chest, and I said, "We'll make them pay, my dear. I swear it."

"Who is it, though?" He sat back and looked at me for the first time since we'd arrived. "That is, surely the Fideles are behind this, but…that laugh. I swear I recognized it."

It hadn't seemed familiar to me, but I didn't doubt him. "Where do you think you heard it before?"

He shook his head. "I don't know. Perhaps I only imagined it. My thoughts were hardly clear at the time."

I didn't know what to say to that, so I merely squeezed his shoulder and let go. The sound of Miss Lester's footsteps came from the hall, and she appeared in the doorway to the parlor. "Grandfather would like to speak with you, Dr. Whyborne."

Whyborne looked as alarmed as I felt. "I…oh. Very well."

I rose along with him. Though the invitation hadn't included me, I wasn't about to let Whyborne venture into Mr. Lester's presence alone.

Miss Lester led us through the house and to the attic. When I'd first glimpsed her grandfather, I'd thought him abused, locked alone in a freezing attic room. It hadn't taken long for me to reconsider…and I'd not even had my shadowsight then.

I tried to brace myself as we climbed the last flight of narrow stairs. But even so, I wasn't prepared for the sight that awaited me.

Moonlight streamed through a round window at one end of the room. Only three objects occupied the vast space of the freezing attic. A shrouded mirror, an old man, and the wheelchair he sat in.

"Grandfather," Miss Lester said, "Dr. Whyborne has come, as you asked. Mr. Flaherty is with him."

To ordinary sight, Mr. Lester appeared an old man—ancient, even. His wrinkled skin seemed almost to sag from his skull, its texture strangely waxen. His toothless mouth gaped open slightly, and hands gnarled by arthritis curled in his lap.

But overlain with the image of the man, I beheld something quite different. Its features were twisted, not quite human and not quite dog. Claws tipped its long fingers, and leathery wings folded along its back. A sense of menace, of eldritch evil far greater than anything human, seemed carved into its demoniac expression.

It looked rather like the talisman that hung about his withered neck.

An involuntary gasp escaped me. Though the old man's head didn't move, the doglike face overlain with his lifted and looked straight at me. Its jaws gaped, and a tittering sound emerged, audible even though the physical body didn't seem to move.

I grabbed Whyborne's elbow, ready to flee down the stairs if necessary. Ival's face had gone pale, though of course he couldn't see anything beyond the ruinously aged man.

"Whyborne," said the doglike thing inhabiting Mr. Lester's flesh. Again, spectral jaws moved, but I could see no tremor of aged lips. "Fear God."

Whyborne blinked in surprise. "I'm afraid I'm an atheist, Mr. Lester." Then his eyes widened. "No, wait. You mean my ancestor, don't you? Fear-God Whyborne?"

I tried to recall the brief history lesson Niles had once imparted to Persephone and me. "He was the one who came from England and helped Blackbyrne found Widdershins, yes?"

The creature spoke again. "The first to take the oath. But the rest of us followed. Renewed each generation."

"The oath?" Whyborne asked blankly. "What oath?"

The old man's breath wheezed, as if the interview took a toll on him. "Stay away from the Draakenwood. If you venture beneath the trees, the monster lurking there will eat you up."

"The hematophage?" Whyborne asked. "But no, it's in Widdershins. At least some of the time. What monster do you mean?"

He received no answer. The twisted face only I could see closed its eyes, seeming to slip into repose.

Miss Lester nodded, as though she'd received a silent signal. "Gentlemen," she said, indicating the open door.

Once we'd returned to the ground floor, Whyborne asked, "Miss Lester, do you know what your grandfather meant? About the oath?"

"No." Her mouth flattened. "As you may have noticed, many of the secrets of the old families are reserved for male heirs alone. Niles may better be able to tell you."

Whyborne sighed heavily. "Blast. I'll call upon him tomorrow, then. Thank you, Miss Lester. And I apologize for the mess in the cemetery."

We took our leave. The walk home wasn't short, but we'd sent away the cart with the others, and there were no cabs so late. Neither of us spoke much, too tired and dejected to make the effort at conversation. As our attempt to retrieve Waite's body had proved a spectacular failure, I didn't know how we'd locate the hematophage now. Certainly not in less than two days' time.

Perhaps Rupert would have some new idea. Or Niles could shed light on this oath, whatever it might have been.

As we rounded the corner to the house, I came to an abrupt halt. A figure waited at our gate, leaning idly against one post. There was no telltale glow of magic, though, so I started walking again, Whyborne alert beside me.

The figure lifted his head when we drew near, and the street lamp revealed Detective Tilton's features. At least he appeared to be alone, though why he'd wait for us through the wee hours of a cold, dark night…well, it wasn't because he came with good news, that was for certain.

"Detective," Whyborne said warily.

"Dr. Whyborne." Tilton touched the brim of his hat. "I'm glad you returned. I need to speak with you."

"Of course," I said, before Whyborne could unthinkingly invite him inside. I had no intention of letting any police in our door again, no matter the circumstances. The memory of Detective Tilton standing by while his men went through our drawers, peered into our cabinets, scalded me. "There's a saloon a few blocks away. You can buy us a round while we talk."

CHAPTER 24

Whyborne

"A BEER FOR each of us," Tilton said, as if we were simply friends who had met at the saloon and requested a back room for a bit of private conversation. He set them down with a thump; foam sloshed over the sides and onto the table.

Griffin hefted his, but I merely folded my arms over my chest and regarded the detective. Weariness gnawed at me; my eyes felt full of grit, and my stomach roiled with acid. I wanted nothing more than to collapse into bed in Griffin's arms.

But I feared the moment I shut my eyes, I'd see Guinevere again. Or whatever remained of her.

"Should Whyborne summon a lawyer to join us?" Griffin asked.

Tilton had just taken a sip of his own beer; he set it down hard. "No! No. I'm not here on Early's behalf."

The detective looked pale in the dim light, and his eyelids had a puffy, bruised quality that suggested sleepless nights. And something else, though it took me a moment to recognize the emotion.

Fear.

"What did you wish to talk about?" Griffin asked.

Tilton took another swallow of beer, perhaps for courage. "I'm a lifelong Widdershins resident. Born and raised in this town. My mother lived here her whole life, too, and her father before her. I learned never to stare too close at the ocean. To look away from cloaked figures. To mind my own business. And above all, never to cross the old families."

"And yet you became a policeman," Griffin observed coolly. "Which, unless I'm mistaken, requires you to ask questions and regularly arrest certain members of the Marsh and Waite families."

Tilton held up his hands, as if to ward off accusation. "Only those from the fallen branches. The ones with no invitation to the family mansion. Oh, they've got secrets of their own, make no mistake. But I'm less likely to end up floating face down in the Cranch River for inconveniencing them."

I remembered Father's suggestion, that we deal with Early in precisely such a fashion. "I don't condone such, er, solutions," I said.

Tilton peered at me intently, as though trying to divine the truth of my words. "Is that so? I suppose that explains why Early is still breathing. I'd wondered."

Griffin cocked his head to one side. "Wondered? Or hoped?"

"Early is ambitious. Ruthless. Ready to take on the world." Tilton took a deep pull from his beer. "And maybe those qualities would serve him well in Boston, or Salem, or anywhere else. But here, they've led him to insert himself into the middle of a struggle between the old families. If it was just him, he could take his chances. But he's the chief of police, which means he's dragged the rest of us into it as well. He's already cost a good man his life."

The jailor the sorcerer had killed. "I'm sorry."

"So am I. He deserved better." Tilton sighed. "So did his wife and children."

Curse it. The sorcerer had come for me; the jailor and my fellow prisoners had been murdered for no better reason than being potential witnesses. "Give me his wife's name and address. I'll speak with Father and see what we can do to make her burden easier, at least financially."

Tilton looked shocked. "Well. That's…that's mighty kind of you, Dr. Whyborne."

"It seems the least I can do."

"Why didn't you set more men to guard the cells that night?" Griffin asked. "Early would never have known, your officer would still be alive, and Whyborne wouldn't have been put in mortal peril."

"That isn't fair," I objected.

"It's a good thing I didn't." Tilton held Griffin's gaze defiantly. "One dead man was enough."

"Sorcerers avoid drawing attention to themselves—"

"Once upon a time, yes," Tilton cut him off. "But whatever the rules used to be, they're gone now."

Griffin started to respond, but I lifted my hand for silence. A look of surprise flickered across his face, but he held his tongue. "What did you mean by that?" I asked Tilton.

He licked his lips nervously. "It used to be sorcery was a thing done in the shadows. A book seller dying unexpectedly in a locked room, torn apart by no human hand. Unexplained disappearances among the dockworkers. The occasional odd light or sound of chanting from a house meant to be abandoned." Tilton shook his head. "The old families stood shoulder-to-shoulder. Whatever quarrels they had were kept to themselves. But now we've battles on the Front Street Bridge, and a Whyborne arrested for the murder of a Waite. We've someone coming into the very jail and brazenly killing four people." He took a sip of his beer; his hand trembled visibly as he lifted his tankard. "None of the rules seem to apply anymore."

He was right, of course. Somehow I'd not even realized things had altered. I thought it had just been me that changed.

But I was a part of Widdershins, wasn't I?

"I'm sorry," I said helplessly.

Tilton didn't reply, only drained the rest of his beer. Griffin watched him closely, then leaned forward. "Surely you didn't just bring us here to chat over a beer. What did you really want?"

Tilton hesitated visibly. "I hope to God this comes as a surprise to you, Dr. Whyborne," he said. "I'm inclined to imagine it will. Though I also hope your evening included something you can use as an alibi in court."

I doubted grave-robbing would incline a jury to sympathize with my case. "Oh no. What's happened?"

The detective winced apologetically. "Chief Early and the family wish it held in strictest confidence. Especially from you or your father. So if anyone asks, you didn't hear this from me. Joseph Marsh was murdered earlier tonight, in the same manner as Mr. Abbott and Mr. Waite."

CHAPTER 25

Griffin

"I DON'T HAVE to tell you how bad this is," Niles said. He poured a measure of brandy into three glasses, then brought two of them to Whyborne and me. We sat together on a large couch in the drawing room of Whyborne House. The previous picture above the fireplace had been replaced with a portrait of Guinevere; from the youthful cast of her face, it must have been painted shortly before she'd left for Europe to find a husband.

Whyborne had taken one look at it and blanched. But he hadn't said anything, merely chosen a chair where he didn't have to view it directly.

We'd come here immediately after leaving the detective. Niles dispatched Fenton to Miss Parkhurst's address, in hopes of either finding Persephone there, or having Miss Parkhurst summon her. Niles settled us in the drawing room while we waited. Servants had brought a round of coffee while he dressed; Whyborne and I wasted no time finishing the pot.

God, this night felt endless.

There came the sound of footsteps from the hall: Fenton's measured tread, followed by the slap of Persephone's batrachian feet against marble. "Miss Whyborne," he announced solemnly at the door. I had to admire the man's composure.

Persephone tossed back the hood of the cloak she wore. No doubt she had borrowed it from Miss Parkhurst. "Father," she said by way of greeting. "Griffin. Brother—you are in trouble again?"

"Not yet. Or, not precisely." Whyborne's cheeks colored slightly. "I'm sorry for, er, disturbing you. But there's been another murder. Joseph Marsh. They haven't accused me of it yet, but I'm sure it's only a matter of time."

"At least with Marsh's death, we know what the Fideles seem to be after," I said.

Whyborne frowned, and Persephone cocked her head. But Niles nodded. "Yes. Abbott. Waite. Marsh. They're targeting the old families."

"Blast it." Whyborne rubbed at his eyes. "We've had an eventful night. It began when we went to steal Sterling Waite's corpse."

He explained everything that had happened, though he left out the part about Guinevere. Niles's expression grew more and more grim throughout.

"This is what comes from burying your dead," Persephone said disapprovingly. "You must eat their hearts, livers, and brains so they can remain with you."

Whyborne didn't bother to hide his expression of disgust. Instead of addressing Persephone's comment, he said, "I don't know how they were able to raise the dead as they did."

"Because of the blood the hematophage consumed?" I hazarded. "If it's draining the old families at the command of the Fideles, and the only corpses who arose belonged to them…"

Whyborne shook his head. "No. They haven't killed any of us, and…"

He caught himself, but it was too late. Nile's skin went the color of cottage cheese, and he glanced almost reflexively up at the portrait.

"She's at rest, Niles," I said, as gently as I could. "I swear to you."

He was silent for a long moment, struggling to master himself. Then he nodded. "Thank you, Griffin."

"The Lesters were among the risen, and none of them have been killed, either," Whyborne said, as if wishing to hurry the conversation along. "Father, do you know what this oath was, that Mr. Lester spoke of? One taken by Fear-God and repeated through the generations?"

Niles frowned. "I can't think of anything. Unless…but no."

"What?" Persephone prompted.

"We all took an oath on joining the Brotherhood, of course." Niles waved a hand. "There was a special one for members of the old families, though. But surely that isn't what Mr. Lester referred to."

"I don't see why not," Whyborne said bitterly. "Do you remember the exact wording of the oath? Or have a copy of it?"

"I'll find a copy. And I think we have a journal belonging to Fear-God somewhere in the library."

Persephone's tentacles lashed. "Whatever the Fideles hope to achieve, if their aim is to murder a member of each of the old families, that leaves the Lesters…and us." She muttered what sounded like a ketoi curse. "It may not be safe for me to visit Maggie."

Niles frowned. "The secretary? What on earth are you doing visiting her?"

I tried to think how to answer his question delicately—or at least less bluntly than Persephone seemed about to. Whyborne leapt in first, however.

"Your youngest children have more in common than you'd probably like, Father," he said. "So I hope you don't have your heart set on any tentacle-haired grandchildren."

Niles pinched the bridge of his nose and sighed. After a pause, he said, "I see. Well. Persephone should be safe, so long as she remains with the ketoi. I doubt the hematophage will be able to attack her beneath the waves. The rest of us are easier targets."

I finished my brandy and set it aside. "I wonder why they didn't bring the hematophage to the jail? Why set the Hounds against Percival instead?"

"Perhaps they need purely human blood?" Whyborne suggested dubiously. "Although if so, Miss Lester has nothing to fear."

"We can't assume," Niles said firmly. "Without more information, we must be on our guards. This horror might be sent against us at any time."

"At least it only seems to be able to strike at night," I pointed out. "Still, you must take precautions never to be alone, Niles. And make certain all of your servants able to handle a gun are armed."

"Yes, yes." No doubt I was only telling him what he already knew. "As soon as the hour is more reasonable, I'll put in a call to the asylum and ask to speak to Stanford. He must be warned as well."

"Stanford!" Whyborne sat up straight. "Father, is he still at the asylum?"

Niles looked at his son as if he thought him mad. "Of course."

"How certain are you?"

I put a hand to my husband's arm. "Whyborne? What is this about?"

"The laughter at the cemetery. I knew it seemed familiar." Whyborne met my gaze, his dark eyes grim. "I'd bet Father's entire fortune that it belonged to Stanford."

CHAPTER 26

Whyborne

"I CAN'T BELIEVE this," I said.

Griffin shut the door behind us. Dawn had broken as we returned home. Father would call the asylum as soon as the hour was decent, but I had no doubts as to what he would find.

"No," I corrected myself, before Griffin could reply. "I *can* believe it. All too well. Of course my damnable brother would be the one behind it all. My only surprise is that he didn't have the hematophage kill me first."

Griffin locked the door and turned to me. He looked tired, his eyes bruised, and I felt another surge of fury toward Stanford. We'd had too many sleepless nights thanks to him.

"We don't know for certain," Griffin said. He crouched down as Saul trotted from his napping place to greet us. "Niles may find Stanford ensconced safely, if not happily, in the asylum."

"No. That was his laugh. God knows, I heard it often enough." Usually directed at me, as his favorite victim. Stanford had been the sort of child to find amusement in pulling wings off flies. No surprise he'd found forcing tears out of me to be the height of hilarity.

"It doesn't mean he's in charge of anything." Griffin followed me into the kitchen, leaning against the table as I fed Saul. "He's no sorcerer."

"Perhaps not. But he could learn." I shook my head as Saul's happy purr filled the air. "He has the same bloodline as Persephone and me, after all. And yes, the Endicotts say twins are the most powerful sorcerers, but that doesn't mean he wouldn't be able to learn more easily than someone purely human."

"True, but it would require intellectual effort. Not the sort of thing Stanford ever seemed to care for." Griffin folded his arms over his chest and stared into nothing. "I suppose his knowledge of the old families would make him useful to the Fideles. But they still wouldn't simply hand everything over to him."

"They certainly found him valuable last July," I reminded Griffin.

My husband seemed unconvinced. "Yes, but at the time he still had a chance at making Niles believe he'd changed, or been cured of whatever made him capable of killing Guinevere and trying to kill you. That opportunity is gone, and the other old families will hardly embrace an escaped lunatic. He's burned every bridge behind him."

"Perhaps." I gave Saul a last pat, then followed Griffin upstairs.

I hesitated slightly in the study. What if Early had men watching our house? Marsh was dead; would Early use the murder as excuse to harass me further?

Griffin paused in the doorway of what was ostensibly his bedroom. His thoughts must have trended along the same lines, because he said, "Perhaps we should sleep apart. Just until this business is resolved."

Maybe I should have let Father do away with Early after all. "If you think it best."

He crossed the room and kissed me softly. "This is only temporary, my dear."

"I know." I kissed him in return. "I love you."

"I'll wake you in a few hours." He stepped back reluctantly. "Today is the first of February. If Rupert is right, and the Fideles' plan will culminate on Candlemas, we don't have much time to stop them."

My room felt cold and lonely without him. I didn't even have the Valentine's Day cards he'd given me over the years for company. As I stood alone, looking about my barren room, anger struggled to fight through my exhaustion.

Damn Early. Damn my brother, and Waite, and Marsh, and everyone else.

I didn't want any of this. I just wanted a quiet life with my husband, and my job at the museum, and my cat. Why couldn't they simply leave me alone? The police, the Fideles, the old families, the Endicotts, all of them.

Wind stirred the curtains, even though the windows were shut and locked. I took a deep breath—no sense in inadvertently wrecking my room with wild magic on top of everything else.

I needed to sleep. As Griffin had said, time was running out.

Time was always running out, it seemed.

I undressed and stretched out on my cold sheets. I'd left the door cracked, in case Saul wanted to join me, but he must have preferred Griffin's company. I didn't blame him. So I lay alone, my mind filled with dark thoughts, and waited for the sound of the alarm.

We met Christine and Iskander at the Endicotts' rented house several hours later. I'd managed to fall into a fitful sleep, but my feet dragged and my eyelids felt made of sandpaper. My separation from Griffin, in the heart of what should have been our sanctuary from the world, left me in a foul mood. Seeing the Endicotts did nothing to improve it.

The maid served us tea, then withdrew. Griffin and I took turns explaining everything that had happened since we'd parted outside the cemetery.

"Father called on the telephone just before we left to come here," I finished. "He contacted the asylum. None of the doctors had the slightest recollection of Stanford being a patient there."

"Their minds were altered," Rupert said. As always, he was neatly dressed and perfectly poised. I rubbed my jaw and discovered I'd missed a spot shaving.

"Yes. The Fideles do seem rather fond of mind control," Griffin said.

"A pattern taken from the masters," I said. The gods and the ketoi, the Mother of the Shadows and the umbrae, the avatar and the rust. "When Father ordered Dr. Hayes to look at the patient records, the man was horrified and confused as to how he could have forgotten such an important patient. Let alone have no idea when he vanished."

Hattie snorted. "Bet he was pissing himself, on the telephone with Niles Whyborne and saying he'd forgotten his son."

"Language, Hattie," Rupert pleaded with a pained look. He turned to me. "So you believe your brother was at the cemetery last night."

"I'm certain of it," I said.

Christine muttered a shocking curse in Arabic. "I know the man is your brother, Whyborne, but if I ever have him in my sights…"

"Don't hesitate to pull the trigger." I stared at my tea, rather than her. "So. The Fideles helped Stanford escape and brought him to Widdershins. They're also using the hematophage to murder someone from each of the old families and drain their blood."

"Not just anyone," Iskander said. "Correct me if I'm mistaken, but so far haven't they killed the head of each household? Abbott was the last of his family, thus head by default. Sterling Waite and Joseph Marsh were the patriarchs of their clans, yes?"

"Which means Niles is the one in danger." Griffin shifted forward, to the edge of the couch we sat on. "And Miss Lester."

Hattie whistled low. "So you think your brother is fine with helping to kill your father?"

"Assuming he doesn't do it himself," I replied sourly. "He murdered our older sister, and encouraged the Fideles to kill me. I doubt he'll draw the line at Father."

"Well that's a right shame," Hattie said. "You'd think even an abomination would be loyal to his family, wouldn't you?"

"A terrible shame," Iskander agreed. Christine cast him a sharp look.

"So why try to capture Whyborne?" Griffin asked. "Given Stanford, I would have expected him to show up at the jail and try to murder Whyborne instead."

"His motives and those of the Fideles may not be completely aligned." Rupert sat back in his chair, cradling his tea thoughtfully. "At any rate, though we weren't able to get any of the hematophage's essence from Mr. Waite's corpse, we can guess where it will appear next."

Griffin nodded. "The Lester mansion or Whyborne House."

"Exactly. I propose we divide into two groups and send one to each location after nightfall."

"I'll take the Lesters," I said, before anyone could volunteer me to spend an entire evening with Father. I already had to return to Whyborne House to examine the journals he'd promised; I wasn't certain either of our tempers could tolerate an entire day in each other's company.

"Hattie will go with you," Rupert said. Hattie made a face at him, but didn't object.

Griffin visibly hesitated. Iskander must have noticed, because he said, "Niles knows you best after Whyborne, Griffin, so it only makes sense for you to stand watch over him. Christine can accompany you. Her rifle will be most useful if she has the high ground, and Whyborne House has both height and plenty of windows. I'll go with Whyborne and Hattie."

Christine looked as though she wished to object, but could find no grounds on which to do so.

Rupert inclined his head. "Very well. I will accompany Mr. Flaherty and Dr. Putnam-Barnett."

I didn't care for any of this, but there seemed no alternative. "Perhaps Persephone should join you as well. I'll summon her."

"I'm certain Miss Parkhurst can do that, if you send word to her," Griffin put in.

I glowered at him. It wasn't that I disapproved, but it seemed to me Miss Parkhurst could have done better than my sister. Not to suggest Persephone had no redeeming qualities, but she was just so...*irritating* at times.

Still, I supposed it was no more nonsensical than Griffin choosing me, when he might have had his pick of other men. "A good suggestion," I agreed. "And you and I can inform Father of our plans. He should have found the journals, and the exact wording of whatever horrifying oath he took that will end up dooming us all."

"People really should be more careful with those," Rupert said dryly.

We took our leave, along with Christine and Iskander. Hattie followed us to the door. "You ought to come by and spar with me some time," she said to Iskander.

His eyes lit up. "I'd love the chance to pit our skills against one another. Perhaps—"

"We have other things to do," Christine interrupted. "Come along, Kander."

Once we were on the sidewalk, Iskander said, "That was quite rude of you, Christine."

Christine spun on him, her hands clenched into fists. "Have you forgotten the Endicotts aren't on our side?"

"We're working together to stop a common threat." His dark eyes narrowed. "Of course they're on our side."

"Oh yes, except for the fact they've already tried to destroy the entire town, and to kill us in Alaska, and—"

"Hattie wasn't responsible for any of that," Iskander shot back. They glared at one another, faces inches apart, both flushed with anger. "And neither was Rupert. You can't go about blaming them for the actions of others. Shall I condemn Whyborne for what Stanford has done?"

"If you think, even for a moment, that they don't plan to stab us all in the back the first chance they get, you're deluding yourself," Christine said. "Just because your mother—"

Iskander's eyes widened. "Leave my mother out of this."

"How can I?" Christine gestured angrily at the Endicott's house. "When she's the entire reason you're so determined not to see Hattie for what she really is?"

I rather thought Christine had a point. Iskander, however, narrowed his eyes. "I see what this is about. You're jealous."

My jaw gaped open. Not only was the accusation entirely unjust, the man must have no sense whatsoever of self-preservation.

Christine took a step back. She paled, save for two spots of angry color on her cheeks. "How dare you. If you mean to dismiss my concerns with childish accusations, then to hell with you. Come home when you're ready to apologize."

She spun on her heel and stalked away. I started after her, but she said, "I've work to do at the museum. I'll see you tonight, Griffin."

I stopped and turned back to Iskander. "Griffin and I have things to attend to as well," I said, making my voice as cold as possible. The wind picked up, an icy breeze that seemed to echo my words.

Griffin sighed and put a hand to Iskander's arm. "I know family is difficult," he said. "If you need to talk, I'm here."

"Thank you, Griffin," Iskander said, pointedly not looking at me.

I cleared my throat and made a show of checking my pocket watch. Griffin took the hint and fell in beside me. But before we'd gotten more than a few feet, I heard the sound of a door opening.

Hattie had come out. No doubt she'd witnessed the whole shameful argument. She gestured to Iskander and said, "Ready for that sparring match?"

"Yes," he said. "I rather think I am." And followed her back inside the house.

CHAPTER 27

Griffin

I LOVED ISKANDER like a brother, which meant I spent the rest of the morning worrying about him.

I'd wasted years trying to win my parents' approval, and clung to the hope of a reconciliation for as long as I could. It hadn't proved possible, and I'd carry a seed of regret within me for the rest of my life. Iskander bore his own regrets, and with his mother dead and the rest of their family vanished into the desert, this was possibly his last chance to reconnect with that part of himself.

Christine had severed ties to her family and never looked back. But Iskander and I had those ties severed for us. In Iskander's case, without even realizing it had happened until after his mother was already gone. Christine didn't understand his desire to try to recapture some part of his heritage, and so—in typical Christine fashion—she reacted in anger.

Which of course made Whyborne angry on her behalf, and led to Iskander feeling even more attacked and isolated. His accusation to Christine had been foolish in the extreme, of course, but doubtless some part of him felt Christine was trying to make him choose between his life here in Widdershins and his legacy as an Egyptian monster hunter.

The thought of heritage caused me to look up from the book I hadn't actually been reading. Niles had located Fear-God's journal, which proved to be encoded in a simple cipher. He'd left us in the library, while Whyborne decrypted the crumbling pages.

Whyborne was like Christine—able to turn his back and walk away. He'd first done it to go to university, then to take a job at the museum. If not for his mother, I doubted Whyborne would have spoken to Niles at all after leaving for Miskatonic.

Had I been in his place, I would have gone to Widdershins University, learned business and law, and shaped my outward seeming into whatever would please my family most. Just as I would have stayed in Kansas and been a farmer, had fate not intervened.

Given Whyborne's power, it was a good thing he had that streak of stubborn defiance. Otherwise, he would have joined the Brotherhood alongside Niles and Stanford. And when Blackbyrne had been resurrected…

Blackbyrne's interest in Whyborne had contained an element of lust. Would the older, charismatic sorcerer have seduced him?

I didn't like the thought, but the idea of the maelstrom's power in the hands of Blackbyrne and his followers was what truly made me shudder. Thank God the necromancer hadn't recognized Ival as anything more than an uncommonly brilliant man.

The door opened, and Niles entered. Fenton followed with the coffee service. "Leave it here, Fenton," Niles instructed. "We'll serve ourselves."

"As you wish, sir." Fenton left the small cart and withdrew.

"I'll pour," I offered, as it gave me something useful to do. "Whyborne? Do you want coffee?"

He hadn't so much as looked up from the crabbed handwriting he puzzled over. At the sound of my voice, he finally seemed to realize he wasn't the only one in the room. He peered at me a moment, blinking like an owl in the sun. "Coffee? Oh. Yes, please."

"You always did get lost in those books of yours," Niles grumbled. "Have you found anything useful?"

I prepared Whyborne's coffee as he liked it and set it at his elbow. He flashed me a grateful smile. "Thank you, darling."

He must have been tired, or distracted, to address me so in front of his father. He realized it as soon as he said the words, and for a moment he stiffened, his expression starting to close off. Then he seemed to deliberately catch himself, and…relaxed would have been precisely the wrong word. But he kept the shuttered look from his face. As though to say he'd made no mistake.

"You're quite welcome, my dear," I said.

"Well?" Niles asked impatiently.

Whyborne sipped his coffee and sighed contentedly. I knew from experience the brew Niles favored was excellent, far better than the brand we obtained from the grocer. "I've learned that Fear-God Whyborne was a sadistic bastard with terrible handwriting, and a disregard for any standards of spelling."

"How enlightening." Niles accepted his coffee from me. "I'm so glad your mother threw away a small fortune for you to attend university."

If Whyborne was annoyed, he didn't let it show. "Then you'll be glad to know that's not all I've discovered. Do you have a copy of the oath you swore when you joined the Brotherhood?"

Niles seated himself across from Whyborne. It seemed an odd reversal of their usual roles, with Whyborne behind the desk and Niles in front. "There are several." Niles took a sheaf of papers from his pocket and gave them to Whyborne. "Basic oaths for those who joined the Outer Circle. Those who could be trusted to act as guards during rituals, or perform various tasks for us. Then the Inner Circle, which included hereditary members, or those who had proved themselves worthy assets. Philip Rice was one of these."

Philip Rice, the young man whose murder had first caused my path to cross with Whyborne's. In over his head, he'd mailed the *Liber Arcanorum* to his father, hoping to stop Blackbyrne's plans. After his death, his father, who knew nothing of the Brotherhood or sorcery, hired me to find out who had killed him. I'd taken the book to Whyborne for translation, and that had been the start of…

Everything, really. The life that had finally brought me happiness.

Well, not quite the start, given what I knew now. That had come earlier, when I returned to Fallow and the reach of the arcane line there.

Whyborne said there were others whose minds had been touched by the umbrae, whom the maelstrom might have chosen. But it didn't; it picked me. Because it knew, somehow, that I would see him in a way no one else did.

Even if there had been no Philip Rice, no scheme of the Brotherhood's, I believed I would have found Whyborne anyway once I came to Widdershins. If I'd spotted him on the street, I surely would have been intrigued enough to contrive a meeting.

Did the maelstrom understand human things like love and companionship? Or had it come to know them through Whyborne's experience of the world? Had his deep loneliness caused it to choose Christine rather than some other archaeologist, me instead of another who wouldn't have loved him as I did?

"Then a third oath, for those who formed the core of the Brotherhood," Niles went on, pulling my attention back from my own thoughts. "The third oath was only for those belonging to the old families."

"That matches what Fear-God wrote," Whyborne said. He tapped the crumbling journal in front of him. "He's the one who created the third oath. But he did it *after* Blackbyrne died. Apparently he had some sort of dream or vision. Until then, there were only two oaths, for the Outer and Inner Circles."

Niles frowned. "Is that significant?"

"Perhaps. It might also be significant that the founding members of the old families were the ones who burned Blackbyrne's house down, after he was killed."

"The Somerby Estate stands where Blackbyrne's house was, correct?" I asked.

But Whyborne shook his head. "I'd assumed…but there was no drawing of a house on the old map, just a label indicating Blackbyrne owned the land. And he never actually said it was in the same location. Judging by what Fear-God writes about going to the house to raze it, it was constructed on a different part of the property."

"And why does that matter?" Niles prodded.

"It might not." Whyborne glanced at me. "But Blackbyrne built his house within the Draakenwood."

"The Draakenwood," I said. "Downing and Mr. Lester both warned us against it. Likely the Fideles are hiding in its depths even now. Are they there by coincidence, simply because sorcerers are involved, or…?"

"I don't know." Whyborne rubbed at his eyes, then picked up the papers Niles had given him. "It looks as though the oaths, including the third one added later, remained consistent over the decades. The first two are mainly superstitious twaddle. They seem to concern keeping the secrets of the Brotherhood of the Immortal Fire, supporting one another in all things. And of course they promise terrible retribution if said oath isn't kept." He paused, and finally looked at Niles. "The third oath includes genuine arcane elements. It might actually be…well, binding."

"Let me see that." Without waiting for an answer, Niles snatched the paper from Whyborne's hand. "Which part?"

"The part where you seal it with your own blood." Whyborne shook his head in disgust. "Honestly, Father, why on earth would you do such a foolish thing? It isn't as though you didn't know sorcery was real."

"It didn't seem terribly different from the first two oaths." Niles tossed the paper back on the desk. "It still doesn't, except for the ritual bloodletting. *I pledge the life, and the lives of all those who carry my blood, even past the wall of death. When the time comes, we will answer the call of the Immortal Fire. Let this promise be renewed with the blood of each generation to come after, until such time as the oath is fulfilled.*"

"Wait," I said, sitting up straighter. "The pledge isn't to the society itself? To the Brotherhood? It's to the Immortal Fire?"

"Whatever that is," Whyborne said sourly. "Some necromantic nonsense, I've no doubt."

"We were told it was a symbol of immortality and Blackbyrne's promise of resurrection." Niles frowned. "But if the final oath was written *after* he died…Fear-God and the others chose not to resurrect Blackbyrne as they'd promised him, but instead took his power for themselves."

How could neither of them see what seemed so obvious to me? "Whyborne, think," I exclaimed. *"I am the fire that burns in the veins of the world."*

He cringed at the reminder—then his eyes widened. "I…you could be right."

Niles looked confused. Whyborne had begged me not to repeat any of the things he'd said in the field in Fallow to anyone who hadn't been there. "Given everything we know, it makes sense." I turned to Niles. "The Immortal Fire the old families pledged themselves to isn't some abstract concept or philosophical allegory. It's the maelstrom."

CHAPTER 28

Whyborne

"BUT WHAT DOES any of this have to do with the dead getting up and trying to kill us?" Hattie asked some hours later.

We sat in Miss Lester's freezing parlor, coffee steaming in our hands. Iskander and Hattie had arrived together, and our greeting was nearly as cool as the air inside the Lester mansion.

I suspected Rupert had ordered her to accompany me tonight because I'd be helpless against her witch hunter's daggers. Ostensibly we were on the same side, but I had no doubt the Endicotts had drawn some line in their minds. Should I step over it, they'd judge our temporary alliance not worth the risk they believed I posed. And Hattie would surely take on the role of executioner.

Iskander's presence was less reassuring than it should have been. Not to suggest I didn't trust him—of course I did. But I wished I knew what Hattie had said to him, away from the rest of us. After all, Theo and Fiona had been damned persuasive, when they'd had me alone with no one to provide a counter to their words.

"If the old families have created an arcane bond with the maelstrom through their blood, that link could be twisted and used for necromancy," I said, careful to watch my words. I didn't wish the Endicotts to know the maelstrom had any sort of sentience. If they knew it could *want* things…

I wasn't certain what they would do. Probably nothing direct, against something so vast. But those it collected to work its will were far more vulnerable. Most likely, they'd renew their attempts to wipe Widdershins off the map.

Iskander wouldn't have let such a secret slip, would he?

Miss Lester's lip curled. "Outsiders, coming here and turning our own power against us. They will regret it…briefly."

"Er, yes," I said. "It's well after sundown, which means the hematophage may be making its way to us at any time. We should ready ourselves."

"Indeed." Miss Lester rose to her feet in a single, smooth motion. In her stark white dress, she looked almost like a statue come to life. "My assistants and I will keep watch within the house. Dr. Whyborne, if you and your associates would care to patrol outside, I would be grateful."

"If we can stop this thing before it gets inside, so much the better," I agreed. Assuming it wasn't making for Whyborne House and my father. And Griffin.

I did my best to set aside my concern for him. Persephone and Christine would both be there. And Rupert, of course. Probably Griffin had less to worry about than I did.

Once we were outside the old mansion, Hattie shivered dramatically. "Lord, Iskander, I can't believe you let that *thing* wander free. Your mum would've taken care of it the moment she stepped off the boat. Not had a bloody tea party with it."

Iskander cast her a startled look. "Do you mean Miss Lester? She is…odd, yes. But hardly dangerous."

"If she's all the way human, I'll eat your shoes." Hattie hastened her pace, until she walked beside me across the yard. "What is she, then?"

"None of your business," I snapped.

"Not a ketoi. Nor a hag." Her eyes went to the mortuary next door, and she came to a sudden stop. "Bugger me sideways. She's got ghūl blood in her."

Blast it. "Of course not," I said, but it was too late. I might have fooled Hattie, but Iskander knew me too well by now.

His eyes widened. "They're…and they handle the dead of the

town." A look of utter revulsion crossed over his face. "How could you never have told me? Does Christine know?"

"It slipped my mind until recently." Since when was it my responsibility to answer for every oddity in Widdershins? "And I don't see why it would matter."

"Of course it matters!" His jaw clenched, and his dark eyes sparked with fury. "This is my heritage."

"Miss Lester is one of our only allies at the moment," I reminded him sharply. "And as I recall, your family in Egypt weren't indiscriminate killers like the Endicotts."

"Oi!" Hattie exclaimed.

"My family aren't murderers," Iskander said. "But they don't hesitate to put down monsters."

"Then you should never have come to Widdershins." I flung my arms out to either side. "We're all monsters here."

"Er, Dr. Whyborne?" Miss Parkhurst asked tentatively. "Is this a bad time?"

She stood beneath the nearest street light, peering at us. She wore a sensible dress and carried a small purse, which she clutched nervously in both hands.

"Miss Parkhurst?" I said blankly. "What on earth are you doing here?"

"I've come to help. If I can." She bit her lip. "Persephone said I could go with her, to Whyborne House, but…I thought perhaps you might need assistance."

More likely, she felt uncomfortable at the idea of spending the evening with my father. Especially if Persephone had told her that Father knew about their relationship. Whatever the reason, I was glad for the distraction from the argument with Iskander. "I understand." I hesitated. "But perhaps it would be better if you retreated somewhere…safer?"

"I'm certain I can be of help," she protested. "I'm not sure how, exactly, but you don't have to worry about me getting in the way."

"Erm…" I scrambled to think of some way to decline and still spare her feelings.

Hattie gave Miss Parkhurst a hard look. "She's your secretary, ain't she? Send her off. She's just going to get herself killed, or one of us killed looking after her."

I stiffened. "Miss Parkhurst is quite competent, I assure you."

Hattie rolled her eyes. "Then you keep an eye on her. Iskander and I will stand watch here in front. You head to the back, and take your *secretary* with you."

"I certainly will," I said with a huff. "Come along, Miss Parkhurst."

I marched toward the rear of the mansion. Miss Parkhurst's skirts swished in the dead grass as she hastened to keep up with me. Lights showed from within, but I'd not thought to bring a lantern with me. As a result, I tripped over the low line of bricks demarcating a garden behind the kitchen.

"Ow." I rubbed my ankle and glared at the back of the house. Originally built in colonial times, it had been added onto more than once over the years. It sprawled across the lot, though from what I'd seen inside, most of the rooms appeared unused. The Lester family had dwindled through the generations as well, it seemed.

"We should find a place to conceal ourselves," I said. A low hedge bordered the property, so I led the way to it. If we stood close enough to its dark bulk, hopefully we wouldn't be spotted.

"I brought binoculars," Miss Parkhurst said in a hushed voice. She took them from her purse.

"Good thinking," I whispered back.

"Thank you." She shifted from one foot to the other. "What are we looking for, exactly?"

"Any sign of someone, or some*thing*, trying to gain entry into the house," I said. "We don't really know much about the hematophage, or how it travels." Other than it managed to gain access to its victims when they were alone, without being spotted by the rest of the house. "That's why we made certain Miss Lester is entirely surrounded by defenders. Even if we don't spot it out here, it won't be able to reach her unseen."

Miss Parkhurst pointed her binoculars at the house. I stared at the surrounding yard, as the cold slowly seeped into my bones. At least if I'd gone to Whyborne House, I would have been out of this accursed wind.

How was Griffin faring? Was he having a quiet night, or had he come under attack?

As if she'd read my thoughts, Miss Parkhurst abruptly said, "Mr. Flaherty has always been very kind to me."

I blinked at the non-sequitur. "Well…yes. That is, I should think so. He's very…kind." My face heated in the darkness.

She didn't lower the binoculars. "I always thought…that is, I was always touched by what good…friends you are."

Oh dear lord, where was the blasted hematophage? Couldn't it attack and put an end to this conversation? "Yes," I agreed. "He's very…friendly."

"And handsome," she added. Perhaps she was like Griffin, and inclined to an interest in more than one gender. "I always thought so."

Thank heavens, there came a faint rustle from our left. Possibly nothing more than a stray cat, but I was desperate for an excuse. "Stay here," I whispered to Miss Parkhurst.

I crept in the direction of the sound as quietly as possible. Holding my breath, I stepped around the end of the hedge.

And found myself staring down the barrel of a rather outsized gun.

"Well, well," Police Chief Early said with a satisfied smirk. "It looks like I've caught you in the act this time."

"Hands in the air, where I can see them," Early ordered. "And don't try to escape. Where's the rest of your gang?"

I lifted my hands, struggling not to clench them into fists. Damn the man! A dozen scenarios ran through my mind. I could lay frost on the gun and cause him to drop it. Try to summon wind before he realized what I was about.

Set fire to the powder in the bullets.

I took a deep breath, striving for calm. The Endicotts would strike him down without hesitation, as would my father.

But I wasn't them. Perhaps he would listen to reason, all prior evidence to the contrary. "I don't know what you're talking about."

"You didn't come here alone." An ugly grin stretched his face. "I've had an officer following you since you left your father's house. You met some woman dressed as a man, and that Arab half breed. It will be interesting to hear what they have to say under interrogation." He took out a pair of cuffs. "Put out your hands. I've officers on the way, but I wanted to make this arrest myself. Imagine the headlines: Heroic Police Chief Nabs Murderous Millionaire."

"I'm not a million—curse it, never mind." I might show restraint, but I couldn't imagine Hattie would do so. "Listen to me. You're putting yourself in danger…"

My words died away as a dark shadow cut across the sky.

For a horrible instant, I thought it was a daemon of the night—an enslaved umbrae, sent to kill us. Then I saw the wings—great, bat-like things that made no sound as they flapped.

It headed directly toward the Lester mansion.

"There—" I exclaimed, pointing at the creature.

Agony burst through my head as Early whipped the butt of his gun across the side of my skull. I staggered, dazed, and found myself on my knees looking up at him.

He stared down at me, not at the silent creature that had landed like a ghost atop the roof. Dear heavens, what was it? It couldn't possibly be the hematophage, if only because it was the size of a carriage, from the barbed tail that lashed and curled restlessly, to its tooth-filled maw. It would never have fit inside Abbott's tiny room. Even from a distance, its skin appeared splotchy with disease or rot. The edges of its wings were ragged, as if eaten away.

A cloaked figure rode on its back.

"You must think I'm stupid," Early said, utterly oblivious to the monstrous thing above us. "Any more pathetic tricks like that, and you'll have more than a few bruises by the time we get back to the station." He firmed his grip on the gun. "You'll stand trial just as easily with a bullet in your leg."

A woman's shrill scream broke the air.

Miss Parkhurst ran up, wailing and sobbing at the top of her lungs. "Thank heavens!" she cried, and hurled herself on Early. Her arms locked around his neck, and she pressed against his chest. "Oh please, officer, you have to save me!"

He was clearly torn between keeping the gun aimed at me and comforting a hysterical woman. "You're safe now, miss," he began.

Miss Parkhurst brought up her knee in a vicious strike. Early's face turned red and twisted into a mix of agony and surprise. He crumpled to the ground, gun falling from his hand as he instinctively clutched at the anatomy she'd just crushed with her knee.

She snatched up the gun in a shaking hand and pointed it at Early. "Are you all right, Dr. Whyborne?"

"Yes. That was quick thinking," I added, as I climbed to my feet. My head ached, and the world spun for a moment, before settling.

Early's face was red, either with pain or rage, or both. "Give me the gun, or so help me, I'll…"

I never learned what he would have threatened, because his gaze went past us, to the roof of the house. All the color drained from his cheeks. "God in heaven," he whispered, eyes bulging. "It isn't real. It can't be real. I was knocked on the head…please…don't let it be real…"

"We have to warn the others," I said to Miss Parkhurst. The thing still perched on the roof like a gargoyle come to life and grown monstrously large.

But of the cloaked figure, there was now no sign. And the attic window stood open.

The attic, where Mr. Lester lurked in his wheelchair.

"Miss Lester isn't the head of the household," I said aloud. "Not for magical purposes, anyway. It's come for her grandfather."

The sound of screams erupted from the ground floor of the house.

CHAPTER 29

Griffin

"I'LL WATCH FROM the upper story," Christine said, hefting her rifle. "It will give me a good line of sight. With any luck we'll put an end to this nonsense tonight."

We stood in the foyer of Whyborne House, accompanied by Niles and Fenton. Persephone had refused a ride in the touring car, and had yet to arrive. Rupert had also not put in an appearance.

"I'll send a footman with you to run messages back and forth, if needed," Niles agreed.

She started for the stairs. "Good luck," I called.

Christine paused. Her attitude had been entirely businesslike, but the tension in her jaw and her complete dismissal of any pleasantries suggested that anger still boiled beneath. I didn't dare ask if she knew Iskander had spent more time with the Endicotts, or if she'd even seen him since their argument.

Hopefully by now Iskander and Hattie were in place with Whyborne. Even more hopefully, any attack would come here, not at the Lesters.

"To you as well," Christine replied stiffly. "I just hope I get to shoot someone."

A footman appeared from the rear of the house. "Sir, Miss Whyborne is here. She's brought…guests. I left her in the drawing room."

"Very good," Niles said. Before he could continue, a ketoi emerged from the same discreet door the footman had used. Scars raked one side of her face, and only a socket gaped in place of the eye on that side. In her hand she held a tall spear, decorated with shells and teeth that rattled as she walked.

I'd met her once before, when the ketoi had found the body of a sacrifice in their waters. "Calls Dolphins," I said with a bow.

She nodded a greeting. The footman stared at her, rather nervously. The servants had seen Persephone before, but Calls Dolphins looked even more ferocious than the average ketoi.

"Sings Above the Waves brought ten of us with her," she told Niles. No wonder Persephone had chosen to come on foot tonight. "We will help defend this place."

"I'll let everyone know," Fenton said. He'd paled slightly, but his voice remained unperturbed. "The footmen are armed, and I wouldn't wish anyone to be startled by an ally."

"Do so," Niles ordered. "Griffin, let's go greet my daughter."

I followed him to the drawing room. Another ketoi had accompanied Persephone, and she turned to face us when we entered.

Niles stopped, the color draining from his face. "Heliabel."

"Hello, Niles." She stood with her arms folded over her chest, her face impassive. Once, she'd been the mistress of this house. Confined by long illness, her body frail and worn, she'd spent most of her life in the upper rooms.

The sea had transformed her. Given her tentacle hair and orca skin, stripped away feminine curves, added fins to her arms and legs. Cured her of pain and illness, and left her lithe and strong. Like all the ketoi, she wore almost nothing save jewelry and a skirt of gold netting, to which she could attach any small items she wished to carry. God alone knew what the servants thought, seeing her again.

I hadn't expected her to return here, to the house where she'd spent so many years watching the world go by outside her window. Neither, from his expression, had Niles.

"You're as beautiful as ever, Bel," he said at last.

"As intelligent as ever, as well," she replied. "Odd how that compliment is seldom made."

It had the sound of an old argument. His mouth tightened slightly, but he only said, "I assume Persephone told you about Stanford."

"Of course she did." Heliabel turned away, pacing across the thick rugs. She stopped in front of the fireplace, tilting her head back to gaze up at Guinevere's portrait. "My poor Guinevere. If only she had come to me, when she learned of our heritage. Of the prophecy, and Stanford's plans. But we were never close. She would always choose to go to the park or visit friends, rather than sit with her sickly mother." A rueful smile tugged at her lips. "I certainly can't blame her for that. Perhaps I should have tried harder…but I had Percival, and he needed me more than the other two. Or at least, he needed somewhere safe to escape them."

Niles shifted uncomfortably. "I tried to do my best by all of them."

Heliabel's tentacle hair slithered over her shoulders. "I can't help but think…if the Endicotts had not cast their spell against the ketoi, if it had not reached me across the Atlantic, if I hadn't been so ill but instead able to take more of a hand in raising Stanford…perhaps things would have been different. I might have been able to balance the worst of your indulgences, at least."

Niles's sharp intake of breath was audible even several feet away. "No one could have predicted what happened."

"That a bullying child rewarded for his most base impulses would grow to be an even worse man?" She turned back to Niles, her face hard. "I couldn't stop Stanford from taking Guinevere from us. But I will not allow him to harm either of the twins."

Fenton cleared his throat from the doorway. "Mr. Rupert Endicott has arrived," he said. The faintest note of disapproval tinged the words, though whether because he knew something of the Endicotts, or because of Rupert's race, I didn't know.

I seized gratefully on the chance to extricate myself from the tense atmosphere of the drawing room. "I'll speak with him."

I found Rupert in one of the smaller parlors. "Ah, Mr. Flaherty." He gazed about the room with an air of interest. "This is quite the example of American excess, I must say. No wonder your heiresses so often find themselves appalled when they marry a duke or an earl, only to discover the family estate is damp, falling apart, and lacking in plumbing."

"Did you meet Guinevere, when she lived in England?" I asked. She'd returned here with Theo and Fiona, though they'd been privy to none of her secrets. Nor she to theirs.

"I'm afraid I never had the pleasure," he replied. "May I ask you a question?"

Perhaps staying in the drawing room would have been less awkward after all. "If you must."

"I know of your background. I imagine your life in Kansas afforded few luxuries." He gestured at a gilded candelabrum, cast in the shape of a cherub surrounded by decorative swirls of gold. "You seem a decent man, and yet you took an abomination for a lover. Is it because he is the heir to all of this, and you hope to someday share in the bounty, as it were?"

I clenched my fists, nails biting my palms. My Ival was a treasure beyond any gold or gems, and fury crackled in my blood at Rupert's dismissive words. "Don't speak of Whyborne that way in my hearing ever again."

"Is it genuine affection, then?" His look became pitying. "I meant it earlier, when I said there is something profoundly wrong with Dr. Whyborne. Beyond his ketoi blood, which alone would be bad enough. He isn't human, and if you expect human emotions from him, you'll be disappointed."

"I used to work for the Pinkertons, Mr. Endicott. I lost my faith in humanity a long time ago. What you view as profoundly wrong, I see as entirely right." I turned away from him and walked to the window. We were on the first floor, looking out on High Street. The electric streetlights caused the marble sheathing the mansions around us to glow in the night. "I will say, for a man who seems so learned, you are shockingly ignorant about some things."

"I see." Rupert sounded a bit nonplussed.

"I doubt it," I said. "Now, if you're done asking insulting questions, we should…"

I trailed off, squinting into the semi-darkness outside. Had something moved, in the shadows of the alley between mansions?

I stepped back. "I thought I saw—"

Before I could say anything further, a spectral, greenish shape appeared just in front of me. It looked like a lizard, or a dog, or something that was neither. I drew my sword cane and lunged at it.

Just as it went from ghostly wraith to solid. The Hound shrieked in surprise and pain. I wrenched the blade out of the hole it had made in the beast's body and struck again. It fell to the floor, collapsing in on itself, until nothing remained.

Rupert's eyes had gone wide behind his gold-framed spectacles. "Good lord! How did you know where the Hound would materialize?"

It took me a moment to understand. He hadn't seen the spectral Hound, because it hadn't yet emerged into our dimension. My shadowsight must have revealed the magic gathering at the point it would appear.

"I'm sure Hattie told you of my magical sight," I said.

"Indeed, but—" Rupert stopped, turning to the door. The sounds of battle echoed from beyond. "It seems our Hound wasn't the only one. Let's go."

CHAPTER 30

Whyborne

"Miss Parkhurst, we need to let the others know what's happening here." I took my keys from my pocket and tossed them to her. "Go to my house and use the telephone to call Whyborne House. Tell Griffin and Persephone to get here as soon as possible."

She nodded. "What about…him?"

Early cowered on the ground, his terrified gaze locked on the winged thing. Soft whimpers escaped his throat.

"Leave him," I said. "I don't think he's going to cause any more trouble."

I ran toward the house. The shouts had grown louder, and greenish light flashed through the windows. Had Early's interference meant we'd missed an obvious attack from the ground, or had the assault begun on the other side of the mansion, where Iskander and Hattie had been on watch?

Either way, it was clear the attack was only a diversion. Whoever—whatever—had ridden in on the winged beast meant to kill Mr. Lester, just as it had already killed Abbott, Waite, and Marsh.

I entered through the kitchen. A serving woman hid behind the door, a meat cleaver in her hand. Fortunately, she recognized me before swinging it at my head.

"Where is your mistress?" I asked.

"She'll be in the thick of the fighting, sir." The servant nodded toward the front of the house. "Sounds like it's near the parlor."

When I reached the front rooms, it became clear how the house's defenses had been breached with us no more the wiser. Hounds blinked in and out of the rooms and halls, passing easily through walls and furniture that would otherwise have provided a barricade. I glimpsed Iskander, his knives slick with the Hounds' ichor. Hattie laughed with glee, her blades flashing as she pinned a Hound in place with one, then finished it off with the other. Miss Lester's attendants fought with oddly archaic weapons: old, tarnished swords, or muskets of colonial make.

Miss Lester stood amongst them all, her eyes blazing with rage. Her fingers and teeth were green with the ichor of the Hounds.

"Miss Lester!" I called. "This is a diversion! Your Grandfather—"

Something screamed.

Or not screamed—the sound wasn't even audible, just something I *felt* deep in my gut. A howl, a cry, the death shriek of something ancient and inhuman.

Miss Lester's eyes widened. "That was him."

I ran for the stairs. The Hounds seemed to melt away from my path, but I didn't question my strange luck. Iskander and Hattie fell in behind me. By the time we reached the final, narrow stair to the attic, my heart pounded from exertion, and I struggled to catch my breath.

I yanked open the door to the attic and was nearly felled by the mephitic stench that rolled out along with the frigid air. The cloaked figure I'd spotted before crouched beside Mr. Lester, who lay several feet from his shattered wheelchair. Pulsing tendrils extended from under the cloak to his body, and horror swamped me as I realized each was tipped with a sucking mouth busily draining away his blood.

The hematophage. I'd imagined it would be something utterly inhuman, and yet it might have passed for any ordinary cloaked figure in Widdershins.

"Stop," I ordered. The scars on my arm ached, and the words of the fire spell burned on my tongue.

To my surprise, the feeding tendrils detached and withdrew, vanishing beneath folds of cloth. The figure rose to its feet, its body strangely disproportionate under the all-encompassing cloak. Its arms and head seemed the normal size for a man, but its legs must have been bizarrely long for it to tower over me so.

Then the hematophage turned to us. Its hands tossed back the hood of the cloak, revealing a grinning face I knew almost as well as my own.

"Hello, brother," Stanford said.

I froze in utter disbelief. For a moment, I wondered if my eyes had tricked me. If I'd actually seen what now lay concealed beneath the heavy folds of robe and cloak. A wild thought flitted through my mind, that he might simply be carrying something monstrous concealed against his body. That he hadn't undergone some unthinkable transformation himself.

But he had. Stanford was the hematophage.

Despite everything he'd done, the lengths he'd gone to, I'd never expected this.

"Not glad to see me?" he asked. Then he reached out a hand toward me and made a strange, twisting motion.

Agony exploded through me, as though my skin was being peeled back and all of my insides dragged out. My back arched, my legs went out from under me, and my poor abused head struck the floor.

Then the pain vanished, leaving me disoriented. I felt as though someone had tried to take me apart, then put me back together wrong.

"Yes!" Stanford's familiar laugh filled the attic. "It worked! The fragment of the maelstrom within you is mine to command."

I tried to stand, but he withdrew a short length of black silk rope from beneath his cloak and flung it in my direction. The rope struck my arm—and stuck.

Sorcery.

Before my spinning head allowed me to react, it began to expand, to lengthen, turning from ordinary rope into a sort of sticky webbing. Within seconds, my arms were bound, then my legs.

Hattie let out a battle cry and rushed at Stanford. Iskander followed on her heels. Stanford flung two more sections of enchanted rope at them. Hattie's witch hunter's daggers sliced through the one aimed at her, but the other struck Iskander's leg as he tried to dodge. He went to the floor, frantically trying to cut through the webbing, but it grew too fast for his ordinary blades to stop.

Before Hattie could reach Stanford, the winged mount that had brought him here thrust its head through the open attic window. At close range, I could see its loose hide was covered in what looked like patches of mold, lending it a furred appearance. Slick, wet skin showed in between, like the flesh of something dead and decomposing.

It snapped at Hattie with long teeth. She managed to avoid being skewered, but its massive head knocked her aside and into the wall. One of the daggers fell from her hand, skittering off across the floor.

"It didn't have to be this difficult," Stanford said. "If you had just cooperated with my emissary in the jail. I would have had you tucked away all this time, and only had the sea witch to worry about. But you always did have to make things hard on yourself." He shook an admonishing finger at me. "As fun as this has been, it's time for us to go. Might as well take the Arab, too. He'll make an excellent meal, after I've ascended and the maelstrom belongs to me."

The door burst open, and Miss Lester charged through. Her dress was ripped and tattered, and ichor coated her hands. Her attendants swarmed in after her, ready to fight.

Hattie rolled to her feet. For an instant, she hesitated, her eyes flicking back and forth from Iskander to me.

The winged creature let out a screeching cry that froze my blood. For some reason, that seemed to decide Hattie. She dove out of reach of its claws and teeth, and her witch hunter's dagger came slashing down at me.

The webbing melted away, the magic destroyed by the edge of the blade. Within seconds, it was nothing more than a short length of rope once again.

"No!" Stanford shouted. "Byakhee—kill the rest, and bring my useless brother to me!"

The winged monster began to tear at the roof around the window, ripping open a large enough hole to fit through. Miss Lester grabbed my wrist and hauled me up with shocking strength. "Go!" she barked at her attendants. "The tunnels!"

"Iskander!" I shouted, struggling against her grip. I reached for the wind, intending to try to dislodge the byakhee from the roof.

Stanford cursed and made the same, twisting motion with his hand as he'd done before. My legs went out from under me, pain spiking through every inch of my body. I couldn't breathe, couldn't even think.

"Carry him!" Miss Lester cried, though her voice sounded very far away. Hands lifted me, bearing me rapidly out the door. I had one last, confused glimpse of Stanford's face, twisted into a hateful snarl, with Iskander at his feet. Then the door slammed behind us, and I was carried away, down and into darkness.

CHAPTER 31

Griffin

THE GRAND FOYER of Whyborne House had transformed into a battlefield. Persephone, Calls Dolphins, and several footmen fought the Hounds across the marble floor. The sounds of fighting echoed from other rooms on the first floor, and I hoped the servants were safe.

A Hound rushed at me—then its image abruptly doubled, splitting from one Hound to a ghostly figure a few feet away, and closer to Rupert.

"There!" I shouted, pointing with my sword cane.

He flung powder on it from his pouch, even as it solidified. Calls Dolphins stabbed at it; deprived of its normal means of avoiding injury, it could only leap back. The jump brought it closer to me, and I skewered it through the back of the neck.

"Persephone!" I called. "My sword cane!"

Fire blazed along the blade. The Hound let out a strangled cry. Its body convulsed, claws shredding the priceless rug, then stilled.

"Well done," Calls Dolphins said. She didn't waste time asking how I knew where it would appear, only turned back to the fighting.

"Block the Hounds down here," Persephone ordered. "They're trying to get to Father. Fenton, have him retreat to the upper rooms.

Christine and Mother will protect him."

Fenton obeyed her without question. One of the Hounds tried to blink past Persephone and follow him, but Rupert cast a handful of powder on it, pinning it in place. The scars on Persephone's face blazed in my shadowsight, and the Hound shrieked as it began to scorch.

Calls Dolphins and I fell in together. She forced the Hounds to blink, and I stabbed them as they reentered our world. Soon my blade was slick with greenish ichor—as was the marble floor. One of the footmen slipped; two Hounds were on him before he could get to his feet. Rupert struck them with the powder, and Persephone sent one flying with a blast of wind. I ran to the footman's side, but he was already dead.

Even so, the tide seemed to be turning in our favor. If we could only hold out a little longer, we'd drive back the Hounds.

Persephone stood at the foot of the stairs, her tentacle hair thrashing as she cast spells. Arcane power poured through her, lighting her up in my shadowsight like a candle. She dashed the Hounds back with wind, scorched their hides with fire, and bent the marble floor around their clawed feet.

Then she froze, her eyes going wide with shock. The light blazing inside her seemed to stretch, past the boundary of her skin. As though someone was trying to rip out her very soul.

She staggered, a cry of pain wrung from her, then collapsed. Whatever force was turned against her seemed to release its grip. The arcane fire that lived within her snapped back into place. She lay gasping on the floor, body shuddering in reaction.

Calls Dolphins raced to her side. The last Hound tried to intercept her, but Rupert's powder already clung to its scaly hide, and I dispatched it with a blow. I sprang over its collapsing body and dropped to my knees beside Persephone.

"What's wrong with her?" Calls Dolphins asked. "Is it some spell?" She turned on Rupert, her tentacle hair poised to sting. "Have you worked some foul magic against her?"

"I don't know what's wrong with the abom—the hybrid," Rupert corrected. He watched from a slight distance, a frown touching his full lips.

"It looked as though something was tearing her soul out," I said.

Rupert's frown deepened. "What do you mean?"

Damn it. Rupert didn't—couldn't—know the truth about the twins and their connection to the maelstrom. I pretended not to have heard him, and instead bent over Persephone. "Are you all right?"

"Yes." Her hand shook, but Calls Dolphins and I managed to get her to her feet. "What happened?"

"I don't know." I squeezed her hand, before letting go. "Some sort of spell, I assume. Turned against the magic inside you."

Her eyes widened in alarm. "My brother."

Could what had happened to her have happened to Whyborne as well? She seemed recovered…but what if he wasn't? Fear slicked my spine with ice, but I forced myself to think rationally. "We've driven back the Fideles here for now. I'll take the motor car to the Lester mansion, and—"

The muffled sound of a rifle shot echoed from above.

"Father," Persephone said. "Calls Dolphins, Rupert—stay here, in case this is only a distraction. Griffin, come with me."

We ran up the grand staircase, making for the uppermost story. The distant sound of shattering glass came from above, accompanied by hoarse cries. As we hit the third floor landing, footsteps pounded down from above.

"Monsters!" The footman Niles had sent to run messages had gone white with terror. "Two of them!"

God—had the hematophage come to kill Niles? But there weren't two such beasts, were there?

I didn't bother questioning the frightened man any further. Instead, Persephone and I ran to the long room on the fourth floor, where Heliabel had once lived.

Where we'd sent Niles to keep him safe, thinking the danger came from below.

Cold air flooded into the room through a broken window. Despite the breeze, a horrid stench clung to the room. Curtains lay in a pile nearby, and the mahogany table had been overturned, the chairs around it scattered.

Two dragonnish creatures clung to the mansion's facade, stirring the air with their rotting wings. Surely it was they who had smashed the windows and overturned the table. Niles and Heliabel lay near the hearth, both of them thoroughly enmeshed in a strange, sticky webbing that glowed with magic. They seemed to be unconscious.

Christine stood before them with her legs braced, a gilded candelabrum gripped in her hands like a club. She faced down a man dressed in the robes and featureless mask I'd come to associate with the Fideles cult.

When we entered the room, she glanced in our direction. It was her undoing. In that instant of inattention, the sorcerer flung what appeared to be a short piece of black silk rope at her.

Christine swung the candelabrum, just a fraction of an instant too late. The rope touched her arm—and instantly adhered, transforming to a sticky web that began to wrap around her body.

"Christine!" I raced across the room, my sword cane at the ready. Before I could reach either her or the sorcerer, one of the winged creatures lunged at me.

Its snapping teeth caught the arm of my coat, ripping through it and scraping off skin. I thrust my sword cane at it. The point of the blade skittered off its bony muzzle, caught on mold-furred skin—then broke free and went directly into an eye.

The monster jerked back with a shriek that forced me to clap my hands over my ears. Its wings spread and flapped as it thrashed.

I saw the spell even as Persephone cast it, the warp and weft of the very universe bending to her will. A blast of wind caught the creature's outstretched wings, sending it tumbling free of the building.

"Now the other one!" I called.

But Persephone's only answer was a shout of pain. Shocked, I turned, and saw she was under a second assault, just like the first. As if something sought to drag the arcane fire free of her very bones.

The sorcerer didn't waste the opportunity. Even as she collapsed, the black webbing began to form around her.

No.

I gripped my sword cane and ran at the man. But before I could reach him, the second creature shoved its bulk halfway through the smashed window. A clawed hand struck me with stunning force. For a moment, my feet left the ground. Then I crashed into the overturned table hard enough to drive the breath from my lungs.

I lay there, struggling to move, to breathe. My sword cane had fallen from my fingers, and I forced my hand to move, searching for it blindly before the sorcerer could act.

Too late. One of the black silk ropes hit me, rapidly growing into the same bonds that covered the rest. I fought, but the strands were implacable, seeming to expand more rapidly the more I struggled. Within seconds, I was thoroughly trussed.

Helpless.

The sorcerer approached and bent over me. My heart pounded with fear—did he mean to kill me now? A wild longing for Ival gripped me, and I prayed he was all right, that whatever had attacked Persephone hadn't affected him.

My captor lifted his mask slightly and blew a palm full of powder directly into my face.

Surprise made me gasp—and draw the substance into my lungs. Instantly, a heavy languor gripped my limbs. I fought against it, but it was no use. My eyes drooped closed on the sight of the winged creature stretching out its hand to grasp me. As I slid into unconsciousness, the last thing I heard was the distant ringing of the telephone.

CHAPTER 32

Whyborne

I SAT ON the ground, my back to the wall of one of the Lesters' tunnels. We'd descended through a basement entrance, into a seeming maze of old diggings. The walls were lined with rough brick, worn from age and the action of water seeping down from above. Where the tunnels led, and what the Lesters used them for, I didn't know. But I couldn't help but be reminded of the catacombs beneath Cairo, where ghūls had made their centuries-old lair.

I glanced at Miss Lester, who paced restlessly not far away. She and her attendants—or cousins, or minions, I honestly couldn't say—had likely saved my life. Whatever Stanford had wanted me for, it would surely not have been pleasant.

And now Iskander was in his hands.

Hattie sat inspecting her knives in the feeble torchlight. As though she'd heard my thoughts, she said, "I can't believe I had to save you instead of a good man. What a cock-up this has been."

"Why didn't you save Iskander?" My voice was rusty from thirst, and I paused to swallow. "I would have thought you'd choose the life of a monster hunter over a monster."

A hiss of frustration escaped her. "It would've been right. I could've told Rupert there wasn't anything I could do. But the family says you're important."

"And you always do what they say?" I asked skeptically.

"Damn right I do." She fixed me with a hard eye. "Family's the only thing you got in this world that you can really count on."

I snorted. "Christine's family disowned her for marrying Iskander."

Christine. God. How was I to tell her that Stanford had kidnapped her husband?

She shrugged. "From what Iskander had to say, it don't sound to me like she did right by them to start with. Went her own way, did what she wanted, and said to hell with what would've been best for her family as a whole. Just like you did."

"If you mean we refused to be pressed into a mold for which we were entirely unsuited, you're quite correct," I snapped back.

Her hands stilled. "My dad ran off to London," she said, eyes focused on her blades. "If he'd stayed where he belonged, maybe he wouldn't have died. But he didn't. And mum and me paid the price. Living in the gutter, fighting and scrapping just to get a bit of bread. Once the family found me, though, everything changed." She tipped her head back and met my gaze. "Maybe I ain't a sorcerer, but they still treated me a damned sight better than anyone else did. They fed me, cleaned me up, got me training. They did right by me, so I do right by them." She shook her head. "Even if it means saving a monster like you."

I didn't know how to respond. If I'd lived her life, I might have a different outlook as well.

"The sun has risen," Miss Lester announced. She'd stilled her pacing at last. "Any creatures from the Outside will have been forced to retreat. It should be safe to return to the house."

How she knew the sun had risen, I didn't ask. From a pocket watch, I hoped, though I'd not noticed her consulting one. Tired to my very bones, I followed her back through the tunnels, Hattie and the silent attendants trailing after.

"I have to get to Whyborne House as quickly as possible," I said once we'd emerged from the basement. I made my way to the front door, stepping over the smears of blood remaining on the floor from the battle the night before. "I have to tell them what's happened. We'll come up with a plan to save Iskander, and..."

I opened the door and fell silent. Miss Parkhurst stood on the walk outside, her eyes red and her cheeks blotchy. When she saw me, surprise and relief transformed her face. "You *are* here! I—I thought they must have taken you too. I didn't know what to do."

Dread pooled in my stomach. "What happened? What do you mean, taken me too?"

"Oh, Dr. Whyborne." Tears of misery gathered in her eyes. "I called your father's house, as you said to do. But it was already too late. The phone rang and rang, and then Mr. Fenton answered, and... your mother and father, Mr. Flaherty, Dr. Putnam-Barnett, and...and Persephone. They've all been kidnapped. There's no one left but you."

I sat alone in the parlor we'd converted to Griffin's office, my head cradled in my hands. The house was utterly silent; worse, it felt empty. As if it knew Griffin was gone.

What was Stanford doing to him even now? To any of them? He'd spoken of Iskander as being sustenance after he *ascended*. Presumably his new form required blood to sustain it. But Stanford was too vindictive to make death easy for Griffin, or our parents. As for what he had planned for Persephone...

From his talk of ascending, he presumably meant to undergo some even more horrific transformation, which would somehow give him access to the power of the maelstrom.

"It worked," he had said. I dropped my hand to my chest, remembering the pain. Somehow, ingesting the blood of the old families, the ones who had pledged themselves to the Immortal Fire, had given him a hold over the fragments within us. Perhaps the binding oath worked in both directions.

Hattie had overheard him. She'd left the Lester mansion rather quickly, saying she wished to confer with Rupert. Once she told him the truth about Persephone and me, they'd probably decide no alliance was worth it, and come to kill me.

Ordinarily, I would confer with Griffin or Christine. Try to come up with a plan to stop my brother before he carried out some monstrous ceremony tonight. I longed for Griffin's steady presence, or even Christine's brash certainty.

Persephone would know what to do. Or Father—he'd give me an angry lecture about being unprepared, but then offer up half a dozen suggestions. Iskander came from a long line of monster hunters, and unlike the Endicotts, I trusted him. Surely he would have some idea of how to proceed. Even if he didn't, he'd offer his quiet support.

Stanford had taken them all from me. Everyone I loved was in the hands of a monster, and it was up to me to save them.

Oh God.

They were all going to die, and it was my fault. Because I wasn't enough. I couldn't *be* enough.

All of the maelstrom's centuries-long plotting, collecting people and bloodlines, fashioning its vessels…and it had come up with me. What a bitter disappointment, assuming such an inhuman sentience could even feel the emotion. Persephone was up to the task, but it would have been better off with almost anyone but me.

I didn't want this. I'd never wanted power of any sort. I just wanted Griffin back. And Christine, and everyone else. My family, even if they weren't all related by blood.

I lowered my hands and stared at them. At my wedding ring, the black pearl rich with hidden colors, just waiting to be brought out in the right light. I loved Griffin, more than I'd ever imagined possible. We'd saved one another, again and again, but it had never just been me. Even when he'd been taken by the Brotherhood, I'd had Christine waiting to lend her support in the form of her rifle.

If I failed this time, they'd both die.

I closed my eyes and took a deep breath. I had to try…something. But what? If I marched alone into the Draakenwood, I'd either get lost and wander until I expired from thirst, or be overwhelmed by Stanford and the Fideles and die alongside my family.

I couldn't do this alone.

But perhaps I didn't have to. I'd stoppered my ears when Father suggested I take charge, gather allies. Order people about. I'd told Griffin the maelstrom had chosen wrong when it picked me as its vessel.

But of course the maelstrom hadn't chosen me at all. It *was* me. Or at least a fragment of it was, so perhaps it would be more accurate to say I was it. Shaped by a human brain, with human emotions and experiences, but still…it.

So it was time I started acting like it.

There came a soft knock on the front door. "Come in," I called.

Miss Parkhurst entered, a bit tentatively. Her eyes were red from lack of sleep, and she twisted her hands together when she halted in the doorway to the parlor. "I just…I wanted to come and find out if there was anything I could do."

I rose to my feet. "As a matter of fact, Miss Parkhurst, there is." I turned resolutely to the instrument mounted on the wall. "But first, I need to make a few telephone calls."

CHAPTER 33

Griffin

I DRAGGED OPEN eyes that felt crusted shut. I lay on my side, at the base of a huge tree. A cage made from its living roots surrounded me, as though it had grown there while I slept. I could still perceive the lingering traces of magic within the wood. Other shapes were within the cage as well, and as I blinked, they came slowly into focus. Iskander sat upright, leaning against the roots and staring out intently. Christine lay unconscious or asleep, her head in his lap. We were unbound, though when I moved, a length of black rope fell from my arm where it had rested.

Memory flooded back, and I sat up. We were in a dark forest, the canopy so thick even in winter it blotted out the sun and left us in perpetual twilight. Other cages had grown at the base of the two nearest trees. One contained Orion Marsh and Fred Waite, huddled together for either warmth or comfort. The other held Niles and Heliabel.

I pressed my face to the living bars, trying to get a better sense of our surroundings. The winter cold had seeped into my flesh while I slept, turning my thoughts sluggish. We were at the edge of a clearing of sorts, surrounded by forest, a heavy mist blotting out the daylight. The trees seemed to crowd together, their bare branches tangled like gnarled limbs, creating a wall of bark all around. Nearer to hand, piles of fallen stone and brick protruded here and there from the uneven ground, covered over by briars and withered grass. Iskander's knives, Nile's cavalry sword, and a small pistol lay piled carelessly atop what remained of a wall. The stone was fire blackened, and I recalled what Whyborne had said, that Fear-God and the other founders had burned Blackbyrne's mansion within the Draakenwood.

In the center of the ruins stood an enormous tree. A dozen men might have been able to encircle its base with their arms outstretched, but only barely. Each branch was so thick it would have formed an impressive tree in its own right, and their dense tangle hid the sky. The lowest branches sank almost to the ground in places, bent beneath their own weight. Lichen crawled over the bark in irregular patches, giving the tree a scabrous appearance.

Weathered charms and bones hung from the lower limbs, and skeletal remains protruded here and there from the thick carpet of rotting leaves covering the ground. Clearly, this had been a place of sacrifice and death for a very long time.

Two gigantic roots, taller than a man in places, curved out from the tree to form a bowl. Nestled against the outside curve of each root was a pair of strange, almost fleshy, pods. Through the thick, gelatinous surface of the left hand one, I could make out Persephone's shape, curled like a seed within a fruit. She seemed to be asleep or unconscious, even her hair still for once. The other pod was empty…for the moment, at least.

Ival. Had he somehow avoided capture?

Both pods glowed with magic, as did the tree. An arcane line cut through the woods, through the ruins of what must have been Blackbyrne's house, and directly beneath the massive roots.

Christine stirred and moaned. Iskander gasped and bent over her. "Christine? Dearest? Are you awake?"

"Good gad, my head," she mumbled. "What the devil happened?"

With a low cry, he clasped her in his arms. "I'm so sorry we argued. I was a fool."

"Yes, yes," she agreed. But she kissed him, which I took to mean she'd forgiven him. "Now let me sit up."

He did so, and some of the color drained from her face as she took in our surroundings. "Oh. This certainly is a fine mess." Taking hold of one of the roots forming our prison, she began to tug on it. "Well don't just sit there, you two. Help me!"

"I have something to tell you," Iskander said as he moved to help her. "It's about Stanford Whyborne. He killed Miss Lester's grandfather. We reached the attic before he was finished, and we saw—"

There came the crunch of leaves, the swish of robes over the forest floor. "You fool," snarled a voice. "How could you let the other one escape? You've ruined everything with your bungling!"

Two shapes entered the clearing, and we quickly left off prying at the tree root. One of them was clearly Stanford...only there was something terribly wrong with the proportions of his body beneath the cloak covering him. Though his arms and face seemed their normal sizes, he'd grown in height, as though his lower half had somehow been stretched out. If he and Ival faced one another, Stanford would be the taller of the two now.

The other figure wore robes with a mask hanging at the belt. He had a plain face, but when he turned his head, I saw one ear had sprouted a host of tentacles. One of Nyarlathotep's sorcerers, just as Downing had warned. Only, unlike Downing, this one had apparently decided it was best to cooperate and keep the rest of his body from mutating.

"It doesn't matter, Kolter," Stanford said. "My useless brother is no threat. In fact, this is even better." His small eyes swept the cages, lighting on me. "Before he dies, I'll rip this one's head free and show it to him. No—not his head. Some other part my disgusting pervert brother is certain to recognize."

Though my heart thudded against my ribs, a surge of hope went through me. Ival was still free.

The sorcerer—Kolter—seized Stanford by the arm. "Idiot! We need both pieces of the maelstrom. If you only take that which belongs to the sea, it leaves your brother in command—"

"You forget your place!" Stanford turned on the sorcerer, his face twisted into a mask of rage. "*I* am the only one who can ascend! *Me!* I will control the maelstrom, the old families, all of it. I'm the one giving the orders, and you're the one doing what you're told."

I sat up sharply. Stanford, control the maelstrom?

Bile rose in my throat at the very thought. I didn't know what Stanford meant to do, but the idea of such power at his command was more than terrifying. It was wrong, in a way I could barely articulate.

Kolter made no reply for a long moment. I could practically feel the rage pouring off of him, but Stanford seemed oblivious. "Of course," he said at last. "Forgive me."

Satisfied, Stanford turned his back on the sorcerer. "Besides, my brother couldn't command toy soldiers. He's probably hiding under his bed, quaking in terror." Stanford drew closer to the cages, bending over to peer through the bars of the one entrapping his parents. "Too bad he can't cower behind your skirts anymore, right, Mother? Of course, you barely even wear skirts anymore. I never thought you'd be a harlot."

Heliabel wrapped her clawed fingers around one of the tree roots. "What have you done to your sister?"

"The fish?" Stanford glanced casually over his shoulder. "If you expect me to have any brotherly feeling for her, don't bother. She's nothing to me. Merely a means to an end. When our spy among the ketoi said she would be on land last night, guarding Father, I knew everything was finally aligning to favor me."

A slight breeze picked up, rustling branches and ruffling Stanford's cloak. A foul stench wafted from him—the same as I'd smelled in Abbott's shabby room when Whyborne and I had gone to investigate his death.

My fear and worry deepened, though I struggled not to show it. "You were there, when the hematophage was summoned. When Abbott died."

Stanford turned to me, and a shudder ran down my spine. His movements were all wrong, as though his oddly elongated legs had no bones in them. "You could say that. I promised Thomas his revenge in exchange for his help. He didn't realize quite how much blood I meant to take."

"Dear God, Stanford, what have you done?" Niles asked.

"I needed the blood of the old families. The ones who took the third oath, who had bound themselves to the Immortal Fire." Stanford cocked his head, a maniacal grin stretching his lips. "That's the thing about bindings. They can go both ways. Once I had the blood of all five families, I could act upon the Immortal Fire itself. Not the great vortex directly—it's too big for that. But two slivers, two little weak fragments chipped away from the whole and stuffed into pathetic flesh…those are entirely vulnerable."

No.

I forced myself to breathe. Stanford didn't just mean to kill Whyborne and Persephone. He meant to turn the maelstrom's attempt to free itself from the masters into a method of enslaving it.

Thank God Ival had escaped. "All five families?" I swallowed against the dryness in my throat, determined to keep him talking. "You fed Thomas Abbott, Joseph Marsh, Sterling Waite, and Mr. Lester to the hematophage. You didn't offer it your own blood, so whose did you use?"

Heliabel gasped. "Not your own sons."

An odd look passed over Stanford's face at the mention of his long-estranged children. "No one," he said, reaching for the fastenings on his cloak. It fell open, and my gorge rose at the horror revealed.

From mid-chest up, he still looked entirely human. But from that point down, his body was a mass of squirming tentacles above thick, elephant-like legs. Each pallid, boneless tentacle was tipped with a hideous, sucking mouth. Needle-like protrusions flickered in and out of some; no doubt the source of the puncture wounds through which blood had been extracted. The stench coming from the heaving mass of inhuman flesh was staggering.

Stanford grinned, as though the horror etched on our faces gave him only pleasure. "The Whyborne bloodline was already inside me, after all."

CHAPTER 34

Whyborne

Rupert and Hattie met me at the Lester mansion. As they had no telephone in their rented house, I'd sent Miss Parkhurst to ask them to join me, when I'd finished my calls. Nervousness churned in my gut when I thought of what I'd orchestrated. I was now not only responsible for the lives of my friends, my family, but of those I'd called upon.

I thrust the thought aside for the moment. One step at a time was the only way forward, else my nerve would fail.

And I couldn't allow that to happen. Griffin, Christine, and everyone else were relying on me. I couldn't let them down.

I wouldn't.

"Mr. Endicott, Miss Endicott," I said, nodding to them as they approached the front step where I waited. At least they didn't look any more murderous than they had before. "I'd hoped you'd come."

"Of course," Rupert said. "It's quite clear your brother must be stopped." He held up what looked like a brass compass, but set into a wooden base carved with arcane symbols. "If he left behind a sample of blood or skin last night, we should be able to use this to track him."

"What do we need that for?" Hattie asked. "We know where he is, don't we? He's got to be in the Draakenwood. You couldn't hide those winged beasties anywhere else."

"They're called byakhee," Rupert said with a slightly pained look.

"And the Draakenwood is huge." I folded my arms over my chest. "I also suspect it isn't as simple to navigate through as an ordinary forest. No one sets foot there lightly. Without something to lead us directly to Stanford, we could end up lost and wandering for hours."

"And time isn't on our side," Rupert agreed with a grimace. "Candlemas begins at sundown, and there's no telling when after that the ritual will begin."

"Yes." I took a deep breath, but I felt we needed to get things out in the air. "Stanford means to somehow take command of the maelstrom. Or, at least make a use of it no one else can."

"Indeed." Rupert's dark eyes watched me carefully. "Hattie mentioned it. She also mentioned he was able to interfere with a fragment of the maelstrom within you."

At least he didn't sound as though he meant to cut my throat on the spot. "Yes."

"Using the blood of the families who took an extremely unwise magical oath. Such magic is a double-edged sword, able to cut in either direction." He pursed his lips. "The good news is, he should only be able to use it a limited number of times. Once for each bloodline, most likely."

"And he's done it twice already."

"Yes. It seemed to affect you and your sister simultaneously, even though she was at Whyborne House at the time."

Damn Stanford. If the magic hadn't struck both of us at once, perhaps Persephone would have driven back the sorcerers at Whyborne House. Griffin might even now be here at my side.

But there was no use wishing the past to be different. I had to concentrate on the future.

I led the way up the stairs and knocked on the door.

"Do you know if Mr. Lester's body is still untouched?" Rupert asked as we waited to be let in. "If he fought back, perhaps we can find some trace of blood beneath his fingernails to use to track the creature."

The door swung wide. "We can do better than that," Miss Lester said. Rather than her usual white, she was dressed in mourning black. "Stanford Whyborne did not escape unscathed. If you will follow me."

She led the way up the stairs to the attic. Though cold air poured through the broken attic window, the space seemed somehow warmer than it had on my previous visits. The entire house did, now that I thought of it.

Nothing had been moved since the night before. The wheelchair lay scattered in pieces, the old man not far from it. His hands were still hooked into arthritic claws and his lips drawn back from his teeth. His clothing had been ripped aside, and the familiar sucker wounds showed on his abdomen. The talisman that the old man had cherished—or perhaps required—lay broken into two pieces in one corner.

A heavy stench still filled the room, emanating from the smears of green-black ichor on the floor near the body. At least the old man had been able to injure Stanford before his death. I vindictively hoped the injuries were causing Stanford a great deal of pain.

"Gah, what a stink," Hattie said, holding a handkerchief to her face.

"By a foulness ye shall know them," Rupert murmured, and I recognized the words from the *Al Azif.* "It seems our cousin Stanford has somehow fused himself with something from the Outside."

"But why?" I asked in bewilderment. "Even if Stanford gave a fig about the Fideles and the masters—which I sincerely doubt—he isn't what one would call the self-sacrificing type."

"No," Rupert agreed. "But from what the family has been able to discover about him, he is greedy and vengeful. Promises of power and retribution have driven men to do many strange things. Now please, let me concentrate on my work."

Rupert took out some of his vials and powders, and knelt by the ichor smears. Miss Lester and I retreated to stand near the door, while Hattie examined the claw marks left behind by the byakhee.

"Thank you for saving me last night," I said to Miss Lester. "I'm sorry I didn't express my gratitude before. I seem to have quite forgotten my manners."

"You can be forgiven." She nodded in the direction of the wrecked window. "You had quite a shock, I imagine."

"Yes." I paused. "And allow me to offer my deepest condolences on your loss."

"Don't bother," she replied. My surprise must have shown on my face, because she said, "The body over there did indeed originally belong to my grandfather. But the consciousness that inhabited it…let us say Blackbyrne wasn't the only one to dream of immortality."

"Oh," I said faintly.

"I've taken many steps over the years to ensure I remained…well, myself." Miss Lester shook her head. "And to ensure he had no access to any other potential host. Fortunately, he could only possess others of his bloodline. I counted on time to eventually solve the problem, but your brother hastened matters along. If Stanford didn't intend to use his blood to do something horrible, I would send him a letter of thanks."

Rupert sat back on his heels, the tails of his elegant coat carefully clear of the ichor. "I believe I have it," he said. Holding one hand above the compass, he murmured a chant in Aklo. The compass needle jerked, spun wildly—then took up a new position on the dial, pointing decidedly northwest.

Toward the Draakenwood.

"Huh," Hattie said. "So I hope one of you gents has a plan. Aside from *charge in and get ourselves killed,* that is."

"Indeed. I've found some reinforcements. They're already waiting to hear from me." I steeled my spine. I'd done this once already; I could do it again. "Miss Lester, I'm very much afraid I will need to use your telephone."

CHAPTER 35

Griffin

Iskander made a gagging sound and put his hand to his mouth. Christine hissed in disgust. From one of the other cages, Orion Marsh let out a shriek. As for myself, I could only gaze on in frozen horror. Stanford had perverted his own flesh, twisted his body into something as corrupt as his rotten soul.

He meant to spread his poison to the maelstrom. Defile it with his touch.

"Stanford," Niles said. "What…what have you done to yourself?"

"Take a good look," Stanford said, spreading his arms wide. "Thanks to my perseverance, my fortitude, I stand on the precipice of becoming far greater than any of you could ever dream."

Heliabel stared, shaking her head back and forth slowly. I couldn't even imagine how she must feel at this moment. "What have you done?" she echoed.

Stanford chuckled, and the sound chilled my blood. Did he have any shred of sanity left? "The Fideles are indeed faithful," he said. "Unlike you, my family. And unlike my dear, dear friends over there."

He gestured to Orion and Fred, who clutched one another like men in a nightmare. "What good friends we were," Stanford crooned at them. "Remember happier times, gents? The clubs, the whores, the drink. Recall the weekend we spent in New York, when you visited me on Fifth Avenue? I showed you a good time then, didn't I?" When neither answered, he took a threatening step toward them. *"Didn't I?"*

"Y-Yes!" Fred cried. Orion seemed too terrified to give a coherent answer.

It satisfied Stanford, at any rate. "Exactly. But did you stand by me, when I was shipped off to the asylum for my supposed crimes?"

"Y-You threatened to kill us," Fred said, as though he believed it might still be possible to have a rational argument with Stanford. "At the museum, I mean. What was your friendship worth then?"

I didn't know if Fred was brave or an idiot. "I asserted my rights," Stanford growled. "I should have been in control of Widdershins from that night on. If you had given me my due, I would have rewarded you. But you stabbed me in the back, just like everyone else. Afraid of my greatness."

Dear God, he'd come utterly unhinged. "So you've turned yourself into a monster in revenge?" I asked. "That seems more like a punishment for you than them."

Stanford turned on me like a striking snake. "Shut up, sodomite. I captured you because I hoped to tear you to pieces in front of my weeping brother. But since he was too cowardly to stand and face me like a man, you're far less entertaining."

I held myself very still. If Stanford decided to kill me out of hand, there was little I could do to stop him.

I had to live. My Ival needed me. *Widdershins* needed me.

"Griffin is only putting into words what the rest of us are thinking," Heliabel said. Drawing Stanford's attention from me. "You were my little boy, once, Stanford. Strong and healthy. Now look at you."

"I could say the same, *Mother*. You've become just as much a monster as me."

The ketoi might be fearsome, but Stanford…his form was *wrong* in a way I couldn't adequately explain. Twisted, foul, and revolting on an animal level.

"This was necessary," Stanford went on. "You see, once my *true* friends rescued me from that prison and convinced the doctors I'd never been there to begin with, they told me just how deep the betrayal ran. Bad enough you gave all your affection to that simpering worm Percival when we were children. Bad enough he ultimately turned even Father against me. But worst of all, he and the sea witch took the power that should have been mine."

"Nonsense," Niles barked. "You aren't even making sense, boy. What the devil do you think Percival has taken from you?"

"The maelstrom should have chosen *me*." Stanford's hands clenched at his sides. "None of this land and sea nonsense. What was needed was a single, strong man who could rule this town with a firm hand. Who could bring the old families into line, and force the ketoi to bend their knee." He shook his head. "But it isn't too late to make things right. I have the same bloodline as the twins do. I can withstand the touch of the vortex's power. Tonight, I'll take what should have rightfully been mine from the beginning."

Dear God. Was what he suggested even possible?

Stanford moved a few feet away, hands folded behind him, then turned back to us. "Nyarlathotep. The Man in the Woods. The architect of the maelstrom, who planned the means by which the arcane lines could be twisted, joined, to serve the will of the masters."

"Oh no," Iskander whispered.

"When he learned of its defiance, he was not pleased," Stanford went on. "But he had a solution—one to which I was key. He shared it with his sorcerers, and showed them the necessary spells and sigils in their dreams."

"And…this?" Heliabel asked, gesturing to Stanford's body.

"The twins were only blobs of flesh within your womb when the maelstrom's fragments settled into them. Malleable enough to absorb the Immortal Fire without damage. But the body of an adult is less plastic. I needed to join something from the Outside. To feed and nurture it, first on Abbott. Then the others of the old blood." Stanford glanced at Orion and Fred. "Despite the betrayal of my friends, I was generous enough to clear the way for them to inherit. I hope you two appreciate it. If not, I'm sure I can find someone in your families who would like to take your place."

Fred swallowed convulsively. "Of-of course we're grateful. A-aren't we, Orion?"

Orion nodded. He looked like a man trapped in a terrible dream, unable to wake.

"Better," Stanford said.

"This is madness." Niles clutched the wooden bars of his cage, staring out at Stanford. "Please, son. You're hurting your friends, your mother. Yourself. Stop this and think."

"I've had nothing to do for two years but think!" Stanford struck the cage with one of his feeding tentacles; had Heliabel not hauled Niles back, it would have made contact with his hand. "But no more. Tonight is my ascension. Nyarlathotep will come forth in response to my summons. He will strip the fragment of the maelstrom from the sea witch and give it to me." Stanford turned away. "And when you see my true power, you'll both finally realize you chose the wrong son."

He departed, anger in every line of his body. Kolter watched us for a few moments, then followed, though not before summoning a pack of Hounds to patrol the clearing.

Niles slumped forward in despair. Heliabel absently patted his shoulder. Her jaw was clenched, though whether from anger or in an attempt not to shed tears for her misbegotten eldest child, I didn't know.

"This is bad," Christine said.

Iskander shook his head unhappily. "I'm fairly certain everyone already knew that."

I stared out at the clearing, watching the Hounds circle. Perhaps I should have felt despair, or fear. As Christine had said, we were in a very bad situation.

But I didn't. All I could feel at the moment was anger.

When I had been at my lowest, lost and broken, drowning in pain…that was when the maelstrom had chosen to collect me. Even though there had been others whose minds had been touched by the umbrae, even though I had barely been able to drag my battered soul from one hour to the next, it had chosen *me*. It had seen worth in me, when I'd not seen it in myself.

And now Stanford sought to pervert a part of it, in order to undermine the whole in favor of the masters. He meant to take the sparks the maelstrom had set in flesh—flesh I loved very much indeed—and use them to make sure it remained enslaved.

I would not allow it. He would not kill my Ival, and he would not turn the maelstrom's bid for freedom into shackles.

Not if I had to rip him apart with my bare hands.

CHAPTER 36

Whyborne

MISS PARKHURST, THE Endicotts, and I waited in the cemetery, at the border of the Draakenwood. I had gone to Whyborne House first, and spoken with the servants and Calls Dolphins, who had remained with a few ketoi. Though I lacked my sister's authority among them, they listened carefully to my plan. The forest was no place for them; they'd never be able to navigate it on their frog-like feet with anything like swiftness. Instead, they would stand watch from the Cranch River. If Stanford emerged from the forest instead of us, it would be up to them to try and stop him.

Before we'd left Whyborne House, Fenton had brought me Griffin's sword cane, which he'd found abandoned on the uppermost floor. I held it now, absently running my fingers over the crystals I'd bound to it, the heavy silver head. I had to believe I'd return it to him soon. That we would somehow find him before Stanford could do anything terrible.

The sun was far more westerly than I liked but there was nothing to be done for it. Though Rupert preferred not to guess precisely when Stanford's ritual would begin, I sensed in my bones that our time grew short.

I sensed, too, the arcane line running beneath our feet and vanishing into the wood. There were others, most likely, crossing through the forest, all of them feeding into the great vortex where land and sea joined. Stanford would surely use one of them to fuel his ascension. Which one, and where, was the question only Rupert's tracker could answer.

"We need to get on with it," Hattie said, shifting from one foot to the other. "There ain't much time left. Where the hell are these reinforcements of yours?"

"There," Miss Parkhurst said, pointing down the hill.

Detective Tilton led a handful of police officers up the slope to where we awaited them. My conversation with him, explaining the situation and what I wanted, had been…interesting. When the call ended, I'd not been at all sure if he would come.

He stopped a few feet away, watching me from beneath the brim of his bowler hat. "Dr. Whyborne."

I took a deep breath and did my best to ignore the nerves souring my belly. "How is, er, Chief Early?"

"He's taking a well deserved rest at the Danvers Lunatic Hospital," Tilton replied. "It seems the stress of his new duties proved a bit too much for him. Naturally that means any cases he was personally involved in—yours for example—will be too tainted by accusations of mania for the prosecutor to even consider bringing them before a judge."

"Oh." Though I was grateful not to have to fear a knock on the door from Early, Griffin's experience with a madhouse made me less pleased to see the man consigned to one than I would have been otherwise.

"Early's problem was that he looked, but he didn't *see*." Tilton scratched his chin. "And then was too stubborn to look away when he should have."

"About that." I hesitated, glancing first at Tilton, then at the men he had brought with him. "You told me things had changed. You were right. Our town is in danger, and the time for turning a blind eye to sorcery is past. Now we must act, to put a stop to my brother and his madness. Confronting him may cost some—or all—of us our lives. But if we don't stand against the plots of the Fideles and the masters, we'll either die or be enslaved anyway. So, er. Who is with me?"

It wasn't the most inspiring of speeches. But Tilton shouted "We're with you!" and his men joined in.

"Here come the librarians," Miss Parkhurst called.

They marched up the hill, Mr. Quinn at their head. The joyful expression on his face seemed more suitable to a picnic than a battle against forces that wished to destroy us all. When the contingent reached us, Mr. Quinn bowed low. "Widdershins. The librarians have answered your call."

Oh dear. I couldn't so much as glance in Tilton's direction, and the tips of my ears grew hot from embarrassment. "Thank you. For, um, joining us."

Mr. Quinn straightened. His pale hands clutched a rather large dictionary to his chest. "We are yours to do with as you please."

"Er…yes." I pointed awkwardly at the Draakenwood. "Let's just go, shall we?"

Even with Rupert's compass, the journey through the Draakenwood wasn't easy. No wonder Stanford and the Fideles had resorted to summoning winged creatures to fly in and out.

The trees closed around us immediately. A short distance in, I glanced back over my shoulder, and was dismayed I could no longer see the verge. Even though it was winter, the thick tangle of branches muted the sunlight. Centuries of rotting leaves turned the ground almost spongy beneath us. Deadfalls and thorny underbrush made it impossible to chart a straight course. Without the tracker's needle pointing unerringly in the right direction, we would have been hopelessly lost within moments. Even so, the going was slow, and the already-dim light began to fade.

The policemen all seemed on edge. I'd warned Tilton against the use of guns anywhere near sorcerers, so most of them clutched nightsticks or clubs, though one carried an old sword. As the forest around us grew older and wilder, the trees taller, Tilton quickened his pace to walk beside me.

"It feels as though something is watching us," he murmured.

Mr. Quinn overheard. "It's the trees," he said. "I lost a grandmother and two uncles to the forest, you know."

I rather wished he'd thought to share this bit of information earlier. "That's…I'm very sorry."

"No need to be." Mr. Quinn smiled dreamily at the trees looming around us. "The Quinns have never been ones to shy away from anything strange or dangerous. I'm quite certain they died happily."

I had reservations about the ability of anyone to die happily lost in a forest while the trees watched. But I kept them to myself.

"Perhaps we'll find one of their skulls," he added. "I could mail it to my sister in Boston. I'm sure my nieces would be delighted."

"Er, yes, there's nothing children like more than skulls," I said. "Mr. Endicott, are we still on course?"

The deeper we penetrated into the forest, the more intense the sensation of being watched grew, until all of us were starting at the smallest sound. As the day gave way to twilight, a low fog rose from the ground, making our footing even more uncertain.

By the time night fell, I was dirty, scratched by briars and branches, and hungry. But growing fear held any weariness at bay. Stanford's ritual might begin at any moment. Might, in fact, have already started.

Would I feel it, somehow, if he succeeded in taking the fragment of the maelstrom that was Persephone? Or was she already dead? And Griffin—had Stanford treated him badly? Sacrificed him to some monster? Fed on his blood?

Surely Griffin knew I wouldn't abandon him. But that didn't mean I wouldn't fail him.

Rupert came to a sudden halt. "Shh. Douse your lanterns."

Everyone else stopped and did as he said. I came to join him. He pointed silently, and I saw the faintest flicker of torchlight through the trees.

"Should I scout ahead?" Hattie whispered.

I nodded. Though I half expected her to turn to Rupert for confirmation, she simply slipped away into the dense trees like a wraith.

What felt like an eternity passed, standing silent in the dark woods, waiting for her to return. I kept my eyes fixed on the distant torchlight, my heart knocking out the seconds against my ribs.

"All right," Hattie whispered at my elbow.

I jumped. "Give me some warning, next time," I whispered back at her.

"We need a bit of light," she said, ignoring me. Rupert cracked the shutter on his lantern. Hattie took up a fallen stick, cleared a bit of the ground as much as she could, and crouched down. "Gather 'round.

"The good news is, it looks like the ritual is about to begin, but we're still in time to stop it." She began to sketch rapidly in the dirt, describing the scene as she did so. "There are two cultists here on the left, one on the right. I couldn't tell if they were all sorcerers or not. Didn't see the byakhee, but they were probably in the giant tree. Hounds circling everywhere. There are growths, or pods, or something. Persephone is in one of them; the other looked empty, far as I could tell."

My blood chilled. "It was probably meant for me."

"Probably. And cousin Stanford is right here." She stabbed a point on the ground forcefully.

"Can we take them?" Tilton asked me. "It's only three men, besides your brother, but they have magic. Or might."

"At least two of them do," I said. "Someone had to summon the Hounds at Lester mansion and Whyborne House, after all." I stared at the sketch, mind racing. If only I had Father here; he'd helped plan battles during the war. "They don't realize we're here. Perhaps if we attacked from both sides, and caught them between?"

Tilton studied the map, rubbing his jaw thoughtfully. "It could work. It would work even better if there was some sort of distraction, to draw off the Hounds and those flying things."

I nodded. "Leave that to me. Tilton, you and your men take the right side. Mr. Quinn, take your librarians and come from the left."

Mr. Quinn hugged his dictionary gleefully. "Yes, Widdershins."

"Miss Endicott, your witch hunter's daggers will be most useful against the two sorcerers, so go with the librarians. Mr. Endicott, it seems you have the best chance of freeing the prisoners, since their cages were presumably created with sorcery."

He nodded. "I have just the thing."

"What about me, Dr. Whyborne?" Miss Parkhurst asked.

I hated the idea of sending her into danger. But in truth, I had little choice. And she'd certainly proven herself more than capable.

I handed her Griffin's sword cane. "Take this. Once there's a chance, try to sneak to the pod where Persephone is being held. Try stabbing it, or cutting, or…I'm not sure."

She took the sword cane from me with a solemn nod. "I'll set her free, if I have to claw through it with my fingernails."

"Let's just hope it doesn't come to that." I cleared my throat. "Good luck. To us all."

Within moments, I was alone. I waited a short time, trying to give them the chance to move into position. When I judged five minutes had passed, I began to walk, keeping the flickering torchlight in sight.

There had to be an arcane line here somewhere…

There. I stopped and reoriented myself. Judging from the map Hattie had drawn, the line ran straight through the center of the old ruins. All I had to do was stay on it.

Well. Not all.

Fear flickered in my belly, though I didn't know what made me most afraid. That I wouldn't succeed…or that I would. That tonight would unleash a part of myself which would change me forever.

That someday I would look in the mirror and see not the man I thought I was, but someone more like my father. More like Stanford.

I pushed the fear aside and instead focused on the torchlight through the trees. Griffin was there. Griffin, and Christine, and Iskander, and my parents and sister. Everyone I'd ever loved, and all of them counting on me.

One monster to save them from another.

I had no more time to be afraid. No more time to dither.

Taking a deep breath, I reached into the arcane line beneath my feet and drew its power into me.

CHAPTER 37

Griffin

The ritual began not long after the sun slipped below the horizon.

All of our desperate escape attempts had come to naught. The roots were immoveable. Digging beneath them revealed only more roots tangled under us. Christine even tried sawing through one with a piece of sharp rock our digging had uncovered.

And yet, here we still were. Helpless. *Useless.* Unable to prevent Stanford from killing Persephone, and probably my Ival, and enslaving the maelstrom forever to the masters' will. I leaned against the roots, feeling sick with grief and dread.

"I'm sorry if I was hard on you earlier," Christine said to Iskander, as we watched the last sunlight fade outside our prison. "I understand you want to reconnect with your heritage. We can go to Egypt, if you like."

If we survived, she meant. But Iskander shook his head. "No. I lived with the shardah-iin before, but I never really felt at home among them. Just as I really never felt at home in England."

"Just here," I said quietly.

He glanced at me, one corner of his mouth lifting in wry acknowledgement. "I suppose it's true. Widdershins really does know its own."

He sighed and turned back to Christine. "Mother wanted me to have a better life than she did, and I love her for it. But…I wish she had given me the choice of following in her path or not."

"If that had happened, you would have been introduced to the Endicotts," Christine said. "Just think, we might have met over crossed blades. You trying to kill Whyborne, me defending him. Naturally I would have won, and been forced to make you my captive. Have you at my mercy."

He chuckled softly. "No doubt."

A sorcerer in a faceless mask went around the clearing, lighting torches. The flickering light threw shifting shadows, giving the great tree a semblance of movement. At least, I hoped it was only a semblance.

Stanford took up position where the two enormous roots almost came together. "Now is the time for my ascension," he intoned. The tentacles sprouting from the thing he'd grafted to his flesh squirmed in excitement.

And the Endicotts had the nerve to call Whyborne and Persephone abominations.

I pressed my face to the gaps between roots, hoping that if Stanford became caught up in his ritual, some opportunity to escape might arise. What, I couldn't imagine, but something. Anything.

The sorcerers flanked Stanford, though they stood well back and to the side. Two held position to the left of the clearing, and Kolter went to the right.

The sorcerers began to chant: low, urgent words in what I presumed to be Aklo. In the charged atmosphere, the sounds crackled imperatively through the air. One sorcerer lit stinking incense. Kolter drew sigils in the air and on the ground before the great tree. Stanford added his own voice to the chant, lifting his arms to the mighty branches.

My shadowsight showed the magic gathering. The spells threaded the air, the ground, until what was almost a seam in reality formed within the embrace of the enormous tree's roots.

The beginnings of the gateway that would let Nyarlathotep into our world.

"What's happening?" Christine whispered. But I couldn't bring myself to answer. It hit me with overwhelming certainty that we were likely going to die here. Throughout the day, I'd clung to the hope that somehow, some way, this moment would be averted. Stanford wouldn't welcome Nyarlathotep into the world. Persephone wouldn't be scooped hollow, the fire in her stolen by Stanford.

But it was happening. We were going to die, probably painfully. Then Stanford would return to Widdershins and Ival.

Ival, who would have to stand against him alone.

Oh God, I wished I could be with him.

A roar came from deep within the forest.

Iskander and I exchanged a baffled look. The roar grew louder, from a distant rumble to a howl. The trees began to wave back and forth, branches creaking, and I had just enough time to realize what caused the sound before the great wall of wind was on us.

The gale screamed through the clearing. The trees bent low, trunks groaning. Branches snapped off and flew through the air, and tiny bits of bark and lichen pelted my skin. The sorcerers shouted in alarm, their cloaks and hoods whipping around them. Half the torches went out, and the others guttered madly.

"What the devil is this?" Stanford shouted. "Keep chanting, damn you!"

Whyborne strode into the clearing.

No—the maelstrom did.

My heart nearly stopped at the sight. The power of the arcane line poured through Ival, turning him from a candle flame to an arc light. The sleeve of his shirt had charred away over his scars, and they boiled with blue fire. His eyes blazed like twin stars.

He was beautiful and terrible as a god, and if I had not already given him my heart and soul, I would have done so at that instant.

"You," Stanford snarled. "How dare you interrupt?"

Ival's stride didn't falter. He moved with a determined gait, as if the very ground belonged to him. As though nothing and no one could possibly stand against the force of his will. "I dare," he said in the voice of something ancient. "And I will dare a great deal more."

Out of the corner of my eye, I saw a shadow detach from the trees behind us. Rupert Endicott crouched in front of the cage of roots holding Heliabel and Niles. He drew out a wand, and I saw the spark of magic, invisible to anyone else.

"You're nothing," Stanford said to Ival. "A coward, who stole what was rightfully mine."

Whyborne laughed, and the sound sent a thrill along my nerves. "I am the maelstrom. You imagine yourself capable of controlling *me?* I will burn you from the inside out, until there is nothing left but ash on the wind."

Stanford's eyes bugged from his head. "Destroy him!"

A byakhee dropped from the boughs of the vast tree, its wings spread and its jaws gaping to reveal jagged teeth. Whyborne didn't so much as glance in its direction, only flung out his hand. A blast of wind caught the byakhee like a leaf in a windstorm, smashing it into the enormous trunk. The thing went limp and began to dissolve into slime even as it crumpled toward the earth.

"Stop him!" Kolter shouted frantically. "You idiot, use the binding, before he kills us all!"

Stanford lifted his hand and made a twisting motion.

Instantly, the surge of raw magic through Whyborne ceased. His body jerked, and a bellow of fury and pain escaped him as he collapsed to his knees. Persephone thrashed in her pod at the same moment.

I yanked fruitlessly at one of the roots caging us. Rupert had freed Heliabel and Niles, the roots slowly retracting, and now worked on our cage, but it was too slow. Not enough. I needed to get out, to get to Ival's side.

"Not yet," Rupert said. Our eyes met, and he shook his head. "As I told Heliabel and Niles, hold until Whyborne gives the signal."

Signal?

Whyborne crouched on his hands and knees, breath coming raggedly. Channeling the arcane fire always left him drained, and combined with whatever Stanford had done, I was astonished to see him still conscious.

"I'm almost impressed at how stupid you are," Stanford said, drawing closer to Whyborne. He made another gesture, and roots exploded up from the ground. Within a moment, Whyborne's body was hauled upright, imprisoned in a straightjacket of tangled wood. "What did you think would happen? Coming here alone to face *me?*"

Despite his predicament, Whyborne offered him a savage grin. "Who said I came alone?"

CHAPTER 38

Whyborne

AT MY SIGNAL, the police and librarians burst into the clearing from either side.

The Hounds and sorcerers had all been focused on me, as the obvious threat. They tried to recover, but one of the sorcerers went down within seconds, bowled over by librarians armed with cudgels and bookbinding awls.

Stanford let out a roar of rage and whipped away from me. The full sight of what he'd done to his body revolted me to my core. He'd called forth corruption from Beyond, grafted it to his own flesh, and let it slowly consume him while he willingly glutted himself on the blood of the old families.

And he wanted to take what lived inside Persephone and me, and cage it within such foulness?

It could not be allowed.

Persephone still curled in the pod, but Miss Parkhurst had found her way to it. She stabbed at the vine-like growth connecting it to the gigantic tree. I'd never used magic over such distance, but I focused intently on the wand and cast the curse breaking spell.

The vine heaved, then fell to pieces. The pod holding Persephone split down its length.

There was Persephone free, at least. I struggled against the roots, but they held me fast. I took a deep breath and pulled flame through the scars on my arm. The wood began to scorch—hopefully I could weaken it enough to escape without setting myself on fire.

"Widdershins!" Mr. Quinn came pelting up, gasping for breath. He grasped the roots and tugged on them, without much in the way of success.

Unfortunately, he managed to catch my brother's attention. Stanford rounded on us, and I began to struggle more frantically. Mr. Quinn, however, took his heavy dictionary in both hands. "Stay back," he warned.

"I don't think so," Stanford said. He moved forward, the feeder mouths on his ropey tentacles opening and closing blindly. "The Fideles have told me of your cult, librarian. I think you and I have much to offer each other."

Mr. Quinn lowered the book slightly. "Such as?"

Oh dear.

Stanford smiled triumphantly. "Soon enough, I will be the one who holds the maelstrom fragments within me. Give me your allegiance, and you will be greatly rewarded. What do you want? Dark magic? Power?" His smile turned sly. "Women?"

Mr. Quinn drew himself up, thin nostrils flaring in affront. "How dare you, sir. I serve Widdershins, not some—some trumped-up, two-bit fake!"

He flung the heavy dictionary with all his strength at Stanford's head. Stanford let out a roar of fury and lashed out at Mr. Quinn with the toothy tentacles.

I shouted, but could do nothing, trapped as I was. Instead, my sister hurtled into Mr. Quinn, knocking him aside. She grabbed hold of the nearest tentacle, and frost spread across its flabby gray surface.

Enraged, Stanford raised his hand and yanked.

Persephone and I both cried out then, pain shocking through our bodies. The roots at least kept me upright. She started to collapse, but Mr. Quinn caught her. Through the anguish, a single thought looped through my brain.

This was the fourth time Stanford had used the binding oath against us. If Rupert was right, he had only one more…and surely he would want to save that until Nyarlathotep emerged. Given all the trouble he'd gone to collect the blood of the old families, it must be critical to the spell to remove the maelstrom fragments from our bodies.

The librarians attacked Stanford en masse: flinging sticks, books, and stones. He retreated from the onslaught, and one of them began hacking at the roots encasing me with a hatchet he'd clearly been using as a weapon.

The moment I was free, I grabbed Persephone's wrist. She was on her feet again, thanks to the beaming Mr. Quinn. "Are you all right?"

She nodded. Something not quite slime and not quite sap clung to her skin, and stuck to me when I withdrew my hand. "Maggie freed me. I told her to stay away from the fighting." She picked up Griffin's sword cane from where she'd dropped it. "She told me to bring you this."

"Thank you." I looked around the clearing that had become a battlefield, searching for Griffin.

I spotted him, just in time to see one of the byakhee drop from the sky and bear him to the ground.

CHAPTER 39

Griffin

The moment the roots withdrew enough to squeeze past, I did so. The few torches which remained lit showed scenes of utter chaos. The ruins echoed with shouts and the terrible cries of the Hounds. A group of men who appeared to be from the Widdershins Police Department, of all things, struggled with them. Rupert must have given his powder to Detective Tilton, who scattered it wildly in an attempt to stop the Hounds from blinking in and out of existence.

On the other side of the clearing, two sorcerers faced a contingent of librarians. Heliabel leapt onto the back of one masked figure, tearing aside his cloak and biting him savagely with her shark's teeth.

And Stanford faced the librarians. At the sight of him, rage howled through me.

He meant to kill my Ival, to kill Persephone—and more. He meant to take their very essence, to pervert the maelstrom. To destroy the only home that had ever welcomed me, and Christine, and Iskander, and God alone knew how many others.

He had to be stopped, no matter what the cost.

I took a step toward Stanford, but our escape had been noticed. A Hound began to emerge directly in front of me, and I had nothing to fight it with.

"Griffin!" Niles called. He'd made it to where our captors had left our weapons piled atop the tumbled wall. Even as I turned, he tossed his cavalry sword to me.

I caught it, bringing the blade down just as the Hound solidified. Luck was with me, and the sword slid through its eye, scraped against bone, and penetrated its brain.

I yanked the sword free even as the Hound began to collapse in on itself. A quick glance showed me Iskander had recovered his knives. Niles took the small pistol, but wisely pocketed it and snatched up a fallen branch for defense instead.

Orion and Fred seemed to have fled. A byakhee tumbled through the air, and I glimpsed Hattie astride its serpentine neck, whooping as she stabbed it over and over again. The librarians had converged on Stanford, and Mr. Quinn and Persephone had reached Whyborne.

I had to get to Stanford. And when I did, I'd kill him, and put an end to his plan once and for all.

I waded into the battle, striking about me with the sword. But before I'd gone more than a few yards, the glow of magic distracted me. Startled, I looked up, just as the last byakhee swooped down and knocked me to the ground.

The byakhee reared above me, bat-like wings spread, jaw gaping open. It stank, its scabrous skin oozing fluid. My fall had knocked the cavalry sword from my hand. I clawed blindly at the leaf mold in search of it, not daring to take my gaze from the monster above me.

Its head drew back, like a snake preparing to strike. A blast of putrid breath issued from jaws filled with rows of jagged teeth. I scooped up a handful of rotting leaves and flung them at it, but it didn't so much as blink at my pathetic attempt at defense.

"Leave him alone!" shouted Heliabel, and leapt onto its back.

The byakhee shrieked in outrage, twisting its head around to snap at her. But she was too fast. Her claws sank into its flesh as she scaled its sinuous neck. It thrashed, trying to dislodge her; she responded by stinging it in a flurry of angry tentacles.

I rolled to the side, searching for the dropped sword. A flicker of orange firelight betrayed the blade, and I snatched it up.

Heliabel had reached the byakhee's head. The creature dropped into a crouch, preparing to launch itself into the air, where it would surely have all the advantage. Wrapping her legs around its thick neck, she plunged her clawed hands into its malevolent eyes.

It screamed, thrashing madly at the pain. Its convulsions shook Heliabel loose; she struck the earth hard. I ducked beneath one ragged wing and thrust my blade into its flank. It let out a shriek like iron nails against glass, stumbled a few feet toward the forest, and collapsed to the ground.

The Hounds were almost gone, and two of the sorcerers lay dead. Kolter sprawled on the ground. Christine and Tilton stood to either side of him, Tilton with a nightstick and Christine with a human femur from some old sacrifice, which she'd used as a club.

The seam that had formed in the bowl of the tree, the gateway to the Outside Stanford had meant to open…had grown larger.

Oh no.

I cast about for Ival, and spotted him even as Heliabel let out a hiss of fear and outrage.

Stanford held Ival aloft by the throat, as though he were nothing more than a rag doll. Ival clawed weakly at Stanford's grip, but the magic that had flooded him earlier was gone, leaving behind only the fire that always burned quietly beneath his skin.

And in front of them stood Niles.

"Choose, Father," Stanford said. "Choose between us, once and for all."

CHAPTER 40

Whyborne

AT THE SIGHT of the byakhee descending on Griffin, I broke into a run. My body hurt, and exhaustion threatened to engulf me—I'd used far too much power in far too short a time. But none of that mattered. I'd burn myself out from the inside if that was what it took to save Griffin.

"Oh, no you don't," Stanford growled.

The familiar pain shot through me, the sensation that the very marrow of my bones was being yanked from my body. My face slammed into the ground, and pain spiked through my nose as the cartilage snapped.

It seemed to go on forever this time. Eventually, though, the agony eased, leaving me panting through my mouth. Blood slicked my face and threatened to choke me.

I'd been wrong when I thought Stanford would hold the binding spell in reserve, it seemed.

Stanford loomed over me. The firelight painted his features red. The unspeakable stench of the Outside threatened to suffocate me. If not for the familiar look of contempt and rage on his face, I would have wondered whether anything of my brother remained at all.

He seized me by the throat and lifted me effortlessly from the ground. My neck felt as though the vertebrae would separate, and I scrabbled madly at his grip, struggling to breathe. My flailing legs made contact with the soft, writhing mass of flesh that formed his lower body. Tentacles seized me, holding me still and taking some of my weight from my neck.

"Cower, you wretched fairy," he said. His gaze bored into mine, filled with hate and madness. "Cower before what is even now approaching. Once Nyarlathotep arrives, you'll die screaming while I suck the magic from your bones."

I felt the horrible feeder mouths through my clothing. Black spots danced before my eyes; I could get a small amount of air past Stanford's grip, but not enough. I tried to burn him with fire drawn through the scars on my arm, but I was nearly drained and did nothing more than leave a scorch mark on his sleeve. If I couldn't break free soon, I'd lose consciousness.

"Stanford!" Father shouted. "Stop this instant."

Stanford lowered me slightly. He grip slackened just enough for me to gulp down more air, though the blood pouring from my nose made breathing even more difficult. My vision cleared, enough for me to make out Father standing a few feet away.

"Stop?" Stanford asked. "And why on earth should I do that, old man?"

The wind moaned through the branches above, sent the torchlight to flickering, and stirred Father's gray hair. The expression on his face was one of such heartbreak as I'd never imagined him capable of feeling.

"Look at what you've done to yourself," he said, gesturing at Stanford. "This isn't right. You know it isn't."

"I don't know any such thing." Stanford's grip tightened again on my neck. "And neither do you."

"I know you're angry with me." Father took a step closer. "I know I failed you, when you were a boy. But your anger is destroying you."

"No. It's purified me," Stanford said.

Father swallowed convulsively. "Listen to me. I may not have understood you as well as I should when you were a boy. Then you moved to New York, determined to be your own man…and I didn't allow it. The drink, the women, the gambling…you were hurting yourself as well as your wife. I couldn't stand by, not because I wanted to control you, but because I love you. And if I failed to make you understand that…then I'm sorry."

The hold on my neck relaxed, and Stanford lowered me slightly. "You locked me away in an asylum."

"I know." Father closed his eyes, then opened them again. "But whatever your grievances are against me, what you're doing now isn't the solution. You're angry because I tried to control you, but if you continue down this path, you'll only end up controlled by the masters instead. For your own sake, don't become their puppet just to spite me."

For the first time in my memory, Stanford seemed struck by indecision. Seeing his hesitation, Father pressed on. "Whatever's happened, whatever you've done to yourself and others, you're still my son. I love you. Stop this madness while you yet can, and I swear, I'll do whatever I can to help you." He took another step closer, and Stanford didn't back away. "We'll find a way to reverse this transformation. With your brother's assistance—"

It was the wrong thing to say. Stanford snarled and swayed back, as if Father had slapped him. His fingers dug into my neck, completely cutting off my air. He was inhumanly strong, and none of my flailing or clawing seemed to have any effect. "Of course. This is a trick to save *his* pathetic life. You don't care about me at all."

Father's eyes grew round with fear, and he held out his hands in a placating manner. "That isn't true!"

"Then prove it." Stanford hefted me above his head. My lungs screamed for air, and blackness threatened my vision. "Choose, Father. Choose between us, once and for all."

Everything seemed to grow very still, though perhaps it was my own failing consciousness that made it seem so. The wind died away, and the flames of the torches became motionless. Father's expression settled into one I could no longer read, a mask of iron.

"I'm sorry," he said.

Then he pulled a pistol from his coat pocket and fired.

Stanford jerked from the impact of the bullet. A hole showed in his chest, above his heart. Black ichor poured from the wound, splattering us both.

His hand went slack, as did the tentacles around my legs. I crashed to the forest floor, gasping and choking. Between my bruised throat and swollen nose, I could barely breathe.

"Stanford," Father gasped. He started for my brother, hand outstretched, agony in his eyes.

"Stop!" Persephone grabbed his wrist, jerking him back. Her gaze fixed on Stanford, and she let out a hiss of warning.

Because Stanford hadn't fallen. He stood, swaying on inhuman legs, clutching the wound with both hands. Even as we watched, the flow of ichor slowed. Ceased.

Stanford let his arms drop to his sides. "You chose him," he whispered, sounding bewildered. And I realized, deep down, Stanford had still clung to some shred of hope. That despite everything he'd done—murdering Guinevere, beating Father, trying to kill me multiple times—he could somehow turn back the clock. Return to what he saw as his rightful position as the beloved son, adored and protected.

But none of us could ever go back to what we were before. No matter how much we might want to.

I would never again sit forgotten in a basement office, happily pursuing my translations, unnoticed by anyone save Griffin and Christine. My quiet life, without magic or sorcerers, without a cult of librarians at my call, was gone forever. The world changed, and I changed with it, and nothing would ever be quite the same again.

Stanford must have come to the same realization, because the stricken look on his face hardened, became one of fury. "Die, then," he snarled. "The two of you will be the first to fall."

He raised his hand and made the twisting motion again, the one that had felled Persephone and me before. I tensed…

But it seemed Rupert had been right, because nothing happened. Either none of the sorcerers had told Stanford the power was limited, or he had chosen not to believe them.

Persephone straightened, her tentacles lashing. I stepped to stand by her, and we faced our brother shoulder-to-shoulder. "Surrender," she ordered.

I could have told her it was a hopeless request. Stanford laughed hollowly and began to back toward the huge roots reaching out from the tree. To my horror, whatever magic Stanford had put into motion had continued throughout the battle.

Even though nothing should have been darker than the forest around us, a blackness hung in the air. A rip in reality, opening onto a place that had never known light.

Something moved on the other side, more sensed than seen. For the moment, it seemed too immense to fit through the tear. But the rip was growing steadily larger.

"You think me defeated?" Stanford demanded. "Nyarlathotep is coming! The Man in the Woods is coming, and he will strip you of every drop of magic. He will lay waste to all of you traitors and shape your bones into the throne I will rule from. I will do his work on this earth, and when the masters return, I will be as a god at their side."

"Somehow I doubt that," Rupert remarked as he joined us. "The godhood part, that is. Not the bit about the rest of us dying horribly."

"Agreed." Griffin slipped his hand into mine. I squeezed it, grateful beyond words that he seemed unharmed. "So how do we stop him from emerging?"

I took a deep breath. My bones felt like those of a bird: fragile, hollow, and easily shattered. My broken nose throbbed, and the taste of blood filled my mouth. The scars on my arm felt tender, as though newly healed rather than years old.

I had spent far too much of my own power. Channeled too much magic through my too-mortal body.

This was going to hurt. But there was no other way.

Persephone clearly had the same thoughts. "He's between us and the gateway."

"Yes," I said. "He is."

Then I let go of Griffin's hand, snatched up his sword cane where it lay dropped amidst the leaves, and ran.

CHAPTER 41

Whyborne

MY HEART POUNDED and my pumping legs ached, but I ignored everything except for Stanford. He'd retreated to stand before the tear in the veil, directly atop the arcane line.

Waiting for Nyarlathotep to save him.

Griffin cried out behind me, but I forced myself to ignore what might have been either plea or warning. Rage ignited in my blood and propelled me forward. Physically, so much about Stanford appeared to have changed—and yet nothing really had at all. He was still the boy who ripped the toy train I'd gotten for my birthday from my five-year-old hands, shouting he wanted it for his own. And when Miss Emily gently chided him, he'd broken it rather than give it back.

And now he wanted to do the same thing to my town.

He would look upon all those the maelstrom had so carefully collected, see their flaws, and despise them as weak. He would never see the beautiful kaleidoscope the maelstrom had made from all the broken souls that called Widdershins home. Never understand that imperfection made them no less valuable, no less important.

He would turn what should have been a place of belonging for them into one of abuse and fear and pain.

I reached into the arcane line as I ran, pulling the magic into my flesh until every nerve screamed. I was fire and magic and righteous fury, and I would die before I let him hurt those Widdershins called its own.

Persephone ran behind me, and I could feel her anger throbbing in my bones. And behind us both, distantly, the great heart of the vortex rotated endlessly.

"Stanford!" we roared, and the voice of the maelstrom howled through our lungs.

Stanford had turned to face the rip in reality, holding out his arms in greeting to the thing lurking on the other side. At our challenge, he whipped around, arm flung up defensively. As he turned, I raised the sword cane above my hands, gripped it in both hands, and leapt.

My brother was much taller than me now, but my jump carried me high enough to reach my target. The blade of the sword cane bit deep, plunging between his ribs and down, angling through whatever human parts remained and into the substance of the Outside.

His eyes widened in disbelief. Clinging to the handle of the sword cane with all my strength, the crystals I'd added biting into my fingers, I said, "You want the power of the maelstrom? Then we'll give it to you."

I let go of every mental block, of every individual need and desire, and made myself nothing but a conduit for the magic. It poured through my body, into the sword cane—and into Stanford.

Then Persephone joined with me. What had been a bonfire turned into an inferno. The crystals on the sword cane cracked from the strain. I smelled burning wood and heated metal.

Stanford screamed in surprise and agony. The Fideles had told him his body could channel the arcane power. But they'd never told him how much it *hurt.*

"We have a message for Nyarlathotep," Persephone and I said in perfect sync, the certainty of the maelstrom flowing through us both. "Tell him the Draakenwood is no longer his. It belongs to Widdershins now."

We shoved Stanford as one. I caught a glimpse of his startled expression as he went flying back, through the hole in reality—and was lost in darkness.

Persephone's near hand linked with mine. We raised our opposite hands as one, connected on some deep level beyond thought or understanding. I could feel the wound in the world, its edges torn open by arcane energy. And beyond it…

Something lurked. Drawing nearer and nearer, its vast power reaching for the rip in the veil. Determined to come through.

But we would not allow it.

Magic surged through us, funneled through our bones and blood and scars, until it reached the tear in the veil. It spanned the growing gap, the warp and weft of reality pulling tight. Suturing the rip shut, until nothing remained.

The gateway to the Outside was gone.

For a long moment, all was silent. I tried to turn to my sister, but my body no longer worked properly. My legs folded under me, and I tumbled into blackness.

CHAPTER 42

Griffin

"IVAL!" I CRIED.

He and Persephone both lay crumpled within the embrace of the tree's enormous roots. I ran to them, falling to my knees at their sides. Thank heavens, both of them still breathed. I reached to pull Whyborne into my arms—

And found one of Hattie's knives at my throat. The point of the other pressed against Whyborne's vulnerable neck.

"No one move," she warned.

"Hattie!" Rupert exclaimed. I didn't dare take my eyes off her to see where he stood. "What is the meaning of this?"

The witch hunter's daggers trembled slightly in her grip. Not enough to be visible, most likely, but I felt her fear through the edge of the blade resting on my skin. "You saw them, Rupert. What they did. The kind of power they have." Her eyes narrowed and her grip firmed. "I know what's at stake, but we'll find another way. They're too bloody dangerous to leave alive."

My mind raced. I couldn't possibly disarm her before she slit my throat. And any move I made risked Whyborne's life.

We couldn't die here, after all this.

"Hattie," Iskander said, "please. Don't do this."

Her mouth creased in annoyance. "They're monsters, Iskander."

He sighed. "They're your *family*. And…they're my family, too. Perhaps not by blood, but that doesn't make the bond any less real." He stepped cautiously closer, then crouched down. "You and I have talked a great deal about what my mother would have wanted. But the truth is, what she wanted most of all was for me to be happy. And I am. Here. With them."

"As am I," I said, though I didn't know if it would carry any weight with her. "The maelstrom called me home. To my real family."

"It called all of us home," Christine said from Iskander's side. "And Whyborne is my brother in every way but parentage, so if you dare touch him, you'll have every last one of us to deal with."

"Let it go, Hattie." Rupert sounded weary. "For the sake of the family."

"I'm doing this for the sake of the family," she said. "How are we to stop Whyborne and Persephone, when the time comes and they turn on us? On humanity? You *saw* them. They could destroy the Endicotts, once and for all."

"They could," Rupert agreed. "But without them…our fate is certain. Don't forget why we came here."

For a long moment she hesitated. Then she resheathed her daggers in a single, almost angry, movement. "Fine. Hope we don't regret this."

She strode away, not looking at any of us. Miss Parkhurst, Heliabel, and Niles rushed to join me. As I pulled Whyborne into my lap, he shifted, blinked, and looked at me. His poor nose was swollen and bruised, and the delicate veins in his eyes had burst and stained the whites to red, but I'd never seen a more beautiful sight.

"How did I do?" he asked.

I smiled tenderly at him, then bent to kiss his forehead, well away from any of his injuries. "You were magnificent, my dear."

CHAPTER 43

Whyborne

A WEEK LATER, Griffin and I met Father on the Front Street Bridge.

We'd just come from purchasing a new desk for my office. Once I was back on my feet, I went to the museum and asked Dr. Hart to allow me to return to my job. The newspapers branded Chief Early a lunatic, and Detective Tilton swore me innocent of any wrongdoing whatsoever.

Even more importantly from Dr. Hart's perspective, the Marsh and Waite families had made public amends, by way of a well-publicized dinner in my honor at Le Calmar. After watching our battle against Stanford and the Fideles from the edge of the forest, Orion and Fred had offered me their full support without reservation. The feud between the old families was ended.

As for me, I was simply grateful to return to the museum. Unfortunately, each time Miss Parkhurst entered my office and looked at my old desk, I turned red, she began to stammer, and our interactions became even more awkward than usual. Hopefully a replacement desk would allow us to put the incident behind us. At least until my sister did something even more outrageous.

Fenton sat in the touring car, which was pulled far to the side so as not to impede the flow of traffic over the bridge. Father stood at the center of the span, his hands neatly tucked behind him.

"How is he?" I asked Fenton.

"Distressed," Fenton replied. "But Mr. Whyborne is a man of action. He has flung himself into his work, rather than dwell on events."

I sighed. Father hadn't killed Stanford…but he had pulled the trigger believing he was putting the end to one of his sons to save the other. And, to be fair, to save Persephone and the rest of the world as well.

But Father hadn't lied when he said he still loved Stanford, despite everything he'd done. His decision to shoot hadn't been made in anger, or disgust, but in grief. It was the sort of moment that would haunt anyone.

Griffin glanced at me. "Should I stay here with Fenton?"

I shook my head, then winced at the ache in my nose. Doctors had set it well enough that it should heal straight, and the swelling had largely gone down. Still, I had to exercise caution when kissing Griffin, let alone doing anything more strenuous with him.

Once we'd had the chance to rest, we'd retrieved our belongings from Christine and Iskander's house. But I'd put an end to the fiction of our two bedrooms. It might prove foolish in the future, but I'd moved all of my things into what had been Griffin's room, and was now simply ours.

"Father asked for us both." I took Griffin's hand and gave it a squeeze. "Shall we?"

It was a cloudy February day, and traffic across the bridge was light at this hour. As we approached, Father turned his head slightly to acknowledge us.

"This is the eye of the maelstrom, isn't it?" he asked.

I nodded. I could sense its magic all around me, the great vortex pivoting about this point. And, of course, Griffin could see it perfectly well with his shadowsight. "Yes."

Father stared out at the river. "So much power," he said. "And yet, I can't see it at all." A sigh escaped him. "But then, it seems there has been a great deal I've failed to see over the years."

I stood beside him, turning my own gaze to the flowing water. It was iron gray at the moment, reflecting the low-hanging clouds. I wasn't certain what to say, but felt I ought to offer some words of comfort. "Stanford might still be alive. The other side of the veil isn't meant for earthly life, but he had a great deal of the Outside in him already. It might make the difference."

"Nyarlathotep doesn't reward failure," Father said simply. "We saw that ourselves."

Though Kolter had been taken alive, he'd died screaming within an hour of Persephone and me closing the gateway. And autopsy showed his heart had been converted to an entirely different organ. Needless to say, his fate didn't bode well for Stanford.

"Don't blame yourself too much, Niles," Griffin said. "Whatever happened when he was a boy, Stanford was a grown man who made his own choices." He paused, then added. "And surely your remaining children would make any father proud."

My face flushed, but to my surprise, Father smiled. "True." He clapped a hand to my arm. "I may have failed Stanford. But I will not fail you, Percival."

"I don't—" I began, but he held up a hand to stop me.

"I've been meeting with Orion Marsh and Fred Waite," he said. "And Miss Lester, of course. We've been making plans. Laying groundwork. Organizing the families, even the branches previously fallen out of favor. Persephone has an army of the sea. When the masters come through, you will have one of the land."

Words deserted me. For a moment, I wanted to frantically deny everything yet again. Tell him I couldn't be what he wanted.

But the words died in my throat. Because it was no longer about what he wanted, really. "Detective Tilton's men will report anything even slightly suspicious," I said. "As that would be a great deal to manage alone, the librarians will pass along anything that actually needs my attention. And Miss Parkhurst will comb through several major papers each day, looking for anything that might hint at the involvement of the Fideles." I paused. "And there is one more thing."

Father arched a brow. "Oh?"

"It occurred to me we have other allies, just as desperate to keep the masters from returning. I asked Griffin to speak with the Mother of Shadows. Another little queen has hatched recently." The decision was not one I was entirely certain of...but certainty wasn't something it seemed I was destined to have. Perhaps no one was. "She will come here, to begin a new colony of umbrae. There's a whole forest they can live in now. When the masters return, the umbrae will fight at our side."

Father's smile widened. "Well done, Percival. I'm proud of you."

Before I could think how to respond to such praise, he turned to Griffin. "Now, I still have a business to run. But before I go, I have something for you."

Griffin cast me a curious look as we followed Father back to his motor car. I shrugged; I'd not the slightest idea. It seemed Father was full of surprises today.

When we reached the touring car, Father nodded at Fenton, who quickly removed a long, thin box from the rear seat. He handed it to Father, who in turn presented it to Griffin. "I hope it serves you as well as the original," he said, climbing into the seat beside Fenton. "Good day to you both."

The motor car chugged away. Frowning, Griffin carefully opened the box.

Inside lay a new cane. Griffin let out a delighted gasp and removed it, sliding the concealed blade easily free of the ebony shaft. "I can't believe it!" He made a few practice thrusts, to the alarm of some of the passersby, then sheathed it again. Holding it close to his face, he carefully inspected the black wood, then the silver head.

His lips parted slightly, and he stilled. "Is something wrong?" I asked.

"No." Griffin shook his head and held out the cane for me to examine. The silver was fancifully engraved, but nestled amidst the pattern of leaves and vines was the unmistakable shape of the Whyborne family crest.

We walked slowly back home, our arms brushing, Griffin's new cane tapping on the sidewalk. I had never loved Father quite as much as I did at that moment. Strangely, his unexpected praise had little to do with it. For all our arguments and bitter memories, Father had always accepted Griffin as my husband. Even when Griffin's own parents had been unable to do so.

I supposed he'd do the same with Miss Parkhurst, if Persephone ever proposed. Persephone had been busy as of late, rooting out traitors amidst the ketoi. And even if she hadn't been, undoubtedly ketoi customs were somewhat different from our own. Miss Parkhurst might be left dangling for an unacceptable length of time. Perhaps I ought to nudge my sister a bit?

My musing ended when we turned onto our walk, and I felt Griffin tense beside me. I looked up, and found Rupert Endicott waiting for us on our stoop. Saul, the traitor, twined around his ankles, purring happily and shedding long hair all over Rupert's immaculate trousers.

"Saul likes you," Griffin remarked as we approached.

"I find animals to be excellent judges of character," Rupert replied.

"Oddly enough, so do I," Griffin said. "Will you come inside?"

"Is Hattie with you?" I asked, glancing around suspiciously. Griffin had told me about her decision to slit my throat, and I didn't entirely trust her change of heart on the subject.

"No. She's busy overseeing the packing of our things," Rupert said.

Griffin led the way to the parlor office. "Would you care for coffee, Mr. Endicott? Tea?"

"No, thank you. I find you Yanks don't have the slightest idea how to properly prepare either."

We seated ourselves. "You say Hattie is packing?" I asked. "Are you leaving already? I thought you wanted an alliance until the masters come back."

"We do. Unfortunately, certain events require we return home." Rupert folded his brown hands in front of him. His nails were carefully manicured. "When I originally said we were sent to secure an alliance with you…I wasn't entirely truthful."

"Of course not," I muttered. "You're an Endicott. Well, out with it. What the devil do you really want?"

"We do want an alliance. However…" He paused, seeming to gather himself to say the next. "That isn't all. We…the Endicotts… need your help."

Griffin stiffened in the chair beside me. "You have a great deal of nerve, asking for that."

"I know. But I don't come empty handed." Rupert fixed his gaze on me. "The Fideles stand for everything we fight against. And many of them have been our enemies since long before the Restoration began."

I bit my tongue against the desire to point out it was the Endicotts' own fault if most of the world's sorcerers hated them. "And I should be concerned, because…?"

"Because we could be potent allies against the masters. But the Fideles have struck at our heart, and we are faltering. As Widdershins is the seat of your power, the family estate is the seat of ours." His lips thinned. "The Fideles…have taken it from us. We are without our resources—our library, our magical artifacts, all of it. We have been scattered to the wind."

I sat forward. This sounded serious. "Including you?" A thought occurred. "Did anyone else know you came here?"

"Yes. We had full authorization from the remaining leadership. I'm afraid I can't say more at the moment." He almost sounded sincere. "Hattie and I came here to discover whether you could be considered…trustworthy is a strong word, but close enough. If you proved such, we were to barter for your assistance. Help us, and we shall help you."

Griffin sat back, arms folded over his chest in obvious skepticism. I had the feeling he hadn't forgiven Hattie for threatening to kill me. "You just said you've lost everything. What is it you have to barter, exactly?"

Rupert glanced at him, then back at me. "The key to deciphering the Wisborg Codex."

I stilled. The secrets of the masters were held within its pages, of that I was certain. Without it, we groped blindly, reduced to reacting to the Restoration and return of the masters, instead of actively preventing it.

If we had the key, there was no telling what I might find within its pages. What steps the Fideles meant to take to further the Restoration. When the masters intended to come through the veil.

How to stop them.

"How do I know you're not lying?" I managed.

"Because that would be exceedingly foolish of me," Rupert replied calmly. "Even if the fate of our entire family wasn't at stake…I know what you are now, Dr. Whyborne. Or at least have an idea. Do you truly imagine I have any wish to face the wrath of a being such as yourself? My only chance for survival would be to strike as quickly as possible. And you have far too many fierce guardians; they would either stop me, or kill me in revenge."

I considered for several long moments. Rupert made no move to prompt me. Neither did Griffin, though I was aware of his solid presence at my side. Whatever I decided, he would support.

"Very well," I said at last. "I agree to your bargain. My assistance in saving the Endicotts, in exchange for the key to deciphering the Wisborg Codex."

Rupert closed his eyes in relief, and a little sigh escaped him. I realized how worried he must have been that I would refuse.

"Thank you," he said, rising to his feet. "I will be in contact soon with details. Until then, may you have a pleasant evening. Cousin."

He held out his hand. Rather taken aback, I shook it.

We escorted him to the door. Once he was gone, Griffin turned to me.

"Well," he said with an arched brow. "It seems things are about to get interesting."

Share Your Experience

If you enjoyed this book, please consider leaving a review on the site where you purchased it, or on Goodreads.

Thank you for your support of independent authors!

About the Author

Jordan L. Hawk grew up in North Carolina and forgot to ever leave. Childhood tales of mountain ghosts and mysterious creatures gave her a life-long love of things that go bump in the night. When she isn't writing, she brews her own beer and tries to keep her cats from destroying the house. Her best-selling Whyborne & Griffin series (beginning with *Widdershins*) can be found in print, ebook, and audiobook.

If you're interested in receiving Jordan's newsletter and being the first to know when new books are released, plus getting sneak peeks at upcoming novels, please sign up at her website:

http://www.jordanlhawk.com.

Made in the USA
Las Vegas, NV
20 November 2023